LIVE FRE

The machine-gunner i
swung his weapon and
wildly. As the Enfield cracked again, he threw
up his arms and disappeared backwards out
of the vehicle. The rear kübelwagen was
struggling to turn, its machine-gun lifting. As
Scully fired once more, the gunner fell out;
then, as the vehicle continued to swing, he
shot the driver. Swinging to the first kübelwagen, he picked off the driver, then the man
who was reaching out to take the place of the
machine-gunner, and used his last shot to
knock over one of the motor cyclists who was
trying to bring his machine-gun to bear.

Kehec was staring in astonishment at the
slaughter. Scully studied the scene below for
a second, then he turned to Hasler.

'Okay,' he said quietly. 'It's all yours.'

Also in Arrow by John Harris

Army of Shadows
Cotton's War
Covenant with Death
Ride Out The Storm
The Sea Shall Not Have Them
Swordpoint
Take or Destroy!
The Fox from His Lair

JOHN HARRIS

Live Free or Die!

Arrow Books

Arrow Books Limited
17–21 Conway Street, London W1P 6JD

An imprint of the Hutchinson Publishing Group

London Melbourne Sydney Auckland
Johannesburg and agencies
throughout the world

First published by Hutchinson 1982
Arrow edition 1983

Made and printed in Great Britain
by The Anchor Press Ltd
Tiptree, Essex

ISBN 0 09 930330 2

Author's Note

Though the Petite-Ville-des-Martyrs, which features promi-
nently in this book, is entirely fictitious, there *are* – or were
– similar small *endroits* in Paris. And though the story is
also fictitious, it is based very solidly on events that actually
occurred in the French capital during that heady summer of
1944, and which were faithfully recorded by those men and
women who took part in them.

PART ONE

To Paris

1

'Hello, sir!'

Sergeant Charley Scully opened one eye and regarded the speaker bleakly. He was in no mood for conversation just then. Especially with a young French boy. At that moment, passing the time of day was a long way from Sergeant Scully's thoughts.

He was in a ditch near the village of Tilly-le-Petit in Normandy, hungry, out of cigarettes, his face black with dirt, his clothes soaked, his rifle in that condition which he – faced with the same object in the hands of a recruit – would have described as 'lousy with spiders, rats, mice, cobwebs and dirty filthy rust and verdigris'. He had eaten his emergency rations and finished off his bottle of water, hadn't washed or shaved for seventy-two hours, and stank like a polecat. Above all, he was alone, because most of the poor bastards who'd been backing him up had been knocked over by a German machine-gun, five had been taken prisoner and the rest had bolted for cover, leaving him up ahead, all his grenades gone, out of ammunition, and deciding, as the German counter-attack had swept forward, that the safest place was in a ditch out of sight.

As an old soldier, Charley Scully was not against bolting. He was all for bolting if there were no sense in staying put. *Reculer pour mieux sauter.* Run back for a better kick at the ball. He'd heard that at Dunkirk in 1940. He'd heard it at Amiens in 1918. He'd even heard it expressed in old soldier's English and a variety of other languages on the North-West Frontier and in Palestine between the wars. Old

13

soldiers knew which side their bread was buttered. They knew what was good for them.

And what was *not* good for them.

And what was not good for Charley Scully at this particular moment in time, with Germans all round him and the allied beachhead line in Normandy temporarily pushed back, was a young French boy in a suit that was too small for him, his overcoat tied over his back like a soldier's blanket, grinning all over his silly face and announcing to the world in general that a British soldier was hiding in the ditch.

'Push off,' Scully said. He had dropped off to sleep despite the din going on all round him. He had even been dreaming of some of the women he'd known: Daisy, for instance, who lived in Durham and had had a husband who was a sailor and never home, but when he had been home had obviously given Daisy a few tips on how to behave in bed; Doris, who was a middle-aged party like Charley Scully himself but had a nice line in cooking; and Edna, who was a corporal in the ATS, worked in the bedding stores at Bossington Camp and could always be relied on to do overtime with the store locked and the lights out. Now Daisy, Doris and Edna had all vanished into the blue and he was staring into the phizz of some half-baked Frog kid who was announcing to the whole bloody Wehrmacht that Charles Walter Scully, Sergeant, DCM, North Staffordshire Fusileers, was there in the ditch trying to fulfil his ambition to survive the war without being killed, wounded or captured.

'Push off,' he said again.

The boy didn't seem to understand. His smile grew wider and he edged closer to where Scully crouched under the brambles.

'I am Ludovic,' he said – to Scully's surprise in English.

'Pleased to meet you, I'm sure,' Scully growled.

'Who are you, sir? You are hiding, I think.' The boy smiled nervously. 'I am also, sir.'

Scully glared. 'Why don't you go home to your mum?' he asked.

The boy pulled a face and his shoulders worked in a vast

14

shrug. 'I wish to, sir,' he pointed out. 'But it is very difficult. My mother brought me to Normandy to stay with my Aunt Madeleine because rationing is very difficult where I come from and it was thought I could be well fed for a while and even take some food home with me. Unfortunately, the invasion has come and it is now impossible.'

'Why?'

'Because my home is in Paris. I was staying with my Aunt Madeleine, who lives in Mésnil-Brouay. Her husband is my Uncle André who is a prisoner in Germany. She had to go to Royan because Uncle André's mother's house was bombed and she was hurt. She left me in Sainte-Honorine-du-Bosq with the mother of Didier Danoy, who is my friend when I am in Normandy. But Didier and his mother were hurt, too, when the invasion started and I was left on my own. I decided to go home. Maman will be worrying.'

Not half so much as Charley Scully, the sergeant thought. Especially if he didn't get away from here before the Germans found him. The allied advance, so certain at first, seemed to have ground to a stop here near Caen and he couldn't see himself living off berries and ditchwater for very long. A pity, he thought, that he couldn't have stayed at Bossington. But for the invasion he'd still have been there, with Edna in the stores. It had been dead jammy, that had. A nice mattress on the floor, with officers' sheets and blankets and a cup of tea in the morning, made on the stores officer's personal stove.

He became aware of the boy still studying him.

'Look,' he said again. 'Why don't you push off!'

'Push off?' He realized the boy had not understood him and tried some of the French he'd learned during the First War. 'Allez. Go on. Hop it.'

'Hop it?'

'Oh, Christ! Look – ' Scully tried to be as explicit as possible, speaking slowly and with great care ' – *ici*, Germans. *Pour vous*, no good.'

The boy grinned and nodded fiercely. 'Oh, yes,' he said.

'This place is good. From here, I will go south and try to get aboard a train for Paris.'

Scully stared at the boy, suddenly aware that if Charley Scully didn't know where he was going, at least the boy did. 'You know the way to Paris?' he asked.

'Of course, sir. I am thirteen. I know where the Germans are, and how to dodge them.'

'To get to Paris?'

'Of course. Then I shall go home to my mother. She is very beautiful.'

No one could have called Charley Scully a slouch. Old soldiers never were. He had joined the North Staffs Fusileers at the age of fifteen, fought through the Battle of Amiens in 1918, then, his age discovered, had been returned to England and told to go home to his mum. Since he was an orphan, he had begged to be allowed to stay in uniform and in the end they'd accepted him as a band boy.

Though his period of active service had been short and sweet, the one thing it had taught him was to grab opportunities as they came because they didn't come twice. As an instrumentalist he'd been a dead loss and had soon been returned to ordinary service with the rest of the battalion, but at least he was in and, come hell or high water, short of disgracing himself and the regiment, they wouldn't throw him out again. Grabbing your opportunities was a tried and trusted precept that, to his knowledge, had only gone wrong once – when he'd married Marjory Birchall. Having let him work his will on her in the woods near Farnham in 1923, she'd told him he'd done her wrong and would have to marry her. He'd been young and soppy enough to believe her.

The colonel had torn him off a strip, telling him he was too good a soldier to get himself tied up to a woman and offering to get him exchanged into a regiment that was due to go abroad. Feeling upright and honourable, Scully had declined the offer. Unfortunately, as the colonel had suspected, it hadn't worked out and when the Fusileers had gone to India she'd disappeared with the Jack Dusty from HMS *Warspite*, which, of course, was why he'd always taken a particular pleasure in rogering Daisy, whose husband was in *Prince of Wales*.

He thought for a moment. Never miss your chances, boy, as the bishop said to the actress as he got her up against a shop door in the blackout.

'What's it like in Paris?' he asked.

The boy smiled. 'It is very nice, sir,' he said. 'But just now there is not much to eat.'

'And this mum of yours?'

'She is very beautiful, sir.'

Scully did a little mental arithmetic. The boy was thirteen, which placed Mum in her early thirties. He was prepared to accept that the boy's insistence on her beauty was probably due to filial fidelity rather than strict truth, but it sounded interesting all the same, especially if Dad was away in the army or, better still, in England or North Africa with the Free French. No, Paris didn't sound at all bad. At least he'd be able to disappear into the walls there. Here, among the Germans, he stuck out like a sore thumb.

It might even be interesting. He could help train the Resistance fighters, because what he'd seen of them so far indicated that they weren't much to write home about. He might win another gong. Maybe when he got back to the regiment he could get himself made company sergeant-major. Maybe – if he lived long enough – regimental sergeant-major, so that the officers had to call him 'Mister Scully'. It was the peak of Scully's ambition.

'Give it us again,' he said.

'Give it us again?'

'Tell me again: how're you goin' to get to Paris?'

The boy indicated the ditch. 'I shall walk along this ditch, sir. It goes a long way and the brambles hang over it all the time. I have been along it before with my friend, Didier Danoy. Near Veltru, there is a tunnel – '

'Railway tunnel?'

'Yes, sir. It is quite long. It goes under the hill. At the other end there are fields and at Mésnil-Brouay, which is the next village, I have a bicycle. That is where my Aunt Madeleine lives.'

Scully looked at the boy. He was tall, at the age when he was all length and no breadth, a long streak of whitewash such as Scully had been when he'd first put on uniform.

'And then?'

'And then I shall cycle to Alençon. I shall get rid of the bicycle there and find a train to Paris.'

'That'll not get you far,' Scully said. 'The RAF and the Yanks are bombing everything that moves. Even some things that don't move,' he added, remembering a bunch of misdirected rockets that a few days before had chased him into a ditch near Tarpiquet.

The boy smiled. 'I shall go via Le Mans or Tours,' he said. 'The trains are running into Paris from the south.'

Scully thought once more of Mum. Women were something you never got cured of. Scully had been cured half a dozen times but he was always ready to be bowled over again. And very probably so was Mum, too. Even if he wasn't Tyrone Power, Scully wasn't all that bad to look at.

He was a squarely built man, his years of service showing in every line of him. In 1939 he'd been thinking of buying himself out and he'd often wondered what he'd have done if he had. Probably nothing. *Cetera Desunt.* That was what the regimental motto announced. The rest are wanting. It meant really that the rest of the army were wanting in the courage the Fusiliers could show, but the Fusiliers liked to translate it more freely. 'Them that are out ain't got nothing.' Or as Lieutenant-Colonel Vaughan, who'd as near as dammit brought Scully up and taught him how to behave as a man, liked to say, 'The regiment's your home, son. Remember it, because when you leave it you'll find you miss it.'

Scully studied the boy again. Going to Paris was becoming a right old possibility, he decided. With the Germans between him and what was left of his company, he hadn't much option anyway.

It would be a bit different from the army, mind, and he'd never known any other life. But he was fit and strong, and, at forty-one years old, in his prime. Brown of skin, his face was deeply lined by the sun of India and Palestine. His nose was a bit bolo because he'd boxed for the regiment in his day, but it was still a good nose, and his head was a mass of dark curls. He'd often thought his father must have been a good-looking bloke to produce the feller Charley Scully was used to seeing in the mirror in the morning.

The boy was still waiting as he turned over his options.

'Suppose this bicycle – ?' Scully began.

'Sir?'

'Suppose *I* rode this bicycle of yours, and you rode on the crossbar.'

'*La barre de traverse*? Exactly, sir. That is a good idea.'

'You could show me where to go.'

'Of course.'

'I could maybe hide till my friends arrive.'

'But of course. Monsieur Virec, who has the apartment below ours, has often had escapers staying with him. RAF fliers. Sometimes Americans. They sleep in his spare bedroom which is empty and sometimes visit maman.'

'Uncles?' Scully knew the term. He'd been 'uncle' to more than one child who'd needed an explanation for the soldier staying in the house.

The boy didn't understand what he meant so he let it go.

'Right, flower,' he said. 'I think you're on. First,' he added, 'we'd better get to know each other. I'm Charley Scully.'

The boy shook hands solemnly. 'I am called Ludovic Connaire. At home I am called Ludovic. Sometimes Ludo and sometimes Lulu.'

'That's nice,' Scully said. But he had an eye for the future, and he could hardly go on addressing the beautiful thirty-year-old who was the mother of this kid, as 'Ludo's Mum'. 'How are you, Ludo's Mum?' 'It's a nice day, Ludo's Mum.'

After all, the kid wasn't bad looking, with nice long legs and a straight nose and large dark eyes. If she was anything like her son, she'd be worth knowing as more than just 'Ludo's Mum'.

'What's your mum's name?'

'Sidonie.'

'That's a nice name, Sidonie Connaire.' Scully nodded approvingly. 'Yes, that's all right.'

The boy gave a gurgle of laughter. 'Oh, no, sir. Not Connaire. You have got it wrong. That is my baptized name. My surname is McCosh.'

2

There was a long silence.

'McWhat?' Scully asked.

'McCosh,' the boy said.

'McCosh?'

'Yes, sir.'

Scully stared. What in Christ's name had he picked up here? Mc-bloody-Cosh. The boy even pronounced it like a Scot.

'McCosh?' he said. 'Scotch McCosh? Like McNab and McGregor? That sort of McCosh?'

'Yes, sir.'

Scully frowned. It was like the time when he and Chalky White, one of his sidekicks, had gone out with two sisters from Poona when they'd been in India. They were as Indian as Gandhi himself but they'd said their names were Siobhan and Shelagh O'Hara. And they *had* been, too. Their father was one of the many Irishmen who worked on the Indian railways and the girls had been two of the hundreds of Eurasians they'd produced after taking Indian wives.

All the same, France was a bit different. They didn't go in for that sort of thing here. 'You're having me on,' he said.

The boy looked puzzled. 'Having you on, sir?'

'Pulling my leg. Kidding me.' Scully struggled to find the word he wanted and remembered the French girl in 1940 who'd been in the habit of exploding into rage when he'd suggested she ate frogs' legs. '*Tourmenter*. French kids don't get called Ludo McCosh.'

'I am not French, sir.'

'You're not?'

'No, sir. I am Scotch. My name is Ludovic Connaire McCosh. Connaire is a Scottish name. My father told me.'

'You don't *sound* Scotch.'

'That is because my mother is French, sir.'

Then Scully understood why the boy's English sounded old-fashioned and stilted. His next question was wary. 'Are there other English people in Paris?' he asked.

'Oh, yes, sir! A few stayed behind when the Germans came. They are not all *truly* English, of course. Madame Rohan is French like my mother, and Monsieur Cléry-Kidder was French. But they all speak English and we think of them as English.'

Scully stared at the boy, his thoughts busy. 'Ludovic Connaire McCosh.' He grinned. 'Well I'm buggered.'

The boy gave a little laugh. 'My father was chief of a great clan. He was at the university, sir.'

'Student?'

'Oh, no, sir. But he had lived in France all his life. His father was a publisher. He printed books in France and sent them to England.'

'What sort of books?' Scully had read a few imported French books and knew what they were like.

'Religious books, sir. *His* father was minister of the Presbyterian Church in Paris.'

Scully eyed the boy speculatively. The little bastard was probably illegitimate, he decided. Some by-blow from a good night out in Paris. Scully knew all about illegitimacy springing from good nights out. His own father had been a gypsy hawker selling clothes pegs in a Staffordshire village.

But illegitimacy surely didn't explain his name! His mother would never have chosen McCosh. Not when she had ten million others to choose from. It *had* to be genuine and she *had* to be proud of it.

'Where's your dad now?' he asked.

'He is dead, sir. He was killed at Amiens in 1940.'

'What regiment was he in?' Regimental ties were sometimes strong – even with mums.

'The 119th.'

'There ain't no 119th in the British army,' Scully said at once. 'The 109th, what had the biggest number, was disbanded in 1922. You don't mean the 19th, the Green Howards, do you?'

'He wasn't in the British army, sir,' the boy explained. 'He was in the *French* army. He had lived all his life in France, sir, and he decided he was French and must serve as a Frenchman. My mother told me.'

It sounded bloody complicated to Scully, but curiously it also sounded genuine. Either way, the poor bastard wasn't around any more and Mum was on her own. It seemed to be time to get on with things.

'Look,' he said. 'This train to Paris: You got a ticket?'

'Only from Caen, sir. But it is impossible to board it in Caen at the moment.'

'You're telling me,' Scully said.

Caen was the key to the break-out from the beachhead and while the allies were busting a gut to capture it, the Germans were busting a gut to stop them. The place had already been smashed to rubble by the bombers and he couldn't quite see the station being the place for a leisurely change of trains.

Scully considered. He'd been trying for four days to get back to his own lines and he was growing hungrier and dirtier by the hour. They had been on the edge of a forest surrounded by burning trees when nebelwerfer fire had caught them and, as the howling and wailing of the electrically ignited mortars had filled the sky, there had been time for one brief ejaculation then a series of shattering explosions all round that had sent them diving for shelter like frightened rats. As silence came again, the German machine-guns had opened and Scully had leapt for the ditch. He had had to stay there as the panzers moved past. That evening, for safety, he'd edged further south towards Evrécy because it had seemed that half the bloody German army was between him and the British lines. Then the place had filled with SS troops who had cut off his route again, forcing him closer to the river Orne, and as he'd made another try at dusk he had found the woods around were still so full of men it had seemed wiser to move even further south.

His mind was moving swiftly, a typical old soldier's mind, working out his means of retreat, thinking of everything, even sorting out his excuses for the questions that would be asked when he returned. He didn't for a minute feel he was dodging the battle by going to Paris. He just didn't see much alternative. The more he thought about it, the more sense it made.

At least, it would take him away from this bloody place where the Germans were so thick on the ground you couldn't move without falling over a Tiger tank.

'There's just one thing, flower,' he said to the boy. 'What happens when we get to Paris? I'll have to eat. You got ration cards in France?'

The boy smiled. 'Oh, yes, sir. But it will be all right, sir. Anything you want will be taken care of. The British Réseau will know what to do with you.'

'What's the British Réseau?'

'It's a cell, sir. Part of the Resistance. It is called the British Réseau because everybody in it speaks English.'

'*They're* British as well?'

'Yes, sir. Well, they are not *all* British. One is Russian, one is half Belgian, one is half American. It is like that, you see. But everybody speaks good English.'

'And what about this train ride? How're you goin' to get aboard if your ticket's from Caen? You got any money?'

'Unfortunately, no, sir. I thought I might slip aboard when nobody was looking.'

Scully made up his mind. You couldn't find better conditions than he was being offered: English-speaking Resistance armed to the teeth, and a mum who was dark-eyed, long-legged and beautiful.

'I think, kid,' he said, 'that we can sort that one out. What you say sounds a good idea. I'll come with you and pay for your ticket.'

The boy grabbed Scully's hand and kissed it. 'Thank you, sir! Oh, thank you very much!'

'And stop calling me "sir".'

Scully became brisk. Removing the short bayonet, he slipped it into the scabbard which he stuck in his belt and thrust his rifle among the brambles. Then, taking off his helmet, equipment, gaiters and battledress blouse, he tossed them after it.

'How's that look?' he asked.

The boy clapped his hands in a curiously un-English way and Scully spat on his palms as he'd spat on them at the beginning of every job he'd ever done, whether it was a day's work, a session at the butts, or even picking up a girl. It was less an indication of heavy work than a symbol of something being about to happen.

'Right,' he said. 'Let's go.'

3

What the boy had said about the ditch was right. It followed the road for what seemed miles, hidden all the time from the passing traffic by the undergrowth.

Behind them, they could hear the racket of battle, the thump of heavy guns, the clatter of machine-guns and the sporadic bursts of musketry. Towards Caen the sky was filled with a towering column of brown smoke that lifted to a height of 500 feet before the top drifted away eastwards in the light wind. The weather was warm and they could hear bees among the flowers. They could also hear flies – thousands of them – moving among the cattle that lay dead in the fields, their bellies swollen so that their legs were lifted into the air like stakes.

Eventually, the ditch with its bramble cover came to an end.

'This is where it stops, sir,' the boy said. 'We go across a field here and through the railway tunnel.'

Scully nodded. 'Okay, flower. Lead on.'

Slipping from the ditch, they crossed a road into a clump of trees. They could hear aircraft overhead somewhere and Scully was wary. But there wasn't a German uniform in sight.

Ahead he could see the black hole of the tunnel and they were just about to leave the shelter of the trees when they saw a German sentry appear. He looked about nineteen, thin and spindly, his helmet like an ugly mushroom on the lean stalk of his neck. He lit a cigarette as he looked about him, obviously a little nervous at being on his own.

'Stay here,' Scully said, pressing the boy down in the undergrowth.

It had always been Scully's boast that he had never gone hungry. He knew how to rob hen roosts and find eggs without disturbing anyone, and now he appeared behind the sentry before the German knew he was there. He was fortunate in that the boy chose that moment to take off his helmet to wipe the sweat from his forehead and Scully hit him hard at the back of the neck with the edge of his hand.

The German dropped at once and Scully bent over him, going through his pockets in search of cigarettes. What he found were German but they were better than nothing and Scully was growing desperate for a smoke. He also found a wallet in the boy's breast pocket that contained a fat bundle of French notes. Stuffing it away, he tossed the wallet into the grass. He was just dragging the body into the undergrowth when he realized Ludo was helping him.

'Git away!' he snarled. 'Them Germans find you, they'll shoot you.'

The boy ignored him and together they pulled the corpse into the bushes and covered it with branches.

'Sir?' The boy looked at Scully. 'Is he dead?'

'Yes.'

'What did you do?'

'I hit him.'

'What with?'

Scully gestured, his hand moving in a half-hearted way because he was vaguely embarrassed to be demonstrating to a mere boy how to kill men.

The boy watched him gravely, his own hand moving in a similar gesture. 'That was very clever, sir,' he said gravely. 'You will teach me how to do that, perhaps?'

'For Christ's sake, why?'

'So I can kill a German too.'

'What do you want to go killing Germans for?'

'They killed my father.'

Oh, Christ, Scully thought, now he was caught up in a sodding blood-feud.

'You leave killing Germans to them what knows how,' he said briskly. 'Come on, let's get through this tunnel.'

They moved quickly through the darkness, walking between the railway lines. It was only when they saw the light at the other end that it dawned on Scully that if there were a sentry at one end, there would probably be one at the other end too.

'You stay here,' he said, pushing the boy into a recess in the brick wall.

The boy stayed in the shadows as Scully moved forward, his bayonet at the ready. As he had thought, there *was* another German, an older man this time, stout and heavy, and smoking a curved yellow pipe. He was sitting on a low white-painted rail, facing the sunshine, his rifle slung, three or four yards from the tunnel opening, staring down the embankment towards a stream as if he were wondering whether there were fish in it.

Scully was on him before he could turn round. He gave a strangled cry as he leapt to his feet, then Scully's bayonet went into his back and he toppled over the low rail and rolled down the bank towards the stream, his body coming to rest by a willow tree.

Scully went through his pockets without a qualm; this time the haul included a packet of French cigarettes, a pouch of tobacco and a wallet with notes, several of them of high denomination. Wondering if the German were an old soldier like himself, working a racket with the French, Scully stuffed the money in his pocket, freed the body from the willow to allow it to roll into the stream, and bent over to wash the blood from his hand.

The boy had crept to the entrance of the tunnel as he reappeared by the railway line.

'Where is the German?' he asked.

Somehow it went against Scully's principles to kill Germans in front of children and he shrugged.

'Wasn't one,' he said, and set off walking at once along the track.

The boy caught him up. 'I heard someone shout.'

'That was me. Fell over that bleedin' rail.'

'Bleedin' rail?'

Scully sighed. He'd have to watch his language, he decided, or he'd have half of the kids in France using English swearwords.

'Wooden thing,' he said. 'Low down. Nearly went in the ditch.'

As they set off across the fields, the boy pointed to a cluster of houses.

'That is Mésnil-le-Petit,' he said. 'Mésnil-Brouay is further on.'

'What about this aunt of yours? Won't she wonder where you are?'

'She will think I am with Didier. And she can't come back, anyway, because the Germans have forbidden all travel round here. My bicycle is still at my aunt's. We went over to Didier's on the bus because I had a suitcase.'

Scully stared about him across the high-hedged, wooded countryside bright in the afternoon sun. 'How far is it to this Mésnil place?' he asked.

'About twenty-five kilomètres.'

Scully nodded. 'We'd better get cracking,' he said.

Towards evening they passed an orchard. There were a few small apples on the trees and Scully eyed them greedily.

'Strikes me,' he said, 'that the first thing we got to do is get hold of some grub.'

'Grub?'

'*Manger*. Food. Then some clothes for me. Perhaps we'll find something on a scarecrow.' The boy looked puzzled and Scully stretched out his arms and tried to explain.

'Oh, no, sir,' the boy said, smiling. '*Epouvantails* don't have clothes on them any more. It is very difficult to obtain clothes in France and old clothes which were put out to frighten the birds in 1940 had all been brought back into the houses by 1942.'

They had moved well back from the fighting by this time, though a few overs continued to drop behind them, and it was as they were debating what to do next that Scully spotted a figure outside a cottage across a field.

29

'I can see an old man there,' he said. 'He's wearing a cap and a jacket. Perhaps I can get hold of 'em after dark.'

'It would be better if I did it, sir. If there are Germans about they will not suspect me. They will just – paf! – ' the boy gave himself a cuff at the side of the head and grinned – 'and tell me to be off. No?'

'You're probably right.' Scully eyed the boy. 'You've got it where you need it, kid.'

'Sir?'

Scully touched his temple. 'Up top, flower. Up here.'

The sun had almost disappeared now and the column of smoke in the distance was showing golden tints on the underside of the coils. The noise of battle seemed to have slackened off, as if the two armies had withdrawn to get their breath back ready for the next day. The night would be full of black-faced patrols creeping about between the armies, probing for openings for the morning, while the men who'd been involved during the day would curl up exhausted in their foxholes, wishing they had the strength to write to their girlfriends or their wives or mothers to let them know they were still alive.

'I think, sir, that I will go now.'

'I'll come with you.' Scully was uneasy at the kid moving off on his own, though he had to admit the little bastard seemed to know how many beans made five. He seemed untiring and able to carry on without resting; considering he was all length and no width, it was surprising.

They crept along the side of the field towards the cottage. From the hedge bottom, they saw the old man light his pipe and stare towards the west where the fighting was, his head cocked. After a while he took off his jacket and cap and started chopping wood. They could hear the whacks as he brought the axe down and could see the white logs split apart.

He seemed tireless and prepared to go on even while it was growing dark. Then, when Scully was just beginning to wonder if he couldn't go forward and try a bit of bargaining, a woman came to the door of the house and called, and the old man put down the axe and moved towards her.

'*Ah!*' Before Scully realized what had happened, Ludo had slithered away along the hedge towards the cottage.

For a long time Scully waited in the growing darkness. A dog started barking furiously, and the old man's voice from the house told it to be quiet. It was still barking when Scully became aware of the boy alongside him once more.

'*Une casquette,*' he said. 'A cap. Also a jacket.'

The jacket was too small for Scully's strong frame but, though it showed a great deal of wrist beyond the sleeves, he managed to squeeze into it.

'It'll do,' he said, 'till we get something else.'

The cap was too big. It hid Scully's eyes and Scully pretended to be blind. Ludo started to laugh. His giggles were high-pitched and Scully grabbed him to shut him up. The boy grabbed him back and they rocked back and forth under the hedge, laughing.

The laughter did them good and restored Scully's confidence a little.

'Right, kid,' he said. 'Perhaps we'd better get away from this place before we're spotted.'

They crept back along the hedge towards the road. It was almost dark now and they began to walk down the centre of the uneven tarmacadam.

'It is better this way, sir,' the boy said. 'The Germans use the verges for ammunition dumps and sometimes at each end they place land mines. Against the Resistance, you understand?'

Scully nodded and the boy chuckled. 'It makes no difference. The Resistance come across the field, and do *pipi* into the petrol tanks.'

He pretended to urinate and Scully grinned.

They passed through a village. It was dark and silent and, apart from the inevitable barking dog, it might have been dead. Striding along, it never occurred to Scully that he might be overtaxing the boy and it was only when he noticed him weaving about on the road that it dawned on him he was exhausted.

He stopped. 'You tired?'

'No, sir. Not at all.'

31

'Come off it.'

'Come off it, sir?'

'Tell the truth. You're tired.'

'I say, look here – !'

'Admit it.'

The boy nodded. 'Yes, sir. I am tired. Perhaps it is because I'm hungry.'

'Git on my back.'

The boy didn't argue and, grasping him round the knees, Scully started marching forward again. It seemed to be time to find somewhere to sleep.

'Look, kid,' he said. 'Suppose we stop at a house and ask 'em to give us a bed? Tell 'em who we are.'

'I think that will be a bad thing, sir.' The boy's voice was slurred with weariness. 'There is much suspicion. There has been for a long time. The Germans have been sending out their agents to do this in the hope of catching people who help escaped fliers – '

The boy's voice trailed off and as he went limp on Scully's back he realized he had fallen asleep.

Some time later, when his own legs were stiff with tiredness, he found a haystack. It was only partly built but there was a heap of hay alongside it, and he lowered the boy down on to it. Taking off the old jacket, he stretched it over him, then leaned back and began to doze.

He was awake as soon as it was light. The boy was still curled under the jacket and Scully looked down at him.

He was a good-looking kid, he decided, and he wondered what his own son would have been like if he'd ever had one, if Marjory hadn't turned out to be such a tart when they'd sent him to India. He sighed. He was a simple man with more understanding than he realized. It couldn't have been easy for her. It was never easy for a woman with her man at the other end of the world, trying to live in England on the few bob they gave them as marriage allowances in those days. The government at that time had been composed of a lot of striped-trousered shits and that was the truth. There was unemployment all over the country and when the Depression had struck they'd even cut the pay of soldiers, sailors and airmen who were already living close to the poverty line. It was no wonder the navy had mutinied. It was a wonder the whole bloody lot of 'em hadn't fixed bayonets and marched down Whitehall to the Houses of Parliament and chased the buggers over the wall into the Thames.

He tried to forget Marjory and think instead of Edna. But thoughts of Edna reminded him that not long before at this time of the morning he'd been in bed in the stores drinking tea – stores officers' tea – and eating biscuits – ATS officers' biscuits – before getting up and marching off to the sergeants' mess for breakfast, leaving Edna to make the bed. Her farewell when he'd left to go to France had been tearful enough to be moving. 'I'll be waiting,' she'd said and he believed she would be.

The boy stirred and sat up, rubbing his eyes. He looked round, bewildered, then saw Scully and smiled.

'Did you sleep well, sir?'

'Catnapped.'

'Catnapped?'

'Napped. Like a pussy. On and off. Here and there. Now and then. It's enough for me.'

The boy nodded slowly, savouring the English phrases he'd never heard before. 'I understand, sir. Catnapped. Like a cat. Of course.'

'Reckon we'll have to get some *manger* soon,' Scully announced. 'I'm hungry. How about you?'

'Yes, sir.'

'I got a bit of cash. They gave us Frog money when we came over on D-Day. In case we needed it, see. No looting. That sort of thing. We can buy a loaf.'

'It is very difficult, sir.'

'Even bread?'

'Even bread, sir.'

'In that case, we'll have to pinch some.'

It was easier than they'd expected. In the next village, a van had pulled up. It was driven by a great bag of gas on the roof, like a balloon, and was collecting bread from a bakery. The smell made Scully's mouth water.

As they drew near, the van driver went into the shop and they saw him leaning over the counter, with his back to the street, talking to the baker's wife, so that it was the easiest thing in the world as they walked past for Scully to slide one of the long loaves from the back of the van and stuff it down his shirt without even halting his stride.

There was no indication that they'd been seen, and at the other end of the village, they found a stream and sat down alongside it, out of sight under the trees, to eat. The stream looked stagnant and none too clean, but they chanced it and drank a little.

'Not much,' Scully warned. 'Gives you the trots.'

'The trots?'

'Gyppy tummy. Bowels.' Scully held his stomach and groaned and the boy laughed.

Kneeling by the stream, they washed their faces and even found an old newspaper in the bushes with which to pack the inside of the vast cap Scully wore. The sun was just growing warm and from the fields the cows mooed a soft welcome.

They were still there when the German convoy appeared in the distance.

'Quick,' Scully said. 'Down the bank!'

As the lorries drew nearer, he decided they weren't sufficiently hidden and indicated the water among the reeds.

'Git in,' he said.

The boy gave him an alarmed look. 'But my clothes!' He was clearly distressed. 'My mother will be angry.'

'Bugger your clothes!' Scully leapt into the water and dragged the boy after him, crouching with him in the green slime among the long grass and overhanging willows as the German convoy roared past, filling the air with dust. They were just about to climb out of the ditch when they heard another convoy approaching.

Scully's eyes flickered about him. A few yards further along, the stream disappeared under the road by a culvert.

'In here!'

Dragging the boy after him, he pushed into the darkness just as the second convoy arrived.

The culvert had been built with a turn in it and the water descended to the lower ground at the other side of the road in a series of little waterfalls. It was stagnant, black and foul-smelling, its surface alive with small moving creatures and spidery insects like water-boatmen. The slime on the surface was covered with worms and leeches, and underfoot they could feel all the broken glass, tins and rubbish thrown there by generations of farm labourers who had sat on the bank to eat their sandwiches and drink their wine.

As they waited, the convoy came to a stop and there were shouts and splashes as men jumped into the stream. They were just wondering what was happening when they heard the howl of aeroplane engines and Scully realized that Typhoons had appeared.

There was a series of shrieks and the crash of explosions. The air was filled with smoke and the smell of cordite, and even in the culvert the air seemed to be sucked out then blown back. Seeing the boy blinking at each new blast, Scully grabbed him and pulled him close.

The attack seemed to go on for hours, though Scully knew it could only have been minutes. As the engines died away, the shouts started again and there was splashing in the stream as the Germans began to climb out. There was the noise of vehicles starting up and they realized the convoy was moving on. As it did so, there was a sound in the entrance to the culvert and Scully saw a German soldier silhouetted against the light. He had thrown away his pack and rifle and was clearly intending to desert. He was only a boy and in the faint light Scully could see the fear in his eyes and the tears on his cheeks. He was alongside Scully before he saw him and, for a moment, he clearly thought Scully was a Frenchman sheltering from the battle. He smiled nervously; then Scully reached out for him and the grin died in a look of sheer terror. Thrusting him under the water, aware of boots kicking at his legs, Scully gripped the squirming youth tightly, watched by the horrified Ludo.

As the body finally became still, Scully dragged it up, streaming slimy water, and felt automatically in the pockets for cigarettes and money.

'I think we'd better be on our way, kid,' he said gruffly.

The boy had a shocked look on his face as they appeared in the sunshine at the other side of the road. 'He is dead,' he said.

'Him or us, kid,' Scully said. It was a lie, he knew. The German boy had been unarmed and as anxious as they were to escape, but Scully's reaction had been automatic. They'd been teaching him for five years to kill Germans and you couldn't change overnight.

'Had to do it, see,' he explained.

Climbing out of the ditch, they saw limbers, guns and bodies scattered about the roadway. An armoured personnel carrier lay nose down in the stream, and for about half a mile up the slope there were smoking vehicles and carts. Dead horses, their carcasses covered with the dust that was drifting down, lay in the shafts, among them the still shapes of men. The cows had bolted to the far end of the field and were still galloping nervously about, their tails in the air. Only one of them was still near the stream, her back broken by a stray splinter, her head up, her mouth open to emit hoarse grating sounds of pain.

'She's hurt, sir.'

'I know.' Scully began to pull the boy away. 'Nothing we can do.'

'We should put her out of her misery.'

'Ain't got a gun, have I?'

'Perhaps one of the dead soldiers has one.'

The boy's face was grey and sick-looking but Scully refused to allow him to remain still.

'Come on,' he said. 'We start shooting, they'll find us, won't they? It's lousy, but there you are; there's a war on. It didn't bother you much killing them Germans, did it?'

Uncertainly, the boy allowed himself to be drawn away and for a while they walked in silence, the boy still occasionally looking back to where the cow dragged its rear limbs agonizedly across the grass.

Mésnil-Brouay was nothing more than a straggling line of low houses built in Norman style with beams set into the plaster. More dead cattle lay in the fields and in one farmyard eighteen cows were lumped together, caught by splinters. A pig was rooting among them, untouched, but the walls were spattered with blotches of what looked like mud and feathers, and Scully realized they were chickens caught by the blast.

A few bewildered French people were just reappearing from the woods to claim their possessions as the boy led him to a house at the end of the street, rather larger than the rest. The windows had all been blown in and one of the walls had collapsed.

'My bicycle!'

In sudden alarm, the boy ran outside and Scully began to hunt through the ground floor of the house. From a photograph on the mantelshelf, an attractive girl with dark eyes and hair stared at him. Alongside it were a pair of thick spectacles with a wire frame, the nosepiece bound round with sticking plaster.

The boy appeared in the doorway, his eyes full of tears.

'My bicycle is broken,' he said.

A shed had collapsed in the bombing and the rear wheel of the boy's machine had been twisted by a falling beam. There was another bicycle among the rubble and Scully yanked it clear. It was old and rusting and lacked a front wheel.

'Who's is this?'

'It was my grandfather's. He died last year.' The boy eyed his own bicycle, his face twisted with grief. 'It had a three-speed gear, too.'

'Stop piping your eye, kid,' Scully said. 'How about we take the wheel out of your bike and stick it in this one? It'll look a bit bolo but it'll go.'

While Scully found a spanner and was wrestling the wheel loose, the boy went into the house. He returned with the pair of old spectacles and the photograph from the mantelshelf.

'Who's that?'

'That is my mother.'

Not bad either, Scully thought. Not bad at all.

'And the specs?'

'Specs?'

'Glasses. Them things.'

'*Les lunettes*? They were my grandfather's. My aunt kept them as a souvenir. I think my mother will like to have them. He was her father.'

They fixed the wheel into the bigger bicycle. It looked odd but it seemed to work and, as Scully was trying it out, the boy disappeared down the road to try to buy some food. While he was away, Scully poked about in the wardrobes and found an old grey jacket and a pair of striped trousers which had obviously belonged to the boy's grandfather. He put them on, deciding he looked more French now than the French.

The boy returned with half a loaf and two slices of ham. 'They thought I looked hungry,' he said. 'They gave them to me.'

'Right.' Scully straddled the bicycle and indicated the crossbar. 'Get on.'

The boy eyed it dubiously.

'Better find something to put over it, or you'll get a sore bum.'

'Bum?'

'Behind. *Derrière*.'

'*Derrière*. Bum. Ah.'

The boy vanished into the house and reappeared with a cushion which he tied to the crossbar with a length of string.

'Fine,' Scully said.

Glancing down the street, he saw they were being studied by a group of men and women and, as he watched, they began to walk towards him. He wasn't sure what they intended but he decided it was safer away from the place.

'Get on,' he said sharply. 'It's time we was off.'

4

The countryside was reasonably flat as they headed south. The rear wheel clattered every time it turned, while the brakes were useless, but they cycled all morning, Scully pushing at the pedals as they moved along the long straight roads and allowing the machine to rattle its way down the hills under its own momentum. Going up the hills, he turned it over to Ludo to push while he walked alongside, recovering his breath. He felt amazingly sure of himself now with money in his pockets and a few cigarettes. The boy seemed happy, too. He had got over his shock and was chattering away all the time.

'You are in the infantry, sir, I think,' he said. 'Have you been in a long time?'

'Ever since Pontius was a pilot,' Scully said. 'The kids what came in when the war started used to ask me where I kept me bow and arrow.'

'Did you like it?'

Scully considered. 'Reckon I did,' he admitted. 'In them days, o' course, it was different. It was hard. Everything had to be shone up, see. They were red hot on shining up in our mob. Join the navy and see the world. Join the army and polish it. You couldn't put your hands in your pockets in them days. You couldn't smoke fags in the street. You couldn't go chasing girls. Not that a girl would have looked at you with the haircuts they gave you, anyway. They rushed at you from the back with a pair of clippers and went straight over the top of your head to the front. Some fellers wept. Buckets. Looked like they'd been scalped. After all, you've got to have enough hair left to comb.'

The boy was laughing at Scully's boisterous description. 'Were you in the Guards, sir? I have heard of the Guards.'

'Guards!' Scully's disgust was unbounded. 'Guards! The Guards is all right – not bad at all – but compared with our lot they're just a bunch of boy scouts. North Staffs Fusileers – spelt with two 'e's – that's me. *Cetera Desunt*. That's our motto. The others are wanting. Means that we're the best. 'Eld the right of the line at Waterloo, didn't we? You know about Waterloo? When we gave the Frogs a pasting.'

The boy's face went taut. 'I think Napoleon was ill this day,' he said stiffly.

From the way he spoke, it was obvious that, despite his claims to be British, he also considered himself French, and Scully changed step quickly.

'Well,' he said, 'the French was on our side in the Crimea a few years later, wasn't they? You'll have heard of the Crimea. Alma and Inkerman and that.'

'There is a Pont de l'Alma in Paris.'

'There was an Alma Road where I was brought up,' Scully said. One end had been occupied by the workhouse and the other, where it joined Sebastopol Street, by the orphanage where Scully had spent his childhood.

The boy was smiling now, his face proud. 'The French won the Crimée, I think.'

'They did *what*?' Scully's education had been sketchy but his knowledge of military history had been acquired through twenty-six years in the army. He knew exactly which regiments had run away and when, and which regiments had stood fast. And he also knew exactly which victories were British victories because he'd seen them on the colours and on the war memorials and regimental rolls of honour. '*We* won the bleedin' Crimea,' he said sharply.

The boy's face became stubborn. 'At school in France,' he said firmly, 'we are taught that the *French* won it.'

'You'll be telling me next they won Waterloo.'

The boy's mixed ancestry was giving him trouble. Through the years when he'd been growing up in France, he'd considered himself French and had shared his friends' pride in what he'd been taught were French victories. Since the war and France's defeat and Britain's solitary defiance of Hitler, however, he had begun to prefer to think of himself as British, and now he found it confusing.

'They *almost* won,' he said slowly. 'Perhaps the English did not play as fair that day as they usually do.'

'We licked 'em fair and square,' Scully growled. 'And no mistake.'

'We did?'

'Yes, we bloody did.' Scully was just about to expound further when he noticed the boy's expression. Mixed with the eagerness to be loyal both to his father's country and his mother's, too, was bewilderment. And with it tension. It was written large on his face, and he was in no mood to be teased or even argued with.

'Oh, well,' Scully said easily. 'The French beat our lot at Hastings, didn't they? William the Conqueror. You know: the feller from that place back there – Caen.'

'Guillaume le Conquérant.' The boy smiled, placated. 'Of course. He taught the English a good lesson, I think.'

Scully sighed and let it go.

It was late in the afternoon when they reached Alençon where they immediately learned that all trains had been cancelled to enable the Germans to move troops to the fighting zone.

'I think we must go to Le Mans,' the boy said.

They slept the night in a barn. It was full of straw and bugs, and Scully woke feeling as if every insect in northern France had been trudging about his person. On the way south, however, they passed the river Sarthe and, taking off their clothes, swam naked in the moving water. As they were climbing out, a couple of village girls saw them and made gestures at Scully with their forearms and fists. He grinned, quite ready to join in the fun, but Ludo's face wore an expression of prudish disapproval, and not for the first time Scully realized that the picture of the French as lecherous and sexy from infanthood was probably wrong.

'My mother is not like that,' the boy said stiffly.

'She's not?' Scully yanked his trousers on.

41

'My mother is good.'

So much the better, Scully thought. More to go at.

They reached Le Mans by next evening. The square near the station was full of German vehicles and men, and at the station they learned that all trains had been cancelled because of bombing.

'We must go to Nogent-le-Rotrou,' Ludo announced.

'Jesus,' Scully was indignant. 'If we go much further we'll have circled the bloody world to get to Paris.'

'Sir – ' the boy was wearing his priggish expression again ' – do the English always call on the name of the Saviour?'

'What you mean?'

'You are always saying "Jesus".'

Scully frowned. Here was something else he would have to be careful about, he realized. It probably meant more to the French than it did to him and the boy had the look of someone who'd been well brought up. Besides, Scottish Presbyterian father or not, if his mother was French the boy must have been raised a Catholic, because that's what they always did. Chalky White had once got himself engaged to an Irish girl and had only backed away at the last minute because he'd not been able to see himself as the father of a bunch of kids reciting a lot of Latin he didn't understand.

'What,' Scully asked with great patience, 'was we talking about?'

'Going to Nogent,' the boy said.

'Yes.' Scully drew a deep breath. 'Well, we'd better go, hadn't we?'

Nogent was smaller and there was a great deal of bustle about the town. A lot of German vehicles were passing through, moving north, and it was obvious the Wehrmacht was withdrawing troops from all over France and throwing them into the fighting in Normandy. There was little food available without ration cards but the boy managed to buy bread and some sliced sausage that tasted like nothing on earth, and they sat at a table outside a bar, eating, and drinking a single beer between them.

Women clattered past on wooden-soled shoes and everybody seemed to be riding bicycles. There were also a few dilapidated horse carriages about, plying from the station, and two-wheeled trailers attached to bicycles; but what few cars and lorries there were towed charcoal gas generators to supply fuel to the engine. The shops contained nothing but portraits of Marshal Pétain and his slogan, *Travail, famille, patrie,* and posters giving directions on how to send parcels to the million French prisoners of war in Germany.

'What do we do with the bike when we catch the train?' Scully asked.

'There is another bicycle in Paris. There is also my mother's which I ride too. We will sell this one. It has two good tyres.'

'Good? Them!'

'Some people ride bicycles *without* tyres, sir. In Paris you starve without a bicycle. With a bicycle you can find food.'

Wheeling the machine to a bar near the station, Ludo propped it against the curb and went inside. There was a great deal of excitement in the air, as if everyone were discussing the invasion, and Scully caught snatches he understood.

'A fortnight,' he heard, 'and *still* they have not driven the Germans back.'

You want to go and try it, mate, he thought savagely, remembering the nebelwerfers and the snipers and the dead cattle. It's harder than you think.

As he waited, a man who was sitting at one of the tables rose and walked towards the bicycle. As his hand touched the handlebar, Scully's big fist fell on top of it.

'Hop it,' Scully growled.

Whether or not the man realized he was English he didn't know, but he gave Scully a sour look and hurried off. Almost immediately, a man wearing an apron appeared from the bar. He examined the bicycle carefully.

'*Mille francs,*' he said.

'*Deux milles,*' Scully growled.

The barman looked up at him. 'Three hundred will take you to the frontier, my friend,' he observed.

'We don't want to go to the frontier,' Ludo said. 'Just to Paris.'

'I am offering mille francs.'

'*Deux milles*,' Scully said again.

The barman shrugged, fished in his pocket and pointedly handed the notes to the boy. As they walked away, he stood holding the bicycle and staring after them curiously.

'He is suspicious,' the boy said.

'He can get stuffed.'

'Get stuffed?'

Scully sighed. 'It's a saying,' he pointed out. 'Go and buy the tickets.'

The boy took two or three notes. 'You ought to come too,' he said. 'They will think it strange me buying the ticket. On the other hand, there is often a German soldier near the ticket office looking for escapers.'

'Is there?' Scully thought for a moment. 'Here, dig out them spectacles of your grandad's.'

Handing them over, the boy watched solemnly as Scully put them on his nose. They were not only made for a myopic old man, but they were twisted and made Scully feel cross-eyed. There was nothing feigned about the way he stumbled after the boy into the station. The German soldier waiting by the ticket office stared at him narrowly and Ludo looked up and smiled.

'He does not see very well,' he explained.

As the clerk issued the tickets, the boy took Scully's hand and guided him down the platform. Crossing the line to the other platform, Scully felt half-witted and was terrified he'd fall under a train; but then it occurred to him that, quite by accident, they'd hit on a good disguise, because nobody would suspect a half-blind man of being a soldier.

Since the invasion the trains had been running more irregularly than ever and a lot of people who had been away from Paris were still trying to get back.

'The railwaymen keep going on strike,' Ludo explained. 'People say it is because they are in the Resistance. It is very difficult for travellers.'

When the train came there was a wild rush to obtain seats, and it began to look as though they weren't going to manage to climb aboard. But there was an open window opposite Scully and, hoisting the boy in his hands, he lifted him feet first through it and scrambled after him, the spectacles cockeyed on his nose, his big feet clearing a space for himself.

The corridors were jammed and, squinting round the corner of the glasses in a way that made him seem more half-witted than ever, Scully blundered along, falling over packages and children and suitcases until Ludo managed to place him against the end of the carriage where eventually a woman slid forward a suitcase for him to sit on.

'He does not see very well,' Ludo explained again.

The journey was slow and, as the train stopped and started, everybody swayed together. Bothered by the old spectacles, Scully pretended to doze. As the train rattled north, he finally fell asleep and almost slid off the suitcase.

The Gare Montparnasse was crowded with people. The invasion had clearly upset the already dubious timetables; nobody seemed to know anything, and there were groups round railway officials, arguing and waving their arms. They all looked tired and pale, and for the first time Scully began to understand what four years of occupation meant. British cities were shabby and paintless and the people threadbare, but here there was a listlessness in the air that indicated despair and undernourishment.

'What now?' he asked as they emerged into the street.

'I live not very far from here, sir. In the Rue Fantin. Close to the Luxembourg Palace. It's not far.'

Ludo had barely finished speaking when a boy hurtled past on a bicycle with racing handlebars. He shouted, stopped dead, lifted his machine round the other way and came back to them at full speed, the tyres screeching as he clapped on the brakes and came to a halt.

'Ludo. C'est toi!'

'Oui. J'arrive.'

Trying to peer round the edge of the spectacles, Scully saw that the newcomer was older than Ludo, a strong-looking boy with fair crewcut hair and a long beaky nose. He had an assured manner and a voice that had begun to break and skated up and down erratically as he spoke. He was looking at Scully with an expression of contempt.

'*Et lui?*' he asked, jerking a thumb.

'*Mon oncle. Mon Oncle Charles.*'

'I didn't know you had an Uncle Charles,' the boy on the bicycle observed, switching to English.

'Oh, yes,' Ludo said, following suit. 'This is he.'

The boy on the bicycle stared again at Scully. '*Il semble un peu fou,*' he commented.

Ludo shrugged. 'He doesn't see very well. He brought me home.'

'Sure you didn't bring *him* home? Your mother's going to be pleased to see him, I'll bet, with the rationing.'

'What's he say?' Scully demanded as the cyclist rushed off.

The boy blushed. 'He said you seemed a bit stupid. But he's all right. It's George Presteigne. He's the leader of the Resistance group.'

'What Resistance group?'

'Ours.'

'*You* got a Resistance group?'

'We have been training. For when the time comes.'

'Kids?'

'We know what to do.'

'Got any guns?'

'Well – no, sir. Not guns. We intend to get them from the Germans when the fighting starts.'

Scully looked at the boy. 'You know how to use a gun, flower?' he asked.

'Not exactly.'

'In that case, you leave 'em alone, kid. Nasty things, guns.'

The boy frowned. 'Perhaps you will show us what to do,' he suggested. 'Perhaps you can even show us how to kill with the hand as you did. When Paris is liberated, there will be fighting.'

Scully gave a bark of laughter. 'If there is, son, the best thing you can do is keep your 'ead down.'

The boy stiffened. 'Honour demands that we free our own capital. Honour is very important to the French.'

'I thought you was English.'

The boy moved the flat of his hand backwards and forward. 'I am a little French also,' he said.

After a while they turned into a broad boulevard which the boy said was the Boulevard Saint-Michel, and from there eventually into a side street.

'This is the Rue Commandant-Sardier,' the boy said. 'He was a French hero in the other war. It leads to the Rue Fantin where I live.'

At the end of the street a German officer was sitting on a motor-cycle. He was young and blond and good-looking in the way the Nazis favoured. His manner was easy, as though he had no fears of anyone attempting to attack him, and he seemed like a symbol of the cowed spirit of the capital.

'Who's he?' Scully asked.

'He's always here. I think he's trying to pick up my mother.'

Scully was alarmed. 'Does she go with Germans?'

'No. But four weeks ago, he knocked her off her bicycle. He's been trying to see her ever since. My mother is pretty, you see.'

The German watched them move down the street until, after a hundred yards, they turned again. Scully was staring round him as he walked. The buildings about him now had a strange lost look, as if the age of the petrol engine hadn't quite caught up with the area. The streets were narrow, planted with ancient acacias which grew through iron grilles set in the pavement, and the roadway was laid with setts in curves and angles that formed patterns, while the shops seemed smaller than anywhere else.

The boy seemed to understand Scully's surprise.

'This place is known as the Petite-Ville,' he explained. 'Its real name is the Petite-Ville-des-Martyrs because some people were once killed here in a riot. You'll be safe here. The Germans do not like narrow streets. Many years ago it was even surrounded by a wall. We're close to the Boul' Mich' and the university, where my father and my mother taught history, yet we are almost cut off from the rest of Paris. It has its own bars – five of them – even its own shops and a cinema.'

They had stopped now by a wide archway leading to a small unevenly cobbled courtyard filled with pots of geraniums.

'This is the Hôtel Bouboulis,' the boy said. 'It used to be the town house of a Monsieur Bouboulis but now it's two apartments.'

The walls of the building were covered with ivy so that they had a curious country look about them, and the ground floor consisted of stables which had been converted into garages and the apartment of the concierge.

'The Bar du Weekend is just round the corner,' Ludo pointed out. He gestured at a narrow opening between the buildings barred by a gate. 'There is an alley through there – the Passage du Chien-Nomade. It runs behind the houses from the Rue Lescaut to the Rue Commandant-Sardier. Everybody has a back entrance and I can get to the home of my friend, Charles Rohan, who lives in the Hôtel Barrac in the Rue Noyelle, which is the next street along, without going into the street.'

As they moved through the archway, an old woman appeared from the doorway of the concierge's apartment and began to water the pots of geraniums. She was small and bony and dressed in grey, and as she saw the boy her face lit up and she cried out in a hoarse croaking voice that made Scully think of a small grey parrot.

'Ludo!' she screamed. 'Holy Mother of God, your maman has been frantic!' She grabbed the boy and kissed him on both cheeks, then she became aware of Scully and gave him a suspicious glance. 'And who is this? What is he doing here?'

'It is my Uncle Charles, Madame Weinspach,' the boy

lied neatly. 'He has brought me from Normandy. We had
to go via Le Mans.'

The old woman grabbed Scully and kissed him too.

'Such courage,' she said. 'Such bravery! And he half
blind!'

They escaped at last and reached a curving staircase.

'It is a very good apartment, sir,' Ludo observed. 'You
will be very comfortable. Monsieur Virec has the first floor.'

As they began to climb, an old man appeared, clutching
a violin, and the performance that had taken place in the
courtyard was repeated on the stairs.

'Ludovic! My boy! You're back!'

'Yes, Monsieur Virec. I'm back. My Uncle Charles
brought me back. This is my Uncle Charles.'

The old man pumped Scully's hand, talking over his
shoulder all the time to the boy. 'And your violin lessons,
mon brave? You have done them every day?'

'No, monsieur. It wasn't possible. I have been in Normandy. There was much fighting and, besides, I didn't take
my violin.'

'Of course, of course!' The old man beamed and introduced himself to Scully as they climbed to the second floor.
'I am delighted to meet you, monsieur. I am Narcisse Virec
– formerly leader of the violins at the Opera House, now
retired. My son, Maurice, is with the Free French forces of
de Gaulle and doubtless now back in France trying to en-
courage the British and the Americans to make haste. He
is also a violinist, but of course at the moment he carries a
gun. But doubtless you will have heard of this in the letters
you will have exchanged with Ludovic's mother, Madame
McCosh.' He glanced up at Scully who was trying to peer
at him round the bent spectacles. 'But perhaps you do not
write many letters, monsieur – the eyes, of course! Permit
me to summon her.'

Thrusting the boy aside, he scuttled up the stairs in front
of them and thundered on a door, beaming round at the
boy as he did so.

'Your maman will be delighted, *mon brave*!' he said. 'She
has been desperate. *Attends*! Here she comes.'

49

The door opened and the woman who appeared was just as attractive as the boy's photograph had indicated. She was small and dark-eyed, with a mass of chestnut hair about her face. She looked neat, spotless and efficient but her face was pale and her eyes were red as if she'd been crying.

'*Lulu! Mon fils! Oh, mon chéri!*' She grabbed the boy and clutched him to her, kissing him fiercely. 'Your Aunt Madeleine telephoned. She returned to find Sainte-Honorine had been bombed and the house damaged and Madame Danoy injured. And then she learned you had gone off with a man and – '

'But he is safe home now, is he not?' The old man with the violin danced round on the fringe of the frantic embracing, gesturing and smiling. 'His Uncle Charles brought him. This is Uncle Charles. But, of course, that is something you will already know.'

The woman's face lifted and, as her eyes sought Scully, he was conscious of his ugly cast-off clothes, soiled with contact with the earth and rumpled from being slept in.

'It was very difficult, maman,' Ludo said earnestly. 'We had to hide in ditches.' He gestured at his chest. 'Once up to here in water.'

The woman was looking at Scully suspiciously. 'Are you all right, my son?' she asked quietly.

'Of course, maman. I am safe, aren't I?'

'Well, kiss him again!' the old man with the violin shouted. 'Kiss his Uncle Charles also! You should be grateful to him. With such eyesight, it must have been very difficult.'

The woman quickly pecked at Scully's face, first one cheek then the other. He was aware of his own stink and her spotless cleanliness, and could hardly refrain from grabbing her.

The old man was still dancing round, offering advice and excitedly playing snatches of music on his fiddle.

'See, I play the "Marseillaise" in celebration! And now, "Madelon!" I will give you "Artilleurs de Metz," if you wish. I was in the army in the last war, you know, monsieur: Verdun!'

'Thank you, Monsieur Virec,' the woman said. 'That is kind of you. But I haven't seen my son for a long time and I was worried. You must forgive us. We would like to be alone.'

'Of course! Of course!' The old man bowed. 'I am all understanding. Now, how about "St Cyr Garde à Vous" or "En Revenant de la Revue?" ' And he immediately began to play again as she dragged the boy inside.

There was a distinct pause, and for a moment Scully thought she was going to slam the door in his face. Then she touched his arm and indicated the interior of the apartment into which Ludovic had already disappeared. As the door closed behind him, Scully wrenched off the ancient spectacles and rubbed his eyes.

'Jesus – ' he stopped dead, remembering the need to watch his manners – 'I'm glad to get *them* off.'

As he turned, to his surprise he saw the woman studying him, her face pale with anger. He had expected smiles and a welcome, but her eyes were like burning coals.

'Who are you?' she demanded in English, her voice vibrant with dislike and suspicion. 'And by what right do you force your way in here?''

5

Concerned as he had been with his eyes, Scully hadn't noticed the woman's expression at first and the tone of her voice startled him.

He came to his senses abruptly. 'I'm not forcing my way in,' he said indignantly. 'He said I could come.'

'Why? What did you say to him?'

'Nothing. Why the hell should I? He's a nice kid and he helped me a lot.'

'It is a dangerous world for children these days.' She was giving away nothing in the way of friendship but her expression had altered a little. 'I suppose you are hiding from the Germans.'

'I suppose you could say that' Scully turned on the old charm, feeling sure that what would work for Daisy and Doris and Edna and the others would work for this one, too. Her face didn't relax, however, and she stood in front of him, her back stiff as a poker, her head up, her eyes on his face.

'You're *sure* he is unharmed?'

'Sure he is. Right little soldier, that.'

'I do not wish him to be a soldier,' she snapped. 'His father was a soldier and he is dead. My father and my uncle were soldiers and they are dead also – at Verdun in 1916, like so many more. My brother-in-law was a soldier, too, and he is a prisoner in Germany. It will be better if he is *not* a soldier.'

Scully lifted his hands. 'All right, ma'am,' he said placatingly. 'That's all right with me.' This first interview, on which he'd always set so much reliance, seemed to be going wrong. She was supposed to fall into his arms with gratitude, as Edna would have, and offer him a cup of tea with a tot of brandy, for bringing the boy home.

'Are you a deserter?' she snapped.

Scully stiffened. Charles Walter Scully had been a few things in his time, and there were a few he sometimes – but not often – felt ashamed of. But deserter wasn't one of them. 'No, I'm not a deserter,' he said angrily.

Old soldiers didn't desert. They'd had it drilled into them that desertion was worse than death. The old soldiers Charley Scully knew were a pretty rough lot on the whole and some of them would have been best in prison – but there hadn't been much desertion in 1914 or in 1940 either, when the old soldiers of the British army had held the line until all the conscripts who'd looked down on them in peacetime could be gathered in, trained and shoved into battle. They probably hadn't much in the way of brains, but they'd known not to desert.

'I got cut off from my mob,' he growled. 'I had to move south. Then I had to move south again to avoid being captured. That's when I bumped into the kid. He said I'd be all right here in Paris.'

The boy had been watching them with a troubled expression. 'The sergeant paid my fare home,' he said helpfully. 'He also killed a German. Two, in fact.'

She rounded on him at once. 'Where? Here?'

'Oh, no, maman! Up near Mésnil.' He demonstrated the chop with his hand. 'I saw him. Like that.'

She stared coldy at Scully. 'And now I suppose the Germans will shoot twenty French hostages.' In her anger, the precise English she had clearly learned from her husband – clipped and with a trace of Scottish accent – flowed easily. 'This is what the Resistance does. This is *all* the Resistance does. They appear with red scarves and their hair cut *en brosse*, swaggering and threatening, and sometimes – not very often – they kill some lonely German soldier or bomb some solitary truck. Then the Germans turn round and shoot people in retaliation, while the Resistance disappear again back to where they came from. They don't take the risks other people take. Monsieur Virec has hidden escapers and boys evading forced labour in Germany for years. *I* have hidden them in my spare room for him. Sometimes I wish to God I hadn't, because the Germans never let up.'

Scully listened, startled. From what he'd heard on the BBC and read in the papers, he'd believed that half France was up in arms killing Germans, and the other half was supporting them.

'Listen, lady – ' he began. He sensed he was in need of a good explanation. She was plainly angry, didn't trust him, and he knew he had to stay in the apartment until he could find somewhere else. The kid had been a bit over-optimistic, it seemed, and Mum didn't want Charley Scully one bit.

He was just about to launch into a lengthy explanation, extolling the needs and virtues of Charley Scully when there was a knock on the door. As she turned to open it, he saw a German uniform on the landing and, realizing it was the German officer he'd seen on the motor-cycle down the street, he hurriedly jammed the crooked spectacles back on his nose.

'Madame,' the German was saying. 'You will remember me. Adam Holzmeier. Leutnant Adam Holzmeier.'

'Of course.' She spoke stiffly, warily, in a way, Scully decided, that would have frozen out anybody but a German.

'I came to see how you were.'

She was holding the door no more than two inches ajar. 'You have already been more than once to ask me that,' she said.

'I was concerned.' The German's voice was gentle, almost pleading. 'How is the bump on your head?'

'I have long since forgotten it.'

'I sincerely regret hurting you.'

'You didn't hurt me. It's all right.' She looked anxiously about her, and, through the crack of the door, Scully could see the old man from the apartment downstairs, still clutching his violin and taking everything in.

'I think I tore your skirt. As you fell.'

'It was soon mended. Please go.'

'I wondered if I might suggest dinner. As a sort of recompense.'

Scully saw her stiffen. 'I don't eat with Germans,' she snapped.

'Madame, I am not like other Germans. I studied here. I speak your language. I love France.'

'So do I,' she snapped. 'And I do not make friends with her conquerors.'

'Madame – !'

'Please go! My son has been missing for several days. His uncle has just brought him back from Normandy. He's frightened and they're both tired and hungry.'

'Permit me to send you some food.'

'No!' The word was almost a shout and she managed to push the door to at last. Leaning against it, she was breathing deeply, pale, angry and frightened.

'Who's he?'

'Some fool who knocked me off my bicycle! He's been trying to get in here ever since.' She drew a deep breath. 'The arrogance! The stupidity! As if any decent Frenchwoman would be seen alongside a German!'

There was a quiet scratching at the door.

'Go away!'

'It is I, madame, Narcisse Virec.'

She opened the door cautiously and Scully saw the old man's face peering in at her. 'I have a little something for your son, madame. As you know, my needs are small and there are now three of you.'

A small packet wrapped in newspaper changed hands and the door closed. She leaned against it again, clutching the packet to her breast, breathing deeply as she tried to regain her calm. After a while she looked at Scully.

'You may stay,' she said. 'With a male relation in the house, perhaps he'll not try again. But only for a short while. I can't feed you. Everything is rationed.'

'I've got money,' Scully said. 'Plenty of it.'

'Thank you,' she said stiffly. 'But you must still go as soon as possible. Who are you, anyway?'

'Scully, ma'am. Charley Scully, Sergeant, North Staffs

Fusileers – spelt with two 'e's. I've got the DCM,' he added
feebly, feeling it might help.

'I do not like the English. Thanks to the desertion of their
English allies, the French army went down to defeat in 1940
and as a result we have suffered four years of humiliation,
misery and oppression.'

It had always been Scully's impression that the French
had had only themselves to blame for their defeat. In 1940
he'd seen hundreds of French soldiers moving towards the
coast, unshaven, dirty, undisciplined and devoid of officers
and NCOs. Having heard from the boy how stories could
be twisted, however, he suddenly wondered which version
was right, because some of the things he'd read about Dunkirk in the papers in England had been sheer bloody rubbish
and he himself had seen groups of men in the back areas,
corrupted by the idle winter of the Phoney War into starting
rackets, who had been more concerned with getting their
ill-gotten gains home than with stopping the Germans.

He said nothing and she seemed to take it for meekness.

'I am Sidonie McCosh,' she said tartly. 'I was born Sidonie
Godard. I am a widow and I have to work for my living.
There is no one else and I have been frantic for days wondering where my son was. My sister must have been mad to
keep him in Normandy after the invasion started. What if
it had happened that he was on one side of the line and I
on the other?' She flung a glance at the boy, her relief at
his return overcome now by anger that he had been in
danger. 'I have spent a fortune on telephone calls and tele-
grams trying to find out where he was. By the grace of God,
my employer is a lawyer and a kind man and he allowed me
to use his telephone and his contacts. He told me to take
time off to find him. I was just wondering where to start.'
She paused and looked at Scully, her eyes full of anguish.
'Why do they not come?'

'Who?'

'The allies, of course. Who else? Perhaps they just do not
try hard enough.'

Still angry, she showed Scully to a room which looked

about as big as a wardrobe. There was a single bed in a corner with just sufficient space to turn round alongside it.

'You may sleep here,' she said. 'Take off your clothes.'

He gave her a startled look.

'Everything,' she said. 'I shall burn them. You may have fleas. In any case, I cannot have someone as disreputable as you are in my flat. People will talk. The bathroom is next door. Ludo will put the water in the bath. It will be cold, of course, because there is no fuel to heat it, but it will have to do. Put your clothes outside the door and use a blanket.'

Scully stared at the door as it slammed, aware that he was face to face for the first time in his career with French suburban rectitude, and that all Frenchwomen did not welcome handsome strangers into their homes and immediately go into a clinch with them. Some were different. By a long way. This one was.

Sitting with a blanket round him and smelling of soap, Scully pondered on his position. Things had turned out a bit differently from what he'd expected. Mum was a bit of all right, without any doubt, but she was far from welcoming. What help she was giving him, he suspected, was purely in return for seeing the boy home and certainly not because she'd fallen for the charms of Charles Walter Scully.

The door clicked and a hand appeared and dropped a bundle of clothing to the floor. Scully picked it up, and found underwear, a white shirt and collar, a blue tie, and a grey suit. He tried them on and they fitted him reasonably well. The late McCosh, he realized, had been a well-made man. But, Jesus – he stared disgustedly at himself in the mirror behind the door – his clothes made Scully look like an undertaker's mute. Charley Scully in civvies had worn trousers with wide bottoms, and Jimmy Cagney jackets with pinched waists and padded shoulders. He'd once even gone in for a pencil-line moustache and sidewhiskers until the regimental sergeant-major had asked him if he thought he was Al Capone.

With the collar half throttling him, and feeling like something the cat had dragged in, he edged sheepishly round the door. Ludo, also scrubbed and clean in fresh clothes, was sitting by the window.

'Is it all right, flower?' Scully asked, more nervous than he cared to admit.

The boy grinned at him. 'Yes, sir, it's all right.'

'Is she always like that?'

'Not always, sir. I think it is the war. Perhaps it is because the German came.'

'Is he always dropping in?' Scully could see Leutnant Holzmeier causing difficulties.

'Only since he knocked her off her bicycle.'

Scully's eyes were moving about the apartment, trying to find things that would tell him what he wanted to know. He indicated the photograph of a man in French uniform which stood on a small table by the window, draped with black crêpe, a small vase of flowers by it as if it were a shrine.

'Who's that?' he asked. 'Your dad?'

'Yes, sir. It is always there. Monsieur Hasler used to laugh and place it face down.'

'Who's Monsieur Hasler? Another German?'

'He's an Englishman. He is hiding in the city. He stayed with Monsieur Virec at first but then he left. He is in touch with the Resistance.'

'Is he – I mean, does she – ?' Christ, Scully thought, how did you ask the kid if Hasler was Mum's lover boy?

The boy supplied the answer. 'Is he her lover?' he said.

Scully's jaw dropped. 'Yeh,' he said. 'That.'

'Oh, no. They are not in love.'

Well, that was a relief, Scully thought.

'Does he come often?'

'No. Not often. She told him about Armande.'

'Who's Armande?'

'Armande Démange. He was my mother's friend. After my father was killed. He was also a lecturer at the university and they knew each other well. After the Americans went into Algeria, he went south to join the Free French army. He has joined General Leclerc. We heard on the BBC. We think he will be among the first to liberate Paris.'

It looked, Scully decided, as if he'd have to get to work a bit fastish.

The boy gestured. 'Pierre does not think he will, though,' he said casually.

There was a very long silence before Scully spoke again. 'Who's Pierre?'

'Pierre Lambrouille.'

'Does *he* come here, too?'

'Of course.'

Christ, the bloody flat was like a posting house for boy-friends! Including Scully, that made four of 'em in competition.

'Doesn't he like Armande?' he asked.

'He says patriotism is a silly sentiment these days.'

'He a collaborator?'

'Very probably.'

'Why doesn't your mum hand him over?'

'He is her cousin. It's a matter of honour. French families are very close.'

By God they were, Scully thought. Literally hanging round each other's necks.

6

Scully sat back, sipping at a glass of wine from a bottle that had been slammed on the table by Sidonie McCosh with an instruction to the boy to give him an apéritif.

Shifting his behind, he made himself comfortable and moved the bottle nearer. The flat had a shabby look, as though carpets, curtains and covers were wearing out, but it was furnished in good taste and was spotlessly clean. Even to Scully who, apart from a brief sojourn with Marjory Birchall in lodgings after his ill-fated marriage, had never lived in a house, the furniture looked expensive. There were pictures on the wall that looked valuable and knick-knacks on the sideboard that had an air of graciousness about them which served to make him faintly uncomfortable.

As he lifted the glass again, Sidonie returned. She sloshed some of the wine into another glass, sipped it, then placed the bottle on the sideboard beyond Scully's reach. He gave her a reproachful look, because he'd been hoping to get down to a little serious drinking.

'It is not a good wine,' she said bleakly, fishing in a drawer and producing a tablecloth. 'The Germans have most of what is worth having, and the collaborators have taken the rest.'

She seemed prickly and ready for a fight and Scully moved warily.

'Their day'll come,' he said.

'Not a moment too soon. It is a pity the British and the Americans do not help the Free French to recapture France.'

Scully's eyebrows shot up. So far he'd not even seen a

Free Frenchman though he knew there were a few around somewhere. People in Europe, he reckoned, seemed to have a funny idea of who was winning the war.

She was setting the table as she talked, and she wasn't talking to Scully, merely throwing comments into the empty air, as if she didn't wish to address him directly.

'You need money these days to eat well in Paris,' she went on. 'The black market restaurants can always find food, of course. But these are used mostly by Germans and the collaborators and the black marketeers themselves.'

Knives, forks and glasses were slammed on to the table. 'Why do not the allies come?' she said. '*Les Anglais ne sont jamais à l'heure*. The English are never on time. But then, of course, they haven't had to live for four years watching the swastikas flapping in the streets.'

'How long did you expect them to take?' Scully asked hotly. 'Two days from Normandy?'

'They have already been two weeks.'

'The whole bl— the whole German army's between 'em! Why don't your Resistance people do something?'

'The Resistance people are very businesslike with their rolled sleeves and red scarves,' she snapped. 'There is a lot of show, but not much in the way of results. They cut telephone lines in hundreds when the landing took place and a lot of the *Milice* and collaborators were shot. Now that the allies are taking so long, they have grown nervous and are going back into the woods, and the *Milice* are taking their revenge.'

The wine was placed in the centre of the table again, and she vanished to the kitchen to return with half a loaf and soup in a large tureen. It seemed to consist chiefly of potatoes, flour and salt, but to Scully, who was hungry and hadn't had a meal sitting at a table for some time, it was like a feast. There hadn't been all that many times in his life outside the sergeants' mess, in fact, when he'd had a meal with a cloth under his plate.

'We are lucky,' she said. 'It is not always possible to get vegetables to make soup.'

'Some people go hunting round the dustbins for potato peelings,' Ludo observed.

Sidonie nodded. 'And coffee is only roasted wheat seeds. Paris has lost her personality.'

So had a few of its inhabitants, Scully thought, looking up warily under his eyebrows and deciding that when she was in a good temper she'd probably be quite a stunner.

'*I'll* get you some food,' he offered. 'I'm good at getting food. I've had two big wars to learn how. I can snatch an egg from under the hen even before it touches the straw. I used to find half a dozen which laid away from the others, and visited them regularly and got three or four eggs daily. In the end they began to develop a harassed look.'

How much they understood he didn't know but the boy laughed. His mother rose quickly and went to the kitchen, returning with three minute portions of liver and vegetables.

'Looks good,' Scully said, feeling he was beginning to make progress.

'You are very lucky,' she pointed out. 'Monsieur Virec is giving violin lessons to the butcher's daughter and sometimes he gets a little extra in payment. He has given it to me in honour of the return of my son.'

'Three cheers for Monsieur Virec.'

'It is very noble of him,' she said coldly. 'Perhaps you had better not let him know who you are. He lost one son when your ships shelled our fleet at Casablanca and he has another son a prisoner of war in Germany. He has no reason to like the English.'

It was far from the easiest of meals. There were long periods of silence when neither Scully nor Sidonie had anything to say. The boy watched them anxiously. He loved his mother and wanted her to approve of his new friend. He also wanted his new friend to approve of his mother. But it didn't seem to be working out that way.

'How long have you been a soldier, sir?' he asked, trying to make conversation.

'All me life, flower,' Scully said. 'Joined at fifteen in 1918, didn't I, and fought through the Battle of Amiens. Then

they found out how old I was and sent me home. They
wanted to chuck me out. I begged 'em to let me stay in.'

'Why?'

'I hadn't got no home, had I? I hadn't a father.' Scully
looked pointedly at Sidonie. 'I hadn't a mother either.'

She looked up quickly at him, then lowered her eyes to
her plate again.

'They made me a band boy.'

'What is that, sir?'

Scully explained. 'You could join for boy service and
learn to play an instrument at the army's expense.'

'What was it like in the army?'

'In them days, not much cop.'

'Not much cop?'

'Rough. Nasty.' Considering that the old soldiers they
were tossed in with didn't consider they'd lived until they'd
had what they called a nap hand – five red entries on their
crime sheet, to say nothing of a dose of clap – it could hardly
be called unexpected. He could still remember himself, a
shrimp of a kid, taking giant strides to keep in step with the
taller men around him, learning to cut the stitches from the
lining of his SD tunics to make a pocket big enough to hold
a packet of Woodbines without a bulge, and how to use
every four-letter in the vocabulary because it was considered
cissy not to. All the same, for Scully, who had come from
an orphanage, and for the other bedraggled youths who had
joined at the same time, it had been the nearest thing he'd
ever known to a home. The army had fitted him out with a
cardboard-stiff uniform and warm greyback shirts and, more
important, had given him a little pride in himself. It had
been a matter of great moment to him the first time he
wrote a letter in the NAAFI on regimental notepaper with
its embossed crest, the first time he had himself photo-
graphed in borrowed blues. Since he had no family, the only
person he could think of to send it to was the warden of the
orphanage.

It was hard to explain this, though, to a boy who'd had
a safe and comfortable home. Whatever the late McCosh
had been or done, he'd left his family with a secure back-

ground, and his wife had given the boy love. For such a boy it was impossible to imagine the starkness of a charity home.

They were still at the table, the boy listening to Scully talk, his mother pretending to read the paper but, Scully noticed, managing to listen as well, when the door rattled.

The man who entered resembled Sidonie. He was good-looking in a dark, regular-featured way, but his face was narrower and lacked her expression of forthright honesty. His clothes, too, Scully noticed, were not so shabby as most of those he'd seen in Paris and he looked well fed.

He placed a small package on the table, kissed Sidonie on both cheeks, and fingered the red bow tie he wore.

'Cousin Pierre Lambrouille's brought you a present,' he said. 'For your birthday.'

As he turned, he became aware of Scully. Straightening up, he stared hostilely, his eyes narrow.

'Who is this?' he demanded.

'This is our Uncle Charles,' Sidonie said quietly.

'We haven't got an Uncle Charles.'

'We didn't know about him.' Her face was expressionless. 'Lulu discovered him in Normandy. He was staying with Madeleine when he turned up. He brought Ludo back to Paris.'

Lambrouille studied Scully. 'He's a deserter.'

'No – ' Ludo interrupted quickly ' – he is not a deserter. He is a good soldier.'

'English?'

'Yes,' Scully admitted.

Lambrouille sneered. 'The French have no reason to love the English.'

'He killed a German,' Ludo said.

'Then he is mad,' Lambrouille snapped. 'And you are mad, Sidonie, for fraternizing with him! And with the others who've been here! Like the officer, Hasler, and the fliers who came. You have little sense; you make enemies of the Germans by fraternizing with the English, and enemies of the French by fraternizing with the Germans. You could do me great harm! Why did you marry that ridiculous Scotch lecturer? Why not me?'

Sidonie's small head came up proudly. 'My ridiculous Scotch lecturer gave his life for France,' she snapped. 'That's something I notice you don't risk!'

'Good Frenchmen follow Marshal Pétain's orders.'

'That old fool! He's a prisoner like Laval! We are *all* prisoners! And the Germans are the gaolers!'

'Of course they are gaolers!' Lambrouille slammed his hand down on the table. 'They have a right to be! They conquered Europe in a matter of weeks!'

'And they're losing it just as fast! The allies will be here soon! It's only a matter of time!'

'They're still in Normandy!'

'You don't expect them to get here in two days, do you?' Scully's head jerked round at Sidonie's words. 'They've got the whole of the Germany army between them and Paris. But when they come, you'll need to consider the things you've said and done. De Gaulle will remember you.'

'De Gaulle ruined my family!' Suddenly, unexpectedly, they were in the middle of a full-blooded quarrel. 'He took away our honour!'

She rounded on him furiously. 'Do you never think of anything else but your stupid honour?' she shouted.

'Your half of the family doesn't know the meaning of it!' Lambrouille shouted back. 'And de Gaulle will *never* come back! France is not stupid! She knows how to ignore charlatans!'

Sidonie's head jerked round angrily. 'Charlatans! In the name of God, what else is Hitler?'

Lambrouille ignored the comment and Scully sat fascinated as he ranted on, his face red with rage.

'The French were never a military race. In the days of Napoleon we dominated only by sheer numbers and since then we've lost our empire three times without much regret! We were defeated in 1870 and again in 1914, though our allies saved us then! It was a foregone conclusion we'd succumb in 1940 unless England made a substantial contribution, and that she was careful not to do! The whole war was a mistake! Why should France have gone to war for Poland? The Germans knew our heart wasn't in it!'

'The only trouble with the Germans,' Sidonie stormed, the anger in the air crackling like electricity, 'is that there are twenty million too many of them!'

'Soldiers can't run away from their country!' Lambrouille yelled. 'They can't fulminate against its government and then expect to be welcomed back! De Gaulle was a deserter in 1940, just as Thorez, the communist, who fled to Moscow, was a deserter! Now he sits in London telling the British to bomb French towns!'

She suddenly became silent and the spectacular quarrel subsided as quickly as it had come, as she made no attempt to answer Lambrouille's arguments with more arguments. In the end, defeated by her silence and realizing he was not going to get any further response, he reached for the door.

'I can see I'm not wanted here,' he said. 'Despite the gift I brought. It's good perfume, too. The best there is.'

'German, I expect,' Sidonie said coldly. 'No good French-man can buy perfume these days. Did your German girl-friend get it for you?'

As Lambrouille wrenched the door open and vanished, she stood by the table, her eyes full of tears and exhausted by the violence of the argument. Ludo, who had listened to the quarrel with a shocked expression on his face, rose silently and headed for his room.

'He don't seem to like de Gaulle,' Scully said quietly.

He had half expected some bitter retort but instead her shoulders lifted in a weary shrug.

'It's a complicated story,' she said almost in a whisper and, because of her earlier antagonism towards him, he was surprised she took the trouble to explain. 'And it's been going on too long. His father, my uncle, ran away in 1915 and de Gaulle, who was his senior officer, broke him for it.'

'Was there bad blood between them?'

She sighed. 'No. My father was there, too, and, before he was killed, he told my mother the story. Then in 1937, when he went to do his own military service, Pierre found himself in a tank regiment commanded by de Gaulle. He was thrown out.'

'Because de Gaulle knew who he was?'

'No. For admiring the Nazis too much. Armande told me – '

'Armande?'

'A friend,' she said simply, offering no further details. 'They were boys together. Armande warned him to hold his tongue.' She sighed. 'Perhaps because it was de Gaulle, he didn't even try. There was an inquiry and the report on him said he had a tendency to unbalanced opinions and the creation of delusive projects. It said he misinterpreted affairs of a complex nature and had the exaggerated self-feeling of a morbid egoist.'

'And does he?'

She shrugged wearily once more. 'I suppose so. It seems so. I don't suppose de Gaulle had any idea he was the son of the man he broke in 1915. I'm sure he'd forgotten. But Pierre hadn't. And now that de Gaulle is coming back as the saviour of France, it is more than he can bear. Pierre regards what he did to him as a slur on the family honour. Honour is important to the French, you see. Especially to Pierre, because his family have been in the army for generations. His grandfather led the last mounted charge of the war of 1870 and his apartment is full of photographs of members of the family who have distinguished themselves. It was a tremendous shock to him when he learned his father hadn't lived up to the standards of the army and an even bigger one when he was thrown out of it himself. I think he thought its leaders were decadent – '

'They probably were.'

She nodded, as though too tired to dispute it. 'Perhaps. But he thought that fascism would save it. They were difficult days then. No one knew where France was going. Hitler was getting all he wanted and many people felt fascism was the answer.'

She was surprisingly forthcoming, as if she were anxious to unload her troubles on someone and felt that Scully, a stranger, would be unlikely to pass them on.

'Was it bad?' he asked gently.

Her hands fluttered over the table, moving things nervously. 'We had cabinet ministers whose mistresses wanted

67

to run the country and for president we had Lebrun, who could think of nothing else but to weep. The French army had fathers who had too much glory, and their sons were the worst equipped in the world. Shirts like sails – I saw my husband's – a capote, no jacket, and boots that had been made in prisons. The army of 1940 was nothing but a mist that disappeared as soon as it was blown on. As they retreated they were baa-ing like sheep.'

A lot of what she said was above Scully's head but he could understand the despair.

She shrugged again. 'Now Pierre's just a toady to the Germans and the Vichyites, and probably even an informer. He's not been sent to Germany to work because he has German friends. He dabbles in the black market and can obtain petrol and tyres and is never short of luxuries. He shoots with one of the German gauleiters in the woods in the Ile de France and has a splendid hunting rifle when no one else is allowed anything of the sort. He has a German mistress with a large apartment on the top floor on the corner of the Rue Saint-Florentin, from where you can see the only traffic in Paris – German traffic in the Place de la Concorde. He uses it as if it were his own. I don't understand how he reconciles his honour with his treachery.'

'He said you should marry him.'

She gave a little broken sigh. 'He is always short of money. And an uncle left me some he'd like to get his hands on. Perhaps there's more to it than that, of course. Perhaps he thinks that if the Germans are defeated, marriage to me might save him. I don't know. Perhaps, even, he loves me. It's possible. But I could never marry him. He frightens me. And if he's known as an informer perhaps people would think I was one too.'

There was a long silence and she looked so distressed Scully endeavoured to cheer her up. 'Forget him,' he said softly. 'When the time comes, people like him will just disappear and then you can all forget what happened.'

Because he had thought her spirits were drooping enough for her to show some friendliness towards him at last, he was surprised when she turned on him.

'If the English think that,' she flared, 'then they are bigger fools than we thought! Too much has happened! France is too divided! Too many people have become enemies! France can never forget! Never!'

7

There were flowers for Sidonie the following morning. Madame Weinspach, the concierge, hobbled up the stairs and, accompanied by the ever vigilant Monsieur Virec, appeared at the door with them.

'They're from him,' she said. 'Holzmeier. He said it's to apologize. He's got it bad, that one, ma chérie.'

'Take them away,' Sidonie snapped. 'I don't accept gifts from Germans.' She stared at the blooms, touched by their beauty in a drab world. 'I can't,' she said. 'What would my friends think?'

The old woman studied her, her head on one side. 'Don't you like him a little?' she asked.

'I detest him. *And* the uniform he wears.'

'He's very good-looking.'

Sidonie's head jerked round angrily. 'Are you trying to test me?'

The old woman gestured. 'Women grow lonely without men.'

'I have a man. I have Uncle Charles.'

'He is not – ' the old woman hesitated ' – not what you would call good-looking, with those glasses and the way he holds his head. And he *is* your uncle.'

Sidonie turned away. 'Throw them in the dustbin. And if he comes back, tell him I want no more.'

Madame Weinspach shrugged. 'I'd take them,' she said. 'After all, he's very polite. Like my German cook from the Prince Eugène barracks who brings me titbits. He's not trying to get me into bed. I'm too old for that and he's too fat, anyway. He just feels sorry for me and thinks we don't get enough to eat. Perhaps this one's the same.'

'I don't want them!'

The old woman shrugged.

'I'll put them in a vase,' she said. 'They'll look nice in my room.'

There were tears in Sidonie's eyes as she leaned against the door, her face twisted with wretchedness and loneliness.

'If only they'd go away,' she whispered. '*All* of them.'

'You ought to be flattered,' Scully said.

'I loathe him,' she spat. 'I loathe them all! You've not had to live for four years with them. You've not heard the firing squads at Mont Valérien or known of the torture that goes on at the SS headquarters in the Rue des Saussaies. You've not had friends who've disappeared. You've not had men like him, conscious of being conquerors, swaggering about, thinking they can pick up any woman they wish.'

'I could remove him for you,' Scully said quietly. 'I know how.'

'No!' The word came out as a cry for help. 'No! There would be reprisals.'

'They wouldn't even know what had happened to him.'

'They would guess. You don't know how cruel they are, how efficient. You haven't lived with the thought that one night there'll be a knock on your door and the words, "*Police Allemande*".'

By the following afternoon, beginning to feel confined and restless in the apartment, Scully decided it was time to explore a little. After all, he thought, he hadn't come to Paris to sit staring at a wall.

'We'll go to the Luxembourg Gardens,' Ludo said. 'Everything that happens round here happens there.'

Following Lambrouille's visit, a shaky armistice had been agreed between Scully and Sidonie. The hostility she felt was still scarcely hidden, but she had produced a pathetic lunch of radishes with a little butter, one hard-boiled egg between the three of them, and a salad consisting largely of dandelions and chickweed.

71

'Is this what you're living on?' Scully asked.

'With food coupons, wine at nine francs a litre, and no meat in the shops, what do you expect? There is no more *soupe à l'oignon* and no more tripe in Les Halles. French wives no longer have bursting bags. Instead they search for cabbage and turnip tops for their families.'

Holzmeier was waiting down the street as Scully appeared with the boy. He was sitting in an open car this time and he looked up with interest as Ludo approached, holding Scully's hand. The boy seemed to shrink inside his clothes and turned very white so that Scully thought he was going to be sick. Then he seemed to get hold of himself with a visible stiffening of the spine and marched boldly past.

'*Bonjour, monsieur,*' he said loudly to the German. 'Say "*bonjour*",' he told Scully.

'*Bonjour,*' Scully muttered, and the German raised his hand in a casual salute.

'Boy!'

As the call came, Ludo stopped and Scully felt his grip tighten on his hand. Lifting his head, he looked round the bent spectacles at the German, who was leaning over the side of the car, his face concerned and anxious.

'The flowers? Did your mother like them?'

Ludo shook his head. 'No, monsieur. She told the concierge to take them away. She has them in a vase. You can have them back if you wish.'

A frown appeared on Holzmeier's handsome face. 'You should persuade your mother that I mean no harm,' he said. 'I only wish to be friendly. She is a very beautiful woman.'

The boy blushed. 'Yes, monsieur. I know.'

The German looked at Scully. 'Can *you* not persuade her, monsieur?'

Caught unawares, Scully wasn't sure of the words he needed and the German seemed to speak good French. Remembering his creed for the occasions in the army when he'd been caught doing something he shouldn't – act daft – he opened his mouth, squinted round the spectacles and shrugged.

There was an awkward silence and Ludo tugged at his hand.

'My uncle doesn't see very well,' he explained. 'Sometimes I think he doesn't think very well either.'

As they moved away, the German was still watching them, a deep frown on his face. Scully allowed a lopsided smile to appear.

'That was quick thinking, flower,' he whispered.

The boy seemed pleased and led him into the Luxembourg Gardens. The sun was shining through the trees, all brass and blue against the dark green of the leaves, the distant mansard roofs slicing the sky into great coloured wedges. The place was full of people – pushing prams, sitting on iron chairs, watching the children on the swings, playing with balls – while the white Paris dust hung heavy in the air beneath the horse chestnuts.

Surrounded by crumbling statues, Scully was enjoying being free again. He was surprised to see how well dressed the Parisians were – as if pride were all that was left to them – and watched them cycling down the long avenues, their cycle spokes glinting in the sun. A plump girl who looked like a tart teetered past, her eyelids heavy with make-up, her heels so high she walked like a pigeon with her toes turned in. He nodded at a group of youths wearing blue berets. 'Who're they, kid?'

'The *Compagnons de France*, sir. They're like the Hitler Youth. They were started by the Pétainists. They are not very dangerous. The dangerous ones are the *Milice*, the auxiliaries of the Gestapo. They are French and know which questions to ask.'

Despite the circumstances, Scully found he was enjoying himself, fascinated by the fact that here he was, a serving British soldier, right in the middle of occupied Paris, watching the Germans and eyeing the girls just as if he were back home in Aldershot, wondering which one to take into Bourley Woods.

Thinking of girls reminded him. He had things to do.

'It was your mum's birthday,' he said suddenly.

The boy looked up. 'Yes, sir.'

'Bought her anything?'

'No, sir.'

'Well, what are you going to do about it?'

'I don't know, sir. Do you like birthdays?'

'Don't go in for 'em much,' Scully said briskly. 'Only cissies and women have birthdays. Besides, I never had no mum and I never had no dad, did I? But women like birthdays. Makes 'em cry a bit and get sentimental. How about buying her some flowers?' Scully's old soldier's mind was working fast and it was less the thought of pleasing Sidonie that made him suggest a gift than that he might get something out of it.

They found an old woman selling violets and the boy walked along with them in his fist, the blooms already wilting a little in the heat. To Scully it was just another sign that, despite his protestations, he was still more French than British. Most British schoolboys would rather have died than be seen carrying a bunch of flowers.

He decided to push his luck.

'Know where the black market is?' he asked.

The boy looked up at him. 'I know where the people are who use it.'

'Show me.'

They walked down the Boulevard Saint-Michel. In the narrow streets near the Seine were several stalls watched by German soldiers and police. It didn't take Scully long to spot which stallholders were keeping goods under the counter and he indicated a man surrounded by minute cuts of meat all labelled with their price and the number of coupons required. Alongside them were a row of lettuces.

'Ask him what he's got that's not on the ration, kid.'

The boy leaned over the counter and whispered. Turning to Scully, he explained. 'Only tired lettuces, he says.'

'How tired?'

Ludo grinned. 'He says they're exhausted.'

'Tell him we'll have one. And ask him what he's got to go with it. Tell him it's a celebration and tell him it's me you're asking for and me who's paying.'

Ludo glanced up at the tall figure alongside him, then at

the stallholder, and whispered again. This time the man whispered back.

'He says *andouillettes*.'

'What's that?'

'Sausages made of chitterlings. They are a delicacy of Burgundy. They are very good.'

'Tell him three.'

Ludo whispered once more, and the man nodded, fished under the counter, produced a small paper packet, slipped a lettuce over it and named the price.

'It is very expensive,' Ludo warned.

'Don't argue.' Scully peeled the money from the large roll he had acquired from the Germans he'd killed. The paper packet went into his pocket while the boy held the unwrapped lettuce.

'Ask him if he's got any spuds?'

'Spuds?'

'Taters. *Pommes de terre*. Good ones.'

The boy whispered again, turned and nodded. 'They are rationed.'

'Tell him we want six.'

The man shook his head. Scully indicated a policeman at the end of the road, rocking on his heels, a bored look on his face.

'Tell him if he doesn't let me have 'em I'll tell the cop over there he's sold me food without coupons.'

The stallholder seemed to grasp what was being said and, without arguing, he pushed forward a parcel wrapped in newspaper. Scully smiled to himself, stuffed the parcel under his jacket and walked off, followed by the boy.

'Now,' he said. 'Wine. All French people drink wine. No birthday meal's complete without it.'

The boy was looking worried now. 'It's very expensive, sir.'

'San fairy ann. Forget it, kid.'

They moved down a narrow street behind the market and by the time they emerged into the Boulevard Saint-Michel again they had a loaf and a bottle of Nuits-Saint-Georges. If Scully couldn't get round Sidonie McCosh with his splendid military presence, he'd woo her, he decided, through her stomach.

'If she'll cook it, flower,' he said, 'we're going to have *one* good meal before it's too late. God knows what's going to happen tomorrow so let's at least enjoy today.'

8

As they made their way home, a cyclist drew up alongside them. It was George Presteigne, the boy who had stopped alongside them outside the Gare Montparnasse, strong, beaky-nosed and confident-looking with a cigarette between his lips.

'*Hé*, Ludo,' he yelled. 'I see your uncle's eyes have suddenly grown better. Who is he? Your mother's lover?'

'My mother doesn't have a lover.'

'Mine does. Or did. What is he then? An American flier or a diver trying to escape work in Germany?'

'He is neither.'

'Deserter?'

'I'm a British soldier, kid,' Scully snapped. 'Sergeant, if you want to know.'

George's face lit up. 'Has he come from de Gaulle?'

'He has come to show us how to fight,' Ludo said.

'I'll tell the others.'

Three streets further on, as they turned the corner, a group of boys was waiting for them.

'It is our Resistance group?' Ludo whispered.

Scully studied the huddle of youngsters with a startled look in his eyes.

'Resistance group?'

'Yes, sir. The British Réseau.'

'The British – ? Is *this* the British Réseau? I thought – For Christ's sake, these are only kids!' Scully's expectations of fierce-eyed warriors disappeared like mist before the wind.

'We all speak English,' Ludo assured him earnestly. 'We

are British to the core. Well – ' he gestured at the bony-faced boy with the bicycle ' – George is. He has a British father *and* a British mother.'

'Which,' George said aggressively, 'is why I am leader of the cell.'

Ludo frowned. 'I thought of it.'

George jeered. 'My voice has broken,' he pointed out coldly. 'Besides, I have had a woman. You haven't.'

'I will,' Ludo said. 'Soon. When I am older. And, anyway, it was only Germaine Guyou. She'll do it with anybody. Everybody knows that.' He looked at Scully and indicated another boy with a stubby blunt face and hair cut *en brosse*. 'This is Auguste Woof. His mother is American.'

Scully accepted the outstretched hand. 'And *his* pa?' he asked.

'Belgian. He is in the Resistance. Nobody knows where he is.' Ludo gestured at a boy leaning against a lamp post, languid and good-looking. 'This is Tom Cléry-Kidder.'

'British?'

'No, sir. Only his mother. His father was French. He is now dead.'

Scully gestured at George Presteigne. 'What about *his* dad? Is he dead?'

'No.' Presteigne snapped the word at him.

'In the Resistance?'

'No.'

Ludo gestured hurriedly at a pale-faced youngster with a shock of yellow hair. 'This is Xavier Lipski. He speaks English but he is really Russian.'

'*White* Russian,' the boy pointed out quickly. 'Not Red. My father had one of the best restaurants in Paris. But when the Germans came, he went into the Resistance.'

'Well, I'll be buggered,' Scully said. 'You're a right old mixture, aren't you?'

A very small boy, much younger than the others, was the last to be pulled forward. He wore a pair of spectacles as crooked as the ones Scully wore, their lenses so smeared with fingermarks they were virtually opaque, their value further reduced by the fact that one of them was cracked.

'This is *Grand Charles*,' Ludo said. 'Charles Rohan. Big Charley. Because he is so small, you understand. Not like General de Gaulle, who is tall and is also called Grand Charles. He will not do any fighting because he is too young. He will just carry messages.'

Scully shook hands gravely, the boy's hand disappearing inside his big fist. He was aware of a pair of owlish blue eyes staring at him.

'Have you met the general, sir?' Grand Charles asked.

'Which general?'

The boy seemed surprised, as if there were only one general in the world. 'General de Gaulle, of course.'

'Oh!' Scully smiled. 'Him! Oh, yes, once or twice. Complimented me on my soldierly appearance.'

'What's he like?'

'What's he like?' Scully wracked his brains. He had seen pictures of de Gaulle but had never taken much notice of them. 'Well – French. He looked French.'

They exchanged prideful glances. Despite their claim to be British, they were all French in spirit, all of them a little odd and sad because not being French made them outcasts; yet, with their stilted old-fashioned way of speaking, they weren't British either and belonged nowhere.

'What's chewing-gum like, sir?' Grand Charles asked. 'Have you ever had any?'

He was pushed aside by Xavier Lipski. 'Never mind him,' he said. 'What's it like being in a war?'

'I'd have thought you knew.'

'Oh, no, sir,' Auguste Woof put in. 'Not here. The Germans are here, of course, and we have heard a few bombs drop – '

'When they bombed the oil depots at Saint-Denis,' George said importantly, 'I watched. I didn't go to the shelter. What is it like being a soldier in the front line?'

Scully shrugged. 'You spend most of your time waiting for something to 'appen,' he said, 'and the rest of the time wishing it hadn't.'

His answer puzzled them. As they digested it, Grand Charles edged forward again.

'I'm a boy scout,' he announced. 'I have a uniform. I have three badges. One for tying knots, one for cooking – I had to cook a slice of sausage; it got a bit burned but they said it would do – and one for tracking.'

Tom Cléry-Kidder jeered. 'Where have *you* tracked? You can't find tracks in a city.'

'It was in the Bois de Boulogne,' Grand Charles said indignantly.

'They helped you. They said "We'll have to help Grand Charles. He'll never see anything. He never polishes his glasses." '

Grand Charles went pink, took off his spectacles and rubbed them carefully with a grubby handkerchief.

'I'm afraid of pushing out the cracked lens,' he said slowly. 'You can't get any more since the Germans came.' He looked at Scully. 'Have you killed any Germans, sir?'

'One or two.'

'Do you know how to fire a tommy-gun?' George asked. 'I once saw a tommy-gun fired. It was a German, who was shooting at some men they said were in the Resistance. They got away. Are you a good shot?'

'Got me marksman's badge, didn't I?' Scully said. He indicated his arm. 'Wore it just there. I could hit anything running, jumping, standing, sitting or flying. Expert with anything that would shoot. A rifle's a good weapon. Easy to clean and a .303 in your tripes stops your gallop as well as anything.'

'Will you teach us how to be good shots?'

'It's not hard, kid. All you have to remember is to cradle your rifle against your cheek and hold it tight. Otherwise, the recoil will break your shoulder. Especially a little feller like Grand Charles here.'

George pushed forward. 'I have more war souvenirs than the others,' he announced importantly. He fished in his pocket and produced a spent bullet. It had been turned into a small metal mushroom after hitting something hard. 'It is from a machine-gun,' he said. 'I also have the tail fin off an incendiary bomb. I got it from a man who lived in Abbeville.'

80

'I have a British pamphlet dropped on the city from a bomber in 1940,' Ludo said.

'I have the nose cone of a shell,' Auguste Woof added.

'And I have a piece of crashed aeroplane.' Xavier Lipski grinned proudly. 'It's aluminium. I've also got a bullet that hasn't been fired.'

'You could get into trouble for that,' Ludo said. 'You're not allowed to carry arms.'

'A bullet's not arms.'

'It is if it isn't fired. The Fritzes shot a student in Montparnasse for having a bullet on him. He was searched when they stopped him in the street. For something else entirely. They were checking papers.'

'We also have a British steel helmet,' Auguste interrupted. 'And a German poster appealing to the French to be friends with them.'

'I got that,' Grand Charles squeaked, squinting through his bent spectacles. 'They stuck it up on the wall near my house and I pulled it off as soon as they'd gone – before the paste was dry. I was only seven at the time.' He grinned at Scully. 'I'm eleven now.'

They were all trying to outdo each other when George Presteigne pushed forward again. 'I know how to make a petrol bomb,' he said. 'To throw at a tank.'

Xavier Lipski thrust him aside. 'I once saw a bomb crater,' he said. 'Out near the Creusot works in 1940. They said there was a body under the wreckage.'

'You forget,' Ludo said aloofly. 'I have just come from Normandy. I saw the Typhoons.'

That silenced them all. George Presteigne frowned. Scully had already put him down as self-important and difficult, and now he tried to draw attention to himself again.

'Our headquarters are in Clichy,' he said. 'They are at the bottom of our garden. My parents are the only ones with a garden. All these – ' he gestured ' – live in apartments.'

While they were arguing, Grand Charles edged between them until he was standing in front of Scully again, staring up at him through his cracked and grubby spectacles. His gaze was unwinking.

'Monsieur, have you met Winston Churchill?'

'Sure,' Scully said cheerfully. 'Plenty of times. Him and me are like that.' He held up two fingers alongside each other.

'And General Montgomery?'

'Often.' Him at the front, Scully thought, doing the talking; me at the back, doing the listening.

'He is French, that one.'

Scully's eyebrows shot up. 'First I've heard of it,' he said.

'Montgomery is a French name,' Grand Charles explained solemnly. 'Like Montrichard, Mont Blanc, Montbard. This is where he learns how to fight. Are there many Americans in England waiting to come to France?'

'Millions.' Too bloody many, Scully thought. They had the money and they had the transport. You couldn't get near the girls for 'em, any more than you could get near the Yanks for the girls. You could hardly blame either side, he supposed.

'They say they are kept in cages,' Xavier said.

'That's right, flower.' Not to keep the Yanks from getting out but to stop the dames from getting in.

The questioning went on for twenty minutes or more. In it there was longing for revenge and the need for reassurance, the need to know that soon their ordeal would be over, that Paris would be free.

'When the curfew starts,' Grand Charles said, 'you have to run to get home. If you are caught out, it is very dangerous. Sometimes, I have to stay with Xavier and they telephone my mother.'

'Nemmind, kid,' Scully assured him, 'it won't always be like that. One of these days we'll have them Jerries on the run, you see. Then it'll be your turn.'

They exchanged glances. 'Then they will suffer,' George said. 'We shall see that they suffer. We have a pistol, monsieur. Did you know that?'

'It's a signalling pistol,' Grand Charles pointed out. 'You can't kill a German with that!'

'If you push it in his face, he will be burned and blinded. That's good enough.' George looked earnestly at Scully. 'When the Germans come, you will not forget us?'

'Not for a moment.'

'You will show us what to do?'

'Of course.'

'We shall need to be expert with weapons.'

'How do you propose to get 'em?'

'That's easy,' George said, his cracked voice skating up and down in his enthusiasm. 'We shall ambush them and kill them and take *their* weapons. There is a perfect place for an ambush near where I live. It's off the Boulevard de Clichy. The Germans have to use the Boulevard Haussmann to get to their barracks and the Rue Mortmain on the left-hand side has a sudden curve where it narrows, and there's a burnt-out house that was destroyed by German bombs in 1940. It's been used since to store bales of rags and you could block the road there with them and force them into the Impasse Saint-Julien.'

'And butcher them!' Grand Charles shrieked.

As they became silent, Scully grinned at them. 'You know what I think?' he said cheerfully. 'I think you're a rotten bloodthirsty lot!'

They seemed delighted by the description. 'The Blood-thirsty Boys,' Cléry-Kidder said. 'That's a good name!'

'Not as good as the British Réseau.'

'I think it's better.'

As the argument developed into a shouting match, Scully moved on again. Ludo tried to explain.

'It is very difficult for George,' he said. 'He always talks big. Il veut faire le Zouave. He has to try much harder than the others because his father will not join the Resistance.'

'Why not?'

'I don't know, sir. His grandfather is a lord or something in England and he pays George's father to stay away. He pretends to be French so the Germans won't touch him but we all know he is British in spite of his false papers. He just does nothing, and uses his money to bribe the police and buy things on the black market. George is ashamed of him.

That is why he is always boasting and why he goes with Germaine Guyou. He makes his cigarettes from dried lime flowers and nettle leaves. He feels they make him look grown-up.'

'And the kid with glasses? What does *his* father do?'

''Grand Charles' father is a painter. He is not in the Re-sistance because nobody will have him. He is so absent-minded nobody *dare* have him. They are afraid he will give them away by accident. He doesn't mind, though, and, anyway, he fought in the other war and was wounded. Now he just paints. But not for the Germans, of course. He is very patriotic.' Ludo glanced back at the British Réseau, standing round George Presteigne's bicycle, watching them, puzzled and whispering. 'They are very impressed,' he said. 'When the Free French come, we will all be behind the barricades.'

Scully stopped and turned. 'You look here,' he said sharply. 'You got no father. That means your mum's got nobody else but you. So don't mix up with no fighting. You aren't old enough.'

'I am thirteen.'

'With muscles like a sparrer's kneecaps.'

'Sir?'

'Nemmind. It don't matter. Just do as I say. And if that kid with the Very pistol starts flourishing it round you, you sling your 'ook. Understand?'

'Sling my 'ook?'

' 'Op it? Push off. I don't want to have to carry you home, blinded and burned. Them things is dangerous. Just remem-ber that. You never point a gun at *nobody*.'

Sidonie was out at work when they reached home and they placed the bottle of wine in the middle of the table, arranged the sausages and potatoes round it and placed the bread to one side.

The apartment was on a corner. From one room it was possible to see the towers of the Sorbonne, Saint-Séverin and Notre-Dame, from another the Luxembourg Palace, Saint-Sulpice and Saint-Germain-des-Prés. From the balcony Scully stared over the plain of stone and iron, with its steeples, domes and cupolas. Away to the north, between the houses, he could see a white sugar-cake fairy-tale edifice which the boy said was Sacré-Coeur.

'It was built after the siege of Paris,' he explained. 'To atone for the defeat of 1870.'

In the street below, a fat German with a pasty face that was damp in the humid heat was just climbing out of a Wehrmacht van. He had a small package under his arm.

'That's Feldwebel Kriss,' Ludo said. 'He is cook at the Prince Eugène barracks. He brings food occasionally for Madame Weinspach.'

'Doesn't nobody ever try to have a go at him?'

'Oh, no, sir!' Ludo smiled. 'Feldwebel Kriss is all right. We have all grown used to him.'

It seemed to Scully that everybody had grown used to a lot of things they shouldn't have grown used to. He could hear Madame Weinspach welcoming the German, and Ludo tried to explain.

'She's Alsatian, you see,' he said. 'And she speaks his language. He comes from Lauterbach just inside Germany and she lived near the forest of La Houve which is just over the border, so they know the same towns and villages. To Madame Weinspach, he means food. To Feldwebel Kriss, Madame Weinspach is a touch of home, I think.'

As the German disappeared into the archway below them, they heard the door click and Sidonie's voice called.

'Lulu?'

'I'm here. Outside the window.'

'I only wished to know you were safe.' The voice sounded a little tired. 'I got the afternoon off and took the train to Auteuil. I thought I might pick up a few vegetables. There was nothing.'

Ludo jabbed at Scully with a sharp elbow and grinned.

They heard the kitchen door open and there was a long silence, then a cry of delight.

'Lulu! What have you done? What a repast! And what lovely flowers!'

She appeared on the balcony, her face all smiles and pink with pleasure.

'It wasn't me, maman,' the boy said. 'It was Sergeant Scully.'

'Oh!'

Her face fell and the smiles vanished. The pinkness deepened as she turned to Scully.

'I thank you,' she said very formally. 'I am grateful.' But she wasn't. She was embarrassed and angry. The thing had gone wrong somehow. Scully made an effort to bring back the life to her.

'Heard it was your birthday,' he said. 'Thought you might like a good meal for a change.'

'What are you hoping for?' she said quietly so that the boy wouldn't hear. 'Repayment? In my bed?'

Scully's face turned red because repayment in her bed was exactly what he had been hoping for.

9

Three days later, Ludo conducted Scully to a house below the slopes of Montmartre. It was surrounded by a high wall and, while Ludo waited by the door, Scully was led down the garden to where a battered hut hid a small printing press and a photographic studio. Scully was seated in a chair and a flashlight exploded, filling the place with smoke.

The following day, Sidonie handed him a set of papers. 'Work permit,' she said. 'Identity card. Certificate from your employer. Without that you might be taken to Germany for the *service du travail obligatoire*.' She gave him a quick look from under the lock of dark hair that hung like a wing over her eyes. 'You might anyway,' she added. 'It doesn't always stop them.'

There was a hint of malice in her words but he was conscious that she was no longer so aggressively hostile as she had been. The meal he had provided had won her round a little, particularly as he had made no attempt to take advantage of it. He was learning a curious restraint that was foreign to all his previous ideas of women, and he didn't have to be told that she was different from Daisy or Doris or Edna.

Now that he could move around with relative safety, Scully took to exploring the city thoroughly, accompanied when he wasn't at school by the boy.

'We will go to the Ecole Militaire,' the boy suggested. 'It's been transformed into a hospital. We go to watch the German lorries arriving with wounded from Normandy. We can see their feet and count how many there are. The Germans know why we come and it makes them nervous.'

The idea of death and wounds providing a peep show was anathema to the old soldier in Scully and he chose the opposite direction. The fact that he had money in his pocket made him restless and he was beginning to grow bored. The news that came to Paris about the fighting in the north came only through German press handouts and what could be gleaned from the BBC news in the late evening. The allies, it seemed, were still halted before Caen and, as Paris grew impatient, Scully determined to move further afield.

Finding a bicycle in a store room on the ground floor gave him an idea and he suggested cycling into the country in search of food. Ludo unearthed his own bicycle, and while they were preparing, George Presteigne appeared and insisted on accompanying them.

'I'm all for cheating the Germans,' he said loudly. '*Système D*: D for *Débrouillez*. D for Diddle the Germans!'

He had an unattractive personality and Scully had no wish to have him with them because his boasting and loud talk were dangerous.

'You'd better ask your dad, kid,' he pointed out sharply.

George shrugged. 'He won't care,' he said. 'He never did. If he had, we'd have gone to England in 1940.'

Near Maunoury on the other side of Bougival there was a farmer Ludo knew from previous visits with his mother who was reputed to have eggs to sell. The countryside was bathed in golden sunshine, the trees straight and green against the blue sky. Somewhere out of sight they could hear aircraft and George stopped and listened.

'Spitfires,' he said.

'You can tell?' Ludo asked.

'You can always tell Spitfires,' George said knowledgeably. 'These days they have cannon, not machine-guns. The American bombers have .5s. I wish we had a .5.' He looked at Scully. 'You have to aim a hand's breadth in front of them to allow for speed. Did you know that?'

'I've 'eard tell,' Scully said dryly.

'You have to guess it. A .5 can shoot through the trunk of a tree. A tank shell will go through a brick wall. Aren't you afraid in battle of being hit?'

Scully shrugged. 'If you're going to get it, kid, it'll have your number on it.'

'They say the Germans chalk names on the bombs they drop. "Best wishes, Winston." That sort of thing. Do the British do that also?'

'You should see *some* of the things they chalk on.'

Straddling his bicycle, George lifted his hands and pretended to fire a machine-gun. 'Paf-paf-paf! Have you ever seen a dead body?'

'I have,' Ludo said proudly. 'In Normandy.'

'What was it like?'

'It was – ' Ludo had been about to boast, then the light went from his eyes and his face fell. 'It was – ' He shrugged and became silent.

'The Germans shot a man in the Rue Réaumur,' George went on. 'Someone chalked his name on the wall and put flowers there, but the Germans threw them away and rubbed it off.' He lifted his hands again to his machine-gunner stance. 'Range one thousand metres. Fire! Paf! Got him! I'm going to be a brain surgeon when I grow up.'

Showing off, he rode ahead, and Ludo smiled at Scully. 'George always has to be the best,' he said quietly.

The farmer at Maunoury not only had eggs but also a skinny chicken. When they returned, Sidonie accepted it without comment but Scully noticed that she kept looking at him in a puzzled way throughout the meal.

She was still aloof and cool, but seemed by now to have accepted that until Scully could be passed along to some Resistance group to be moved to a place of safety or until Paris was liberated, she was stuck with him. Growing in confidence he moved freely in and out of the apartment, wearing the thick spectacles which gave him the look of an amiable idiot, becoming part of the teeming life of the Petite-Ville, enjoying the shops despite their emptiness, savouring the smell of new bread from the bakery in the Rue Noyelle, sampling the bars.

When he could, the boy went with him, probing, wanting to know what it was like being a soldier, what battles had he fought in, how many Germans had he killed? Then the rumour came – no one knew where from – that when the Americans came the Germans intended to fight for Paris. It alarmed the inhabitants of the Hôtel Bouboulis and the Petite-Ville and Scully heard Madame Weinspach, Sidonie and old Virec discussing it anxiously. Then Grand Charles's mother and father appeared through the alley that led to the Rue Fantin from the Hôtel Barrac and added their sixpennyworth. They had married late and Grand Charles had arrived unexpectedly when they had already reached middle age. His mother was thin and fragile-looking, his father a vague man with a self-consciously Bohemian air about him.

'They can't fight in the streets of Paris,' Madame Rohan said nervously. 'They just can't.'

Having fought through a few towns in his time, Scully couldn't quite see why not. Sidonie tried to explain.

'Paris was destroyed in 1870,' she said. 'First by the Prussians and then by the Commune. It has ever since been a fear of the Parisians that the city would be destroyed again.'

'London got a bit destroyed,' Scully pointed out quietly. 'By German bombers.'

She dismissed that with a wave of her hand. 'London is different,' she said. 'It has little beauty. Paris is Paris. In 1940 it was declared an open city.'

'And look what it got you.' Scully couldn't resist it.

As he moved about the streets, he noticed that the Germans had suddenly begun to appear in tighter formations, marching or riding in lorries, their faces wearing harassed looks. The old easy-going custom of strolling on the boulevards seemed to have ended and there was a new brusqueness, as if the fact that the allies were still in Normandy and not thrown back into the sea, as Hitler had promised, was giving them bad dreams.

The money he had acquired still a thick wad in his pocket, Scully watched them with interest, as often as not surrounded by the members of the British Réseau.

'You've got to hand it to them,' he observed. 'They're smart.'

'Germans?' They found it hard to believe he was offering praise. In their youthful world such a thing was impossible.

'Not as good as British soldiers, o' course,' he conceded, 'but all right. For smartness, you should see our lot. The Fusileers. We're the boys who make no noise. The boys who know how many beans make five.'

They became silent. Grand Charles was frowning. 'How many beans make five?' he said.

'Yes. You know?'

Grand Charles frowned again. 'There can only be one answer, sir,' he said. 'Five.'

'No, flower. The answer's two-beans-two-half-beans-a-bean-and-a-half-and-half-a-bean.'

Scully rattled off the saying as fast as he could and Grand Charles stared at him. Slowly his expression melted and he began to grin.

'That is good, sir. Say it again.'

'Two-beans-two-half-beans-a-bean-and-a-half-and-half-a-bean.'

Grand Charles's small moon face was delighted. 'I shall try that on my mother,' he said. 'Two beans, two half-beans, a bean and a half, and half a bean. That is very clever. And did all the Fusileers know the answer?'

'That they did, flower. We came back from Dunkirk marching in threes and carrying our weapons. And when we reached Dover we didn't go to the station in buses like all the rest. We marched – in step and swinging our arms. That's what knowing how many beans make five means. We was called fusiliers because originally we was armed with a lighter weapon than the old musket, see. You'll know what a musket is, o' course. Fusiliers is different. Especially our lot, the North Staffs. We even spell our name with a double *e*. I told you about that. Like the Royal Welch, who spell their name as if they wasn't Welsh but something else entirely. *Cetera Desunt*. That's us. The others are wanting. We're the only fusilier regiment to wear an elephant in our badge. Because we served longer in India than any other regiment ever. They forgot us, see.'

'Why?'

'Well, they did now and then in them days. They left us there so long, we was all so burned black by the sun they called us niggers. So, just to show what we thought o' them, we took to wearing a little black edge to our buttons. We wear it to this day. We're allowed to march through Stafford with bayonets fixed. You know that?'

'Why?' Grand Charles had a disconcerting habit of wanting to know the reason for everything.

'Tradition. You got to have tradition. You got to think that your regiment's better than all the others. It makes you try harder.'

'We'd better do that with our réseau,' Auguste Woof observed.

'It won't do any harm, that's for sure.'

'They've got a réseau in the Rue Ruffalt,' Tom Cléry-Kidder said. 'They're older than us and they're being used already to carry messages. Of course, their fathers are all communists and it's the communists who are thinking of rising against the Germans. We're not communists. My father was an officer at Verdun. Xavier's had his own restaurant.'

'And mine,' George said, 'is a gentleman. And that's all.'

As he watched and listened, Scully became aware of a man in a leather jacket approaching. He was fair and good-looking and was walking with a slouch, his hands in the pockets of his trousers. Stopping by Scully, he jerked his head and the réseau melted into the background.

'You Scully?' he asked in English.

'Yes.' Scully released cigarette smoke from the side of his mouth.

'Heard about you, old man. Mind if I share your pew?'

'Help yourself.'

'I'm Hasler.'

Scully had expected someone younger, an air-force type with blond curls and a lost expression. This man was tall, lean, hard-faced, intelligent, self-confident, smiling and tough. He looked like a native of France and he had the air of self-assured command about him that Scully knew from the army. This one was used to telling people what to do, not the other way round.

'You air force?' he asked.

'You must be joking.' Hasler seemed shocked at the suggestion. 'I've got better things to do than float about up there dropping bombs. I'm Rifle Brigade.'

Scully said nothing. Even a North Staffs Fusileer had to admit that the Rifle Brigade was special.

'I was sent here to do a job,' Hasler went on. 'I suspect I've done it, judging by the way the Germans are looking for me. A train at Chartres, a bridge at Meaux, and a couple of staff colonels and their drivers at Nogent isn't a bad start, is it?' He smiled. 'The city's full of British and American agents. Been arriving for some time. My area runs from Montparnasse to Clichy. I've got it all buttoned up.'

'You going to get me back to England?'

'Use your loaf.' Hasler laughed. 'You're a soldier, they said. Could use a few good soldiers. You a regular?'

'Sergeant. North Staffs Fusileers.'

Hasler smiled. 'Good mob, sergeant.' It was 'sergeant' now, Scully noticed, not 'old man'.

'How did you get here?' Hasler asked.

'No alternative. Got cut off in Normandy. Only one way to go. South-east.'

'You'll be useful. City's full of people wanting to slit the Germans' throats. It'll happen, too, when the time comes. They say the Americans don't want to get tangled up with Paris, but they're going to, like it or not. We're going to see they do. Communists are planning a rising. And the Gaullists are planning to arrive before they can get control. It'll come to a fight.'

'Which side are you on?'

Hasler gave him a hard look and changed the subject. 'What do you think of the McCosh woman?'

Scully made a non-committal sound and Hasler smiled. 'Lucky to be staying in her apartment. Wouldn't have me. In spite of the Germans knowing I was around. Still, I have my spies out doing their recces and when they come snooping I disappear. Got a safe hiding place.'

'You must speak good French.'

Hasler gave him a cold look. 'I also speak good German, good Italian, good Spanish, good Portuguese and good Russian. You name it, I speak it. After I left university I lived over here for a long time. Even joined a circus for a while. Afterwards in the diplomatic corps, but I left to go to Spain when the Civil War started.'

'To fight for Franco, I suppose.'

'No, old man. For the wrong side. Lot of us did. See politics differently now. When *our* war started they recruited me because I could speak every blasted language under the sun. Used me to instruct the boys. Then some clever clot said "Why use him to instruct? Why not send *him*?" '

He pulled out a packet of French cigarettes, extracted one and offered it to Scully.

'Growing a bit tired of Paris now,' Hasler went on. 'Knew it in the old days. Even the women's tits have lost their aggressiveness now. There's too much bloody "France" these days and not enough "amour".' He shrugged. 'Still, there's a circus at the Grand Palais. Jean Houcke's. He's a Swede. Some of my old friends are there.' He gave a cold smile. 'God knows who wants to watch a circus horse these days, though. Most people would prefer eating it. But if you'd like a ticket I can get you one.'

There was a pause then Hasler spoke again. 'You met that cousin of La McCosh? Pierre Lambrouille.'

'Yes.'

'Watch him. He's an informer and he's dangerous. Unbalanced as hell. Probably a lunatic. We know him. His apartment's full of *la gloire*. Makes you think of the muffled roll of Bonapartist drums. God knows how he reconciles it with his toadying to the Germans, but, then, how do Pétain and a few others? You talked to him?'

'I've heard him talk.'

'His bloody lost honour. I lost the whole of my family, never mind my honour. In the blitz on London. He's obsessed with his bloody ancestors. Had a go at me when I was there. The blood *they* shed seemed to be a whole lot bloodier than anyone else's.'

'Why didn't he turn you in?'

'Scared of upsetting La McCosh. But he'd not hesitate now. I've been responsible for the removal of too many of his German friends. He probably won't turn *you* in because he's hedging his bets these days in case the Germans leave. Besides, he wants La McCosh and he knows he won't get her that way. Commies have their eye on him. Think he's turned over more than one of their friends. *I* think he has, too, and I'm keeping it by me in case of trouble.' He pushed the packet of cigarettes across. 'Keep it. Black market. FFI have plenty. Raid tabacs. So far, that's about *all* they do. Be gettin' in touch with you.'

'What for?'

Hasler's wintry smile came again. 'Been watching you. Thought you might carry messages for us. Notice they never look twice at you with those glasses of yours.' He rose, slapped Scully's shoulder and strolled off. As he disappeared, the British Réseau returned. Ludo sat on the bench at one side of Scully, Grand Charles on the other.

'That's Hasler,' Ludo pointed out.

'He's in the Resistance,' George said. 'I know. I've seen him with Jean-Pierre Rou's father. Jean-Pierre Rou's father runs an organization at Clichy.'

It occurred to Scully that if George Presteigne knew about the organization at Clichy, it might well be known to a few other people, too, and it would pay to be careful.

Grand Charles edged closer. Being so small, his clothes were always too big for him because, with the clothing shortage, he had to make do with everybody else's cast-offs.

'Sir,' he asked. 'How do you fire a German anti-tank gun?'

Scully's eyebrows shot up. 'Who wants to know?'

'The time will come,' George said importantly, 'when the Germans will have to fight for Paris and *we*'ll want to know.'

'Son,' Scully said seriously. 'You forget it.'

George stared at him, then pointedly changed the subject. 'They say the 88 is a good gun,' he said.

'You got one in the backyard?' Scully asked.

95

'Is the Bren a good gun, sir?' Xavier asked.

'Chief killing weapon of the infantry, kid.' Scully could handle a Bren like a bored mechanic with his tools. 'One to each section and manned by two men. Fires over a bipod up to six hundred yards. Can also be fired from the hip with a shoulder sling for support. Used principally in defensive positions where they need to be fired accurately over greater ranges and over previously aligned fixed arcs at night or in fog or smoke.'

'I think you know a lot about it, sir.'

'I taught it, didn't I? I can make a Bren talk. But what are you wanting to know for? Same as him?' He gestured at George. 'Because you might have to shoot one?'

'Yes, sir.'

Scully grinned. 'Son, if them Germans start shooting, you get behind something. A cigarette packet'll do. You'll be surprised how small you can make yourself when some feller's trying to hit you.'

'Could you teach us how to drill?'

'Sure I could. But you don't want to worry with that rubbish.' Scully had never been a drill man. 'It never did anybody much good, and I can tell you anything you want on guns. What's the killing range of a 2 inch mortar? How many rounds does a Bren take? Why does a Sten fire 8 millimetre ammo? I know it all, kid.'

'I wish you'd teach us,' Ludo said.

Conscious of having lost the limelight, George jeered. 'We don't need to know *that*,' he said. 'Just how to pull a trigger and look through the sights. I know how to make a petrol bomb. Jean-Marc Pusy told me. His father's one of Rou's men. You use sulphuric acid and potassium chloride.' He paused doubtfully. 'I *think*,' he added. 'In any case, you can always fill a bottle with petrol and stuff a paraffin-soaked rag in the top ready to light. The Resistance use them to knock out tanks.'

Scully studied him placidly. 'If you see a German tank, son,' he said firmly, 'the best thing you can do is 'op it. Fast. Little kids can't do anything against that lot.'

'I'm not a little kid,' George snapped. 'I'm fourteen!'

To Paris

'You're still your mum's only son,' Scully said sternly. 'And she wouldn't want you to stand up to a tank with a bottle full of petrol, would she?'

10

It was growing clearer every day that the Germans were coming off worst in the fighting in the north. The Third Reich, which had expanded so fast in 1940 and 1941, was shrinking twice as fast.

The push in the west had been held up, however, by a great storm which had wrecked allied shipping off the Normandy coast and broken up the floating piers, erected with so much energy and expense, so that in the few areas where there had been organized resistance there had been savage reprisals: a massacre in Gascony and another at Oradour-sur-Glane in the Haute-Vienne. Only on the Vercors Massif, near Grenoble, was there any real success. There, Resistance leaders, army officers and a few others had simply hung out French flags and challenged the Germans to attack.

All this, however, had no effect on Paris. The streets remained empty of traffic save for German Mercedes cars and commandeered Citroëns, and a few vehicles whose owners were clever enough or collaborated enough to possess petrol or *gazogènes*, which were powered by gas from the wood that burned in the wash boilers they towed behind. Only horses – and old ones at that, because the Germans had taken all the others – and bicycles occupied the streets. Even the Métro was closed through all the middle hours of the day and when it was open it was overcrowded, the air fetid with packed bodies.

As the fighting in Normandy intensified, food grew more scarce and there seemed little else but swedes fit only for cattle and artichokes that were almost uneatable.

'How can I bring up a growing boy on what we get?'

Sidonie demanded. 'The honey's abominable, the sweet-meats are made from rotten dates and the coffee's nothing but roasted wheat. Why?' she asked despairingly. 'France grows everything.'

'There are a lot of Germans in France, maman,' Ludo pointed out.

'There are more French in Germany,' she snapped. 'Either prisoners or forced labour.'

When Bastille Day arrived it provoked gatherings and flags in the working-class areas. The Germans felt it was safer to leave well alone, and demonstrations were held unmolested in the Place de la Bastille and at Belleville. The *Milice* were heckled and shots were fired at Gentilly and Vitry, while the crowd sang the 'Marseillaise' and insisted on laying on monuments wreaths shaped like a V or the Cross of Lorraine.

With the German grip tightening nervously on the city, Scully made several more trips into the countryside for food, even as far afield as Chartres. With the warm weather, he was untroubled by the need to find a bed and spent the night in the fields. Unlike working Parisians, he had the time to search and was old soldier enough rarely to return empty-handed.

Holzmeier had still not given up. One day a bag of coffee and a box of Swiss chocolates arrived. Sidonie gazed at them with longing, but firmly pushed them aside, and Madame Weinspach and Monsieur Virec happily shared them. During the evening, Holzmeier himself appeared.

'I hope you enjoyed the coffee, madame,' he said.

'I didn't drink it,' Sidonie pointed out coldly. 'I gave it to the concierge.'

'Don't you like coffee?'

'I like *French* coffee.'

'German coffee is no different.'

Sidonie drew a deep breath. 'I don't like the flavour of German coffee,' she said.

'How about the chocolates?'

'I gave those also to the concierge.'

The German frowned. 'You don't like chocolates?'

'I have to watch my figure.'

'But your son? Surely *he* likes chocolates?'

'He doesn't like German chocolates,' she insisted.

'These weren't German chocolates. They were Swiss.'

'They had been handled by a German.'

Holzmeier's voice grew pleading. 'Why are you so harsh, madame?'

Sidonie's answer was short but unambiguous. 'Article four of chapter twenty-five of the Constitution of 1793,' she said curtly, 'states "The French people do not make peace with an enemy who occupies its territory." There is no answer to that.'

'Madame – Sidonie – !'

Holzmeier's voice was pleading but the answer he received was unrelenting. 'Don't call me Sidonie!'

'It is a lovely name.'

'Not in a German accent.'

For a moment, Scully thought Holzmeier was going to try to push his way in but he was still only a shy and rather desperate young man conscious of the hatred that surrounded him and eager to find some chink in the unrelenting refusal to accept him.

Baffled and frowning, he backed away and Sidonie closed the door hurriedly and locked it. As she turned away, Scully touched her hand, and she grasped his fingers quickly.

'Oh, God,' she whispered. 'When will they go? When will the Americans arrive to save us?'

Rather to his surprise, Scully realized he was changing. He no longer swore so much – not in English, out loud or even in his mind when he was alone – and he was developing traces of good manners.

For the first time in his life, he was living in a house where manners were considered important and, having noticed the first wince of disapproval from Sidonie as he clutched his knife and fork like daggers, he had watched her carefully and was now trying to remember to hold them the way she did. To his surprise and pleasure, he realized she was changing also. Occasionally he heard her singing quietly to herself in the kitchen – the nostalgic 'Je Suis Seule Ce Soir' – and she no longer talked of his leaving. She was also no longer sharp with him, and she introduced him to Auguste Woof's American mother with an unaffected willingness that contrasted markedly with the way he had met Grand Charles' parents. And when Ludo took a photograph of him, he noticed that it took its place on the mantelpiece with other members of the family, and did not disappear like the rest of the reel after a few days.

The apartment was full of books, which revealed her interests and those of her dead husband, and from the way she talked about them he realized that when she read a book it stayed read and didn't vanish into the limbo of the lost, like the books – none of them much to write home about, anyway – which Scully had read in his time. For the first time in his life he found himself enjoying good music – not the heaviest, to be sure, as if she had chosen it carefully as a beginning – and he noticed now that, instead of listening alone to *Les Français Parlent Aux Français*, the BBC programme that came on every night, she had taken to suggesting that he listen too, and translated for him what he failed to understand.

He was in no doubt that initially she had allowed him to remain in the apartment only as a defence against Holzmeier and probably Lambrouille and even Hasler, but he didn't bother to question it, only remaining grateful that she had become friendly. He was going up in the world and was growing ambitious. As his sidekick, Chalky White, had once said – 'I'm going to put in for a commission. You get to drink whisky.' Scully felt the same.

Occasionally, he saw Lambrouille with his red bow tie and smart clothes. It was obvious he was in love with Sidonie and that it was this which prevented him running to the Gestapo with the information that she was sheltering a British soldier.

Then Scully found a new shirt on his bed, with a pair of trousers and a pullover.

'For me?' he asked.

101

'They were my husband's,' she said, avoiding his eyes. 'He put them on when he was not working. They are more comfortable.'

'They're very smart,' Ludo smiled, happy at the new atmosphere. 'Is it true, sir, that soldiers put on clean clothes before they go into battle?'

'Yes. It's true. Dirty clothes lead to dirty wounds.'

Ludo considered for a moment. 'Will there be a battle for Paris, sir?' he asked.

Scully smiled. 'You'd better ask the Germans,' he said.

Sidonie looked at him anxiously. 'God forbid there will,' she said.

Unaware of the city's potential, the main event of Scully's day-to-day life remained the meetings with the British Réseau in the Luxembourg Gardens. He was amazed how little they knew of the games he had played, even in the orphanage, as a boy – cat's cradle, five stones, even cricket.

'Everybody in England plays cricket,' he said.

'My father,' George announced, 'says it is a fool's game.'

But when Scully carved them a bat from a piece of wood George was the most vociferous at insisting his wicket had not been struck.

Never having had any children of his own and having always carefully avoided women who did, Scully had little experience of youthful minds or behaviour, and he was surprised to find he could deal with both and even manage to understand them.

Despite the conditions, they were always in high spirits. Like most youngsters, they seemed to be untouched by the Vichy propaganda and remained set against Pétain and the Germans. Even the air raids didn't bother them because the men who were bombing them were held to be their friends, and when the sirens sounded, they regarded it as a game of cops and robbers, repeating the wail – Grand Charles with his high-pitched voice being particularly effective – and cowering in mock terror against the walls.

They scrawled additions to the Pétainist posters appealing for *Travaille, famille, patrie*, so that they read 'Work (forced), (far from) family, (against the) country.' Like their

102

adults, they referred to the Germans as 'Fritzes' or '*ces messieurs*,' and when they weren't pretending they didn't exist, they mimicked their movements. When the Germans asked the way, they listened with exaggerated politeness before finally sending them in totally the wrong direction, and their great pleasure was to pretend to be going fishing with two fishing rods, so that if they were asked 'Why two?' they could answer 'Because I like deux gaules,' a play on the name of the man they regarded as the saviour of France.

It was just one more act of defiance, like that of the waiter who deliberately put his thumb in German soup, the printer who printed insulting posters, the men who stuck them on walls after dark. It was resistance, just as much as the men who shot German officers in the Métro and escaped in the crowd.

Eventually, Scully was privileged to be allowed a visit to their headquarters at the bottom of the Presteignes' garden in Clichy. The district where they lived was a backwater like the Petite-Ville but of larger, older houses set in their own grounds and surrounded by high walls, with gates which were closed at night against intruders. The Presteigne house was smaller than most, but it looked in good repair, as if there were no shortage of money. Further along the road on the other side was another house of a similar type, with a cobbled courtyard where carriages had once waited, and a wide glassed doorway well protected by sandbags.

'That's the Hôtel Saint-Breille,' George said proudly. 'It used to belong to the Marquis de Saint-Breille. My father knew him. He used to come to have drinks.'

'He was always drunk,' Tom Cléry-Kidder said bluntly. 'Like your father. You said so.'

With a great show of secrecy, George led the way to a ramshackle old greenhouse at the bottom of the garden. It was half obscured by tall weeds, and was black with mould and the droppings of birds roosting in the trees that overhung it. They had rigged up an electric light and arranged their souvenirs on a shelf which had once held flowerpots. On the wall was a notice with the réseau rules neatly inscribed. Underlined was one in large letters that was visible at once. 'Penalty for informing parents – Death.' Alongside was a poster showing a German soldier holding a child, above the words, '*Populations abandonées. Faire confiance aux soldats allemands.*'

'Nice old place you've got here,' Scully said cheerfully.

'This is where the British agent, Hasler, stays,' George said. 'He comes when the police are looking for him.' He indicated an old bench seat from a car. 'He sleeps on that and I smuggle blankets out to him.'

Hasler, Scully decided, was playing a dangerous game with a lot of idealistic kids.

'We all have *noms de guerre*,' George went on. 'Everybody in the Resistance has a *nom de guerre*. Ludo is called "Marcel", Xavier is "Thomas", Auguste is "Xenophon", Tom is "Guynemer". Grand Charles is – well – Grand Charles. I am "Bernard". After General Montgomery. We'll now sing the National Anthem. We always sing it before we start our meetings.'

Standing in a circle, they solemnly raised their voices.

> '*Allons, enfants de la Patrie,*
> *Le jour de gloire est arrivé . . .*'

Scully listened in amazement. 'But you're the *British* Réseau,' he said. 'Why don't you sing "God Save The King"?'

They looked faintly shamefaced and it was Ludo who spoke for them. 'Sir, we don't know it.'

'Anyway, I'm not British,' Xavier said. 'I'm Russian. *White* Russian.'

'You look pink to me, like everybody else,' Grand Charles said and reeled away, laughing.

George gave him a contemptuous look so that he pulled himself together quickly and jerked a hand at the poster on the wall. 'I got that,' he said. 'I've also got a revolver.'

'It's no good,' George sneered. 'Your father found it on the battlefields of the First War. Wait till we get a real gun.'

'Can I hold it when we do?'

They had made a wooden rifle from a plank and painted the breech, stock and barrel in brown and black.

'We drill with it,' Ludo explained. 'We take it in turns.'

'They won't let me,' Grand Charles complained. 'They say I'm not big enough.'

'How do you fire it?' Xavier Lipski asked.

Scully took the rifle, performed a few evolutions with it, then held it to his shoulder, cradling the stock to his cheek.

'Left hand well forward,' he said. 'Butt tucked well in to the shoulder and up against the cheek, right eye behind the rear sight, left eye closed, right hand gripping the stock at its narrowest part. Firmly but not too tight. Forefinger on the trigger ready to press gently – not pull, because pulling jerks and spoils your aim. You take what's known as first pressure, when you have your sights on your enemy. Second pressure's when you hold your breath and gently squeeze, so that the rifle goes off without moving.'

'Were you an instructor, sir?'

'That I was. Before the war. I wasn't bad either. Good-hearted but I could be a swine when I had to be.'

They were still discussing rifles as they headed back towards the Luxembourg Gardens.

'I wish we had a *real* rifle,' Auguste said. 'Then we'd be able to protect ourselves against the Germans.'

Scully was scornful. 'You don't get given a rifle to protect your silly little life,' he said. 'You get it given for the destruction of the King's enemies.'

'The French haven't got a king. They chopped his head off in 1793.'

'Well, their bloody republic then. It's all the same. You look after your rifle. You clean it and oil it and you never stand with your hands on the muzzle. Your hand might be perspiring and perspiration's damp and spoils the barrel.'

'They teach you this in the army?'

'It's one of the things you learn. Like you mustn't whistle the Dead March in barracks. Death's considered important in the army and we don't think about it lightly. It's one of them things – like breaking step across a bridge, because the shock of marching can damage the structure.' Scully didn't believe it, but that was what he'd been told, and what he'd been told in his recruit training had become gospel to him.

'It's training,' he explained. 'That's all. Like when we was caught in Palestine when Chalky White got the DCM. They was all round us. You couldn't see 'em. You couldn't hear 'em. But they was there. We knew they was there. Them Ay-rabs could hide behind a grain of sand. All you could see was sun. We'd lost our scouts – both of 'em stabbed – and the roadblock we'd put up had gone.'

They were hanging on to his words, entranced, and he held their attention as he'd held the attention of recruits more than once, telling them tall stories to accentuate the importance of discipline and training. 'Then, all of a sudden, my right' and man goes down. Pop! "Aagh," he says, and then we see them Ay-rabs coming at us. Yelling. Somethin' to do with Allah. We thought we'd 'ad it, but never say die, that's our mob, and we just remembered everything we'd been told and fired like we was on the range at Aldershot. We'd just about run out of ammo and was growing a bit worried because the vultures had arrived and was waitin' just above, like a lot of black widders, when the Black Watch appeared. You'll know of the Black Watch, o' course. All checked skirts and bagpipes, yowling like a cat what's got its tail trod on. We'd 'ung on. Discipline, see? Without it, we'd have been wiped out. You've got to have discipline.'

'It was very dangerous, I think,' Ludo said. 'This fighting against the Arabs.'

'Good practice,' Scully said. 'It's that what's 'elping us give Hitler his coating. Taught us to keep to the high ground. Never to get into valleys where you can be over-looked. Very important that.' He grinned, enjoying teasing them, but they listened utterly straight-faced. 'Very important to know where you can enfilade your enemies and bring crossfire to bear.'

They were still quiet and thoughtful as they crossed the Pont des Arts, solemnly making sure that they were not in step.

'It don't matter on bridges as big as this,' Scully reassured them.

'Nevertheless,' Xavier said, 'it is a good idea to practise, just in case. What else do they tell you?'

Scully wracked his brains as they settled on a seat in the Luxembourg Gardens. He was beginning by this time to feel drained of information. 'There's lots of things,' he said. 'Like all fusilier regiments have a little bomb-burst on their collars. Like the little verses what go with the bugle calls. So you can recognize 'em when you hear 'em. "Officers' wives eat pudden and pies. Soldiers' wives eat skilly." "Come and do a picquet, boys, come and do a guard. You think it's ruddy easy, but you'll find it's ruddy 'ard".'

He became aware of their looks of blank astonishment.

'Yeh, well,' he said airily. 'It don't matter anyway. It's rifle firing that's most important. Learning to hold your breath as you squeeze the trigger. And never firing over your shelter, only round the right-hand side.'

'Why, sir?' Ludo asked.

'Because, for Christ's sake, if you stick your silly chump over the top you'll get it shot off, won't you?'

Grand Charles manoeuvred himself forward. 'Can you shoot a pistol, sir?'

'I could teach you to get two rounds off quick as light,' Scully said. 'Until you can shoot straight by instinct – out of your pocket, backwards, under your arm, while you're lying in bed – you're not a shot.'

'Is it very hard, sir?'

'Not if you regard your pistol as a pointing finger.' Scully's arm swung. 'Don't dwell on it, though, or you're dead. Two rounds in the target. Bang bang! Change mags. Practise in your sleep.'

'Did you have a Sten gun, sir?' Xavier demanded.

'I've fired 'em,' Scully said. 'Made in bicycle factories, they say, outa the bits left over after they've finished the bikes. You 'ave to mind you don't shoot your own foot off because they have a habit of going off when you don't expect it. So don't point 'em unless you intend to kill. Not even in fun. Never. You can either fire single shots or put him on automatic and let the whole mag go off like a horse farting.'

Grand Charles rolled on the ground, shaking with laughter. George tried to look important and lit a cigarette. 'I'll have to learn how to use a pistol,' he observed.

'Then you'd better give up smoking, kid,' Scully said gravely. 'It slows your reaction and unsteadies your hand.'

They never let up. The following day, when Scully reached the gardens, they were playing football but they stopped immediately and flooded round him.

'How many beans make five?' Grand Charles asked.

'Go on. How many?'

'Two beans, two half-beans, a bean and a half, and half a bean.' Grand Charles' round face split in an angelic smile. 'My mother did not know that one, sir.' He frowned. 'I tried it on a friend in my class at school but he was not amused. I think it sounds different in French.' He touched Scully's hand. 'Our leader's not here today. He went off to see Germaine Guyou.'

'Her father works on the Métro,' Xavier explained. 'And her mother's got a boyfriend. She visits him when her father's at work.'

'And then the flat's empty,' Auguste Woof grinned. 'She asked me one day but I didn't go.'

'Germaine Guyou,' Ludo said, 'isn't important.' He spoke slowly, almost resentfully, as though he longed to be as adult as George Presteigne, to smoke, to go with girls, to have a broken voice.

'Sir, have you ever been wounded?'

'Once.'

'Where?'

Scully bent to show them where a bullet had nicked his ear at Dunkirk and left it with a small fillet missing. It led somehow into a long discourse on gas-operated machine-guns and explanations on how the breech was returned and the bullet pushed into the barrel by the return spring. Scully could strip machine-guns with his eyes closed and had spouted the spiel to recruits so often he recited it now without thinking, his voice rising automatically to the high strangulated tone of an instructor who had learned his lines off pat.

They stared at each other, barely comprehending what he was talking about.

'What about a French Hotchkiss?'

'Top-mounted. Box feed. 303. Bipod and flash suppressor.'

'What about German guns?'

'Maschinengewehr 34's a good gun. Seventy-five-round drums. 1219 millimetres long. 627 millimetre barrel. Fires at a rate of 900 rounds per minute. If you see one coming, get out of its way.'

They were still gasping at his erudition when George appeared, a look of determination and importance on his face. As he skidded his bicycle to a full stop, he threw up a salute.

'Bernard reporting, sir,' he said. 'I've got something for you. It's a message. You're to take it to Maunoury.'

He began to fiddle with his front tyre, making a great deal of show of it. Then he took the pump from its stop and began to unscrew the end.

'What's wrong?'

George was poking about with his finger inside the pump, red-faced and angry. 'It's the message.' His face was flushed with fury and humiliation. 'It's stuck.'

'Give it here.' Scully took the pump, removed the rubber connection and blew through the hole. A small piece of thin paper fluttered out which George snatched up at once.

As he handed it over, the other boys crowded round, eager to know what it contained. Scully shoved them aside and opened the folded slip.

The message was scrawled in English. It said, 'There is a man in a leather jacket, blue beret and red scarf waiting at the Bar de l'Ouest at the end of the bridge off the main square at Maunoury. He will be there this afternoon and tomorrow afternoon. Tell him you've come from Jacquot and he'll ask if you want eggs. Tell him the answer is yes, we're ready.'

Scully stared at it. 'Is that all?'

'There is also a letter. It contains numbers of the Resistance and possible strongpoints. It must not be found by the Germans.' George fished in his pocket and, as he produced the envelope, Scully grinned.

'Why stuff *that* in your pocket,' he asked, 'and the other bit, which ain't very important, in your pump?'

He enjoyed taking George down a peg or two and, as if he realized it, George looked resentful.

'Jean-Marc Pusy suggested it,' he said. 'He's the son of Pusy, who is deputy to Jacques Rou, the leader of the Clichy Réseau. He passed it to me in the pump. We're at the same school.' He gestured at the other boys. 'I'm older than this lot, you know. I'm at lycée. We swopped pumps. Right in front of the bar with everyone watching. The English officer, Hasler, sent it. He was in the Bar du Destin at Clichy. He can't take it himself because he's being watched night and day by the Germans and the communists, and he knew you cycled to Maunoury from time to time to buy vegetables.'

11

When he announced his intention that evening of going to Maunoury to seek eggs, Scully was surprised to hear Ludo asking if he and Grand Charles could take a picnic and go with him as far as Bougival.

'You can fish there,' he explained. 'And it's hot enough to swim.'

Sidonie was not disposed to let the boy wander far but it was impossible, while she was working, to keep him in the narrow confines of the Rue Fantin. 'Somebody has to look after the apartment,' she said uncertainly, looking for excuses.

'There's Madame Weinspach,' Ludo pointed out. 'It's her job.'

'Well, there's your violin lesson.'

'That's not tomorrow.'

Her objections didn't stand up and she flung a worried glance at Scully.

'Forget it,' he said. 'I'll take care of 'em.'

The next morning Scully rose as usual before her to prepare the coffee and fetch the bread from the baker's in the Rue Noyelle round the corner, allowing her to do nothing before she left for work.

'You are very good, sergeant.' Her voice sounded troubled but the expression on her face was curiously gentle.

'Old soldiers,' he said, 'make wonderful wives and mothers.'

She was still dubious about Ludo, however, and Scully looked down at her. 'What's the ration?' he asked.

'Two eggs for the month. Three ounces of cooking oil.'

'And the meat ration?'

She gave a twisted smile. 'It could be wrapped in a Métro ticket – so long as it's not been used. If it has, it might fall through the hole punched by the conductor.'

'You can get eggs at Maunoury for forty centimes each. Don't worry, I'll bring 'em back safe and sound.'

Ludo was delighted. 'You'll be able to show us the lie of the land,' he said. 'Where the Germans can be ambushed and where we could bring crossfire to bear.'

'Sure,' Scully said easily. 'I'll do that. Heights. That's what counts. You've got to capture the heights.'

As the boy went to get his bicycle, Sidonie took Scully to task. 'You should not talk to them of war,' she said.

Scully smiled. 'They're only playing.'

She frowned. 'Playing,' she said gravely, 'is the one thing they are *not* doing.'

It was a comment that left Scully thoughtful. He was still thoughtful as they pedalled along the Boulevard Lefebvre, crossed the Seine, and then began the climb out towards Saint-Cloud. The wide street was empty. There were no buses, and the taxis had long since disappeared. Beyond the city boundaries, however, there was a great deal of German military traffic heading towards Bougival. It roared past, heading north and west, covering them with clouds of dust and filling their eyes and nostrils and mouths. There was a grimness about the German soldiers these days which suggested to Scully that they were all busy working out their chances of survival, a pastime of which he had plenty of experience himself.

'I wonder,' Ludo said suddenly, 'when we shall see the traffic going the other way.'

'Soon, kid,' Scully reassured him. 'Have no fear.'

The fight round Caen was still going on, a wearing sort of battle where men were constantly killed but little progress was made. Scully had taken part in enough similar actions, however, to know that sooner or later it would *have* to come to an end, and that when it did it would be the Germans who would give way.

112

At Bougival, he took the two boys to a ration-free restaurant and bought them a meal of sausage stew that was tasteless but filling, and afterwards saw them to the river. Leaving them unpacking their rods, he headed towards Maunoury, driving hard at the pedals, half hoping to be back at Bougival earlier than he'd planned. It was not his job to worry over them, but something nagged at him and told him he ought to.

He was able to buy a skinny chicken, six eggs and a few chitterlings from an illicitly killed pig and, riding back to the road, he almost ran into Ludo and Grand Charles sheepishly climbing from a ditch. They had put their bicycles in the hedge bottom and were watching the farm. They clearly hadn't expected his return so soon and they rose from the long grass shamefaced, and pink with trying to keep up with him.

'What are you doing here?' he snapped.

Ludo gave him a sheepish look. 'We wanted to see where you went and what you did.'

'You've seen what I do before. I bought eggs. I left you in Bougival.'

'We were interested.'

'In the message,' Grand Charles added.

'It's none of your business,' Scully growled. 'You keep your noses out of this. I've told you before. War's for men not kids.'

'I'm not a kid,' Ludo said stiffly. 'I am thirteen. Nearly fourteen.'

'You're still too young. Now beat it!'

He made them cycle ahead of him, and, re-entering the centre of Maunoury, watched them head round the central traffic island for the road to Bougival and waited until they were out of sight. Then he cycled slowly past the bronze statue of a General Etienne Elié, sculpted in bronze with bicorne hat and curved sabre astride a cannon. '*Né à Maunoury*,' the words below his feet announced. '*Mort à Waterloo. 18 Juin 1815. Soldat de Napoléon*.'

Funny stuff, glory, Scully thought. It looked smashing on a monument, but was never quite the same in fact. The good people of Maunoury probably thought their favourite son had died neatly while leading his troops. From a bullet in the brain, perhaps, to be carried from the field by his sorrowing soldiers. What had probably happened was that he'd been torn apart by a cannon ball, had his tripes spread all over the field of honour by a shell, or been skewered by a British lancer.

As he circled the far side of the statue, he almost bumped into the two boys once more. They were sitting astride their bicycles, trying to see the Bar de l'Ouest at the far side of the square.

'Now what the hell are you up to?'

Grand Charles pointed. 'He's there,' he said excitedly. 'I can see his red scarf.'

'Beat it,' Scully roared. 'I shan't tell you again.'

He watched them cycle hurriedly away down the road to Bougival, making sure they didn't stop or turn back, then he remounted his machine and continued circling the square. The man sitting outside the Bar de l'Ouest was reading a newspaper with a glass of beer in front of him. At first he didn't appear to notice Scully, but eventually he lowered his paper and watched as he disappeared again beyond the monument.

Picking his way through the sparse traffic, Scully took a seat outside the bar and, sipping at the pale, soapy beer which arrived, he looked warily round the crooked spectacles.

'Nice day,' he said in his careful French. 'Jacquot said it might rain but I said not.'

The man with the red scarf put down his drink, took a drag at his cigarette, and glanced at Scully.

'You from Jacquot?' he asked quietly.

'He sent me to see if I could get some eggs.'

The man with the red scarf paused and took another drag at his cigarette. 'I've got some eggs,' he said. 'Do you want some?'

Scully grinned. It was as easy as falling off a log. 'Yes,' he said. 'The answer's yes. We're ready. For anything in the way of food. He sent a list of what he wants.'

As Scully handed over the letter, the man with the red scarf finished his beer and dived into a brown American cloth bag that stood alongside him. 'Got somewhere to put them?'

Scully pulled his haversack round, and six eggs, wrapped separately in newspaper, appeared.

As he paid, the man in the red scarf studied him. 'Who're you?'

'Nobody. I've just come for eggs, that's all. Who're you?'

'That doesn't matter either. Tell them the answer will go where it'll do most good.' As the quiet voice dropped, it was hard for Scully to catch what was said. 'Tell them they're not to move. The orders are that there's to be no rising. The Americans intend to bypass Paris.'

Scully rose and picked up his haversack. The boys were waiting for him a kilometre along the road.

'Did you give it to him?' Ludo asked excitedly.

'Yes.'

'Did you get anything in return?'

Scully eyed him. 'Yes,' he said. 'Six more eggs.'

12

Sending the two boys home ahead of him, Scully headed for Nanterre, where he had heard of a man who had sausages for sale. As he stuffed them in his haversack, he was warned that Germans were stopping people on the bridges over the river on the south-west side of Paris, and, heading further north, he found himself approaching the Etoile from Courbevoie. Guessing he was going to be caught by the curfew, he left the bicycle at a bar where he knew it would be safe and set off on foot.

As he walked along the Avenue de la Grande Armée, intending to turn down the Avenue Marceau towards Montparnasse, he was keeping carefully to the shadows but, near the Etoile, he became aware of something happening ahead. Hearing the rumble and clatter of tank treads and the low throb of engines, he melted into the darkness of a doorway. German lorries and tanks loomed in front and further down the street he could see German soldiers carrying rifles and machine-pistols.

As he watched, another man fell into the doorway, bumping heavily against him. Immediately, there was a low curse and a hand grabbed for his throat. Scully brought down a fist like a maul on the top of the other man's head and the fingers at his throat relaxed long enough for him to tear himself free and grab the newcomer's throat in his turn. For a while they struggled in silence, neither daring to shout out, until it dawned on each of them at the same time that the other was also hiding from the curfew. As their grips relaxed, they rubbed at their throats.

'You have a strong grip, my friend,' the newcomer said. 'Who are you?'

'Never mind who I am. Who're you?'

The other man's teeth showed in the dark as he smiled. 'Let me answer the same way, *mon brave*.'

'You in the Resistance?'

'What's it to you, my friend? Are you?'

It was Scully's turn to smile.

'You're not French?'

'No.'

The other man was silent for a moment; then he switched to a thickly accented English. 'A flier?'

'No.'

'Escaper?'

'You could call me that?'

'What have you in that bag, my friend? Weapons?'

Scully grinned. 'Eggs, chitterlings, and a chicken.'

'You're lucky.' The Frenchman glanced out of the shadows into the street. 'What's going on down there? Can you make it out? There are tanks in the triangle formed by the Avenue Foch, the Boulevard de l'Amiral Bruix and the Avenue de Malakoff.'

As he stopped speaking, a motor-cyclist roared past, heading towards the Avenue Foch.

'Motor-cyclists, too?' the Frenchman said. 'Darting about like mosquitoes at Le Vésinet after the rain.'

'I can see guards with sub-machine-guns,' Scully pointed out.

'So can I, my friend,' the Frenchman said. 'And, in case you aren't aware of the fact, inside the triangle formed by the Avenue Foch, the Boulevard de l'Amiral Bruix and the Avenue de Malakoff are buildings occupied by the Gestapo.'

The two of them were leaning together against the wall now, peering out. A car moving down the road was signalled to stop by the men with the sub-machine-guns and, as it halted, the driver and an officer, both Gestapo men, climbed out and lifted their hands. A covered truck appeared and they climbed into it.

The Frenchman turned to Scully.

'Now what, my friend,' he asked, 'do you make of that? The Gestapo being arrested? It's usually the other way round.'

There was still a great deal of coming and going down the road. Vehicles were parked hurriedly at an angle to the curb, and occasionally they heard shouts and the tramp of feet. It remained impossible to move and after a while they sat down on the steps in the shadows.

'I suppose,' the Frenchman said, 'that you wouldn't have any of those eggs for sale?'

'I might have,' Scully said warily.

Four eggs changed hands and were carefully wrapped in the Frenchman's handkerchief. As the money was handed over, they heard lorry engines starting up.

Peering out, they saw two tanks moving towards them. As they clattered past, they were followed by several trucks filled with men and guarded by motor-cycle combinations mounted with machine-guns.

'Gestapo!' The Frenchman's eyes were wide and puzzled. 'All Gestapo. What in the name of God's going on? Has someone finally discovered the bastards are as corrupt as everybody else?' The grin returned. 'That's the only thing that's made us realize we can beat them in the end. When they first came they behaved themselves, but when we found it was possible to bribe them – to dodge the curfew, to obtain food, to get petrol – we realized they were as venal as anybody else and began to think they could be defeated after all.'

There were still Germans about and, as they watched, more lorries appeared, filled up and vanished after the others.

'SS and SD men,' the Frenchman breathed. 'Mother of God, they must be arresting the whole Nazi organization in Paris!'

They remained huddled in the doorway until the darkness began to give way to the thin grey light of approaching dawn. Peering out, they found the Germans along the road

had vanished and that there were only a few soldiers in
Wehrmacht uniforms standing near the Avenue Foch.

'Wehrmacht guarding Gestapo buildings?' the Frenchman
said. 'I think, my friend, it's time we were off. I see people
on their way to work.'

He held out his hand. 'If you ever need anyone, Englishman,' he said, 'I am Yves Kehec. I'm a Breton, at present
living at 214 Rue Joufre. Having survived a night like that,
I think we can call ourselves comrades.'

Scully stiffened. 'Charley Scully, Sergeant, North Staffs
Fusileers.'

At the Etoile, there were more Germans, all Wehrmacht
men, all heavily armed, and lorries standing in the side
streets. A few cars were being stopped, but men and women
on foot making for their place of work were allowed past
without interruption. Kehec grinned and shook hands once
more before vanishing down the Avenue de Friedland.

Collecting his bicycle from the bar, Scully ate a madeleine, a patent breakfast cake that tasted like sawdust, cost
five francs and could be bought without coupons, and drank
a cup of the nauseating *café national*, then he rode slowly
on towards Montparnasse, skirting the area where he had
spent the night.

Ludo greeted him with a smile as he appeared in the
apartment but Sidonie, who was preparing to go to work,
said nothing and Scully was aware of tension in the air. She
remained edgy as the boy ate breakfast but, as soon as he
had disappeared, she slammed the door and spun round to
face Scully.

'You were working for the Resistance,' she accused. 'I
trusted you and you took my son!'

Somewhere along the line, Scully decided, Resistance security was a pretty poor bet.

'You were carrying a message,' she went on furiously.
'How dare you? How dare you?'

Her small fists thumped on Scully's chest until he grabbed
her wrists and held her close to him. In her rage, she spat
at him, the spittle landing on his cheek.

'They were in no danger,' he said, his strong hands restraining her struggles as he explained what had happened. 'And it wasn't me who was to blame. Somebody'd failed to teach them to do as they're told.'

As he released her, she became silent and stood in front of him, her face white. Then she turned away abruptly.

'I'm sorry,' she apologized. 'I shouldn't have made such accusations. But you can't believe the fear I have in knowing that my son is British and that the Germans might take him away. I've lived with it for four years. Ever since they rounded up the English in 1940. Governesses, showgirls, Irish nuns, Australian spinsters. Old widows even, who were completely French but had married British soldiers in 1918 and never bothered to change their passports back.' She looked up at Scully. 'They treated the Germans like dirt. Some of them even called out "God Save the King". They were sent to a camp at Besançon.'

'Why didn't *you* have to go?'

'I had a small child, and still had my French passport.' She sighed. 'But they *will* take him soon. They take them all when they grow up. It terrifies me and he is growing too big for me. I cannot beat him any more.'

'He's a good boy, Sidonie.'

It was the first time he'd called her by her name and she raised her eyes quickly to his before blushing and turning away to the kitchen. Scully stared at the closed door for a moment then he swung the haversack from his shoulders and followed her. Opening the sack, he took out the chicken, the chitterlings and the eggs.

'There's enough there for two good meals,' he said.

As Sidonie descended the stairs to go to work, Scully followed her. She said nothing as she left, but the tears that had sprung to her eyes and the look of gratitude she gave him for the food were recompense enough.

Madame Weinspach and Monsieur Virec were in the courtyard as Scully dragged out his bicycle again. They had watched with interest as Sidonie had waved at Scully before disappearing through the wicket gate and he had seen the old man whisper something to the concierge. It was clear they were beginning to put two and two together.

'It's good to see you safe, *mon brave*,' Madame Weinspach said. 'The Germans are growing nervous and shoot at shadows.'

'And tanks have been seen near the Etoile,' Virec added. 'My good friend, Marcel Didot, telephoned me. We pass messages to each other. We both played with the orchestra at the Opéra and he retired at the same time I did. We remain in contact and we have many friends strategically placed about Paris. The exigencies of the family, you understand. My wife came from Montparnasse so I live here. He had a daughter who married well and lives near the Porte Maillot. He says the area round the Avenue Foch, the Boulevard de l'Amiral Bruix and the Avenue de Malakoff is guarded by motor-cyclists.'

'Lorries, too,' Scully said cheerfully. 'They were disarming the Gestapo.'

Aware of the old man's startled look, he pushed the bicycle into the street and headed for Clichy. Hasler was in the Bar du Destin and Scully backed him into a corner and made sure he knew how he felt.

Hasler smiled his cold smile. 'The McCosh been at you, sergeant?'

'Never mind what the McCosh thinks. Don't you ever send messages to me by kids again. I know you're an officer but I've spit better officers than some I've met. I'll take your bloody messages if you wish but next time let's do it without involving infants.'

Hasler was unmoved. 'You managed to worm your way into her bed yet?' he asked.

'I haven't tried.'

Hasler's eyebrows rose. 'Brutal and licentious soldiery don't seem to be what they used to be. Then I suppose it must be what you saw near the Etoile last night that's bothering you.'

Scully glared. 'How did you know what I saw near the Etoile last night?'

Hasler smiled again and Scully decided he knew too

much. When he returned to the apartment, old Virec appeared, his eyes bulging with excitement. It was clear that what Scully had said had started him telephoning his contacts about the city and he was full of a story he'd picked up that the Germans were leaving.

'What else can be the meaning of what you saw?' he said. 'And what my friend Didot saw through his blackout curtain? They are *going*. Didot says even that he's heard that people are dancing in the streets.'

As the morning progressed, however, there was no sign of the exodus the old man had been prophesying. Paris seemed the same as ever, drab under its wartime neglect, though there was a sudden strange absence of German vehicles on the streets, and it wasn't until Ludo appeared for his evening meal that they learned what had been happening.

Sidonie had just arrived home, her manner shy and uncertain after the quarrel that morning. For a long time she seemed to be about to say something, but, just as she squared her shoulders and faced Scully, they heard the boy's feet clattering wildly up the stairs and she turned in alarm, wondering what new emergency had arisen.

Ludo burst in, his shirt saturated, dark patches down his spine and his armpits, the perspiration on his face smeared with dust where he had rubbed it from his eyes.

'Maman!' he yelled. 'They've assassinated Hitler! Jean-Marc Pusy told me! They killed him with a bomb in East Prussia!'

PART TWO

To arms

1

For a moment they were all silent, breathless at the incredible news. Sidonie's eyes were on Scully's face and he saw that she had gone pink with excitement.

'Are you sure, Lulu?' she asked. 'You're not making it up? You're not fooling?'

He had torn his trousers in the Luxembourg Gardens and seemed far more concerned with the damage he'd done than with what had happened in East Prussia.

'I'm sorry, maman,' he said, twisting his head to see his rear. 'I know they're hard to get and it wasn't deliberate. It's true all right. It was on the Swiss radio. Jean-Marc Pusy's father says they've declared a state of emergency and the German army's captured all the Nazis.'

'Mother of God,' Sidonie breathed. 'Can it be possible? Have the Germans come to their senses at last?'

It certainly gave meaning to the events of the night before, and it was equally certain that everybody in Paris was going to hear it before long. Going to the Bar du Weekend on the corner of the Rue Fantin and the Rue Lescaut, where the landlord was in contact by telephone with other bar and café owners across Paris, Scully found a crowd of men and women outside on the pavement.

'They blew him to bits.' One of the men breathed brandy in his face as he appeared. 'Scattered him all over East Prussia. Now they're in control in Munich, Vienna and here in Paris. They've been stuffing the Gestapo into lorries for hours and taking them to Mont Valérien and shooting them in batches.'

With the wary caution of an old soldier, Scully found it

125

hard to believe. Germany was so regimented the thing seemed impossible. But it was clear *something* was happening.

When he returned to the Hôtel Bouboulis, Virec was in the courtyard playing the 'Marseillaise'. 'It's all over,' Madame Weinspach shouted. In the parlour on the second floor, Sidonie had opened a precious bottle of brandy she'd been saving and her eyes were sparkling as she looked at Scully. She was alive and beautiful with happiness and, as if she'd never been anything but friendly towards him, she pushed a glass forward as he entered.

'We must celebrate.'

Gently he took the bottle from her and put it back in the cupboard. 'Later,' he said. 'Later, when we know for sure.'

She seemed deflated but made no attempt to argue, and they all waited impatiently for the evening radio announcement. It destroyed all their hopes.

'An attempt has been made on the Führer's life,' it stated. 'But he has received only slight burns and bruises and no other injuries.'

'What does it mean, Charley?'

He turned, surprised, as she used his name for the first time.

'It means,' he said, 'that the boys who arrested the Gestapo must be gettting a bit hot under the collar by now.'

As they talked the telephone rang. Sidonie answered it, and her face went taut as she listened. Eventually she replaced the receiver silently.

'It was Holzmeier,' she said slowly. 'He says it's true. In spite of the radio. He says they've had a signal by teleprinter signed by some field marshal whose name I didn't catch. It stated quite categorically that Hitler is dead and that power's been seized by a party which intends to make peace. It says there's a state of emergency in Berlin.' She looked at Scully in an anguished way. 'Doesn't *this* mean it's ending, Charley? Without him, surely they'll give up.'

'Wait,' Scully counselled. 'Wait. People celebrating now might wish they hadn't tomorrow.'

They waited on tenterhooks all next day. By morning,

despite the German attempts to keep it quiet, the whole city knew what had happened near the Etoile. The same thing had happened at the Rue des Saussaies near the Elysée Palace but, to anybody daring enough to inquire, the Germans explained merely that it was a military exercise. It fooled no one and by mid-morning, the Resistance had learned that the Germany army had arrested practically the whole bestial Nazi apparatus in Paris.

It seemed incredible and it also seemed to be genuine. But even as they digested the good news, bad news arrived alongside it, and rumours flew round that the Germans had attacked the Resistance on the Vercors massif. Bombers had gone in and the Waffen SS had got inside the mountain citadel by glider. Somehow the very ruthlessness of the attack made the other news seem doubtful.

The tension in the city was marked. There was no mention of the assassination in the daily newspapers, but late in the afternoon the word went round that Hitler was not dead after all. Scully was aware of Sidonie's eyes on him, the expression of desperate hope that had been on her face all day gone as her eyes grew moist with disappointment. He touched her hand, trying to comfort her; she made no attempt to move away and her eyes lifted to his face, full of anguished pleading.

As she turned, the telephone rang. She stared at him, startled, and snatched it up. Once again it was Holzmeier and Scully put his head close to hers to listen, aware of her hair brushing his cheek and the sense of warmth and comfort that came from the fragrance of her perfume.

'He's alive!' Scully could hear Holzmeier's voice quite plainly. He sounded shocked and depressed. 'I've heard his voice. The bomb killed several men, but not him. They're already rounding up the plotters, and the SS are being released and they're out for reprisals. They say Stülpnagel, the senior German officer in Paris, is implicated. Don't do anything! Keep quiet and stay indoors! It might be dangerous to go out.'

Sidonie's eyes moved to Scully's. 'Thank you, Herr Leutnant,' she said slowly. 'I am very grateful.'

She put the telephone down slowly and looked at Scully. 'Perhaps he is not a bad man,' she said quietly.

'Perhaps he isn't,' Scully felt a faint twinge of jealousy. 'But he's not being kind for any reason but his own.'

'No.' She stiffened. 'Of course! Of course! This is something we must always remember. It was the same when they came in 1940. They were quiet and polite then, too, and seemed to carry nothing worse than cameras so that we had to keep reminding ourselves they were not tourists.' She looked at the telephone again, then once more at Scully. 'He'll come again,' she said uneasily. 'He'll expect to be rewarded.' Her face twisted. 'I have accepted something from him. It makes me like all those people at Auteuil, the collabos who go to the races with them, who dine with them in the city, who use their cars and accept presents.'

Two days later, the newspapers carried the news of Hitler's escape and the execution of the plotters, and with it the news that the Vercors citadel had been overcome. With no movement from the Normandy bridgehead, the city was in despair. Despite their losses, the German capacity for recovery still seemed enormous.

The Germans were stony-faced and edgy, however, and Scully noticed that in the streets they had all started to use the Nazi salute instead of the army salute. It could only mean that the Nazis were in full control again and tightening the screws.

With the failure of the assassination attempt, survival became the most important thing in everybody's mind once more. Gas and electricity appeared in even shorter spasms, and milk had almost vanished because the milk lorries were being attacked by Typhoons in mistake for German transport. But there was still no sign of the Germans leaving and Tom Cléry-Kidder suggested they should go to the Champs-Elysées to see if the daily march from the Etoile was taking place as usual.

Every day for four years the Germans had driven home the fact of the occupation with a march down the Champs-Elysées to the Place de la Concorde. Normally the Parisians boycotted it but now they watched minutely for any sign of the disintegration of German authority. But there was no difference. Led by a drum-major with a baton, the grey-green column moved past, the people standing under the trees. The air was full of the scent of the acacias, limes and chestnuts that ringed the Place de l'Etoile and an old woman was feeding the pigeons with crumbs, her eyes blank, the male birds strutting and showing off in front of the females. The day was heavy with summer torpor, a huge swastika banner hanging listlessly from one of the occupied buildings, a red splash against the cloudless sky.

The sun was shining on the east face of the Arc de Triomphe as it towered over the Etoile, sombre and grey. Napoleon, crowned with the stone laurels of victory, stared sightlessly at the reds, yellows, blues and greens of women's dresses. The names on the Arc – Aspern-Essling, Eylau, Austerlitz, Wagram – meant nothing to Scully because they weren't the battles of the British army, any more than the names of the men who had fought them – Lannes, Soult, Davout, Ney, Masséna, Murat – were British names, but he was aware that history was bursting out of the stone in a link that tied the imprisoned city to a long-dead glory.

The Germans were still circling the Arc, kettledrums beating the step. A curious cow-horn standard decorated with horse-tail tufts preceded the band, followed by an officer on a horse who headed the main body of men. File on file of them, rifles on their shoulders, bayonets fixed – a polished, spotless, unhurried column, symbolic of France's humiliation – they moved on down the Champs-Elysées towards the Place de la Concorde where the striped Wehrmacht sentry boxes barred the entrance to the Tuileries Gardens.

Trailing behind them were French units, the *Milice* and one or two youth organizations, and George Presteigne watched them with an expressionless face.

'They've also organized the Jeunes Gardes,' he pointed out. 'They wear a uniform with a dark shirt, crossbelt and boots.' There was a faint hint of wistfulness in his voice, as if he, too, would have liked to wear a uniform of some kind.

As they headed homewards down the Avenue Marceau, two German officers were in front of them, upright and immaculate. As Xavier Lipski began to mimic them, affecting the same stiff walk, Grand Charles giggled and Auguste Woof gave a strangled yelp of mirth before he managed to muffle his mouth with his hand.

Encouraged by the laughter, Xavier was pretending now to be Hitler; with a finger under his nose, his strut changed to a goosestep. Grand Charles was crouching helpless with laughter against the wall and Ludo was clutching George Presteigne and Auguste Woof. But passers-by were grinning, too, and it suddenly dawned on the two officers that something was happening behind them.

Xavier was so engrossed in his act he failed to notice the Germans' suspicion, and suddenly one of them stopped and turned. Grabbing him by the arm, he delivered such a clout at the side of his head, that the boy went staggering to the wall.

'Keep your pupils in order, *monsieur le professeur*,' the German said in excellent French, clearly imagining Scully was a teacher. 'Or next time perhaps it will be you, not him.'

There was still no restriction on moving beyond the city boundaries and Scully continued to visit Maunoury, carrying messages as he sought eggs. But by now the Germans were asking questions and it was growing more difficult, and the day came when he was turned back and told to go home.

Wondering if they'd arrested the man with the red scarf, he learned that the Americans had captured Cherbourg and reached the end of the Contentin peninsula, and their Third Army, after probing deep into Brittany, had now turned west and was sweeping towards Le Mans and Chateaudun to the south of Paris.

Driving at the pedals, he clattered down the Boulevard Saint-Michel and finally turned into the Rue Fantin. Sidonie had clearly also heard the news. As he opened the door, her face was flushed with pleasure.

'They're coming to Paris,' she said. 'They're coming to liberate us!'

Scully had found eggs near Bougival and they were eating

a colossal omelette when Pierre Lambrouille arrived, his bow tie crisp, his suit neat, his collar spotless. It had been so long since Scully had last seen him that he had almost forgotten his existence and he guessed it was the news they'd heard that had brought him out.

'Good evening, Uncle Charles,' Lambrouille said sarcastically. 'I see you're still here.'

He seemed nervous and on edge, as if, as Hasler had suggested, he were beginning to wonder about his future. When Sidonie offered him a drink, he refused brusquely and sat watching them eat.

'So our friend, de Gaulle, has sacrificed the men of Vercors to his ambition,' he said sharply. 'He has allowed the Germans to destroy them, just as Stalin is allowing them to destroy the Polish patriots in Warsaw.'

Sidonie sat silently, her face pale, her lips tight, and he went on in the same jeering tone. 'You know, of course, that he doesn't intend to allow any rising in Paris and that the British and Americans are expecting to bypass us.'

Sidonie's head turned as she glanced at Scully.

'You didn't know that?' Lambrouille smirked. 'Well, it's true! They're afraid of being involved in street fighting and losing a few precious American lives. The Jews who run their country don't like their people dying for France and they don't like de Gaulle. His ambition will be the death of the invasion, the death of France, the death of him, and the death of Paris. The communists consider the city worth 200,000 dead and they'll fight. And, because the Americans will not come to their help, the city will be devastated.'

'You would make a good politician,' Sidonie said bitterly. 'It amazes me that you know so much about the communists.'

'I have friends among them.'

Her eyes flashed. 'France has always been a country of strange politics,' she snapped, 'but you must be the only left-wing fascist between the Mediterranean and the Channel.'

His face took on a sly look. 'You know, of course, that this apartment is being watched? The communists know our

English friend here carries messages to the allies for the Gaullists, Pusy and Rou. They've also noticed the German who comes to call.'

As Sidonie's eyes flew to Scully, Lambrouille smiled.

'Oh, I know old Weinspach has a fat German visit *her*,' he said, 'but that doesn't mean a thing. Everybody knows about him and she's so old nobody cares. But you're different. You're young and you're suspect. People are envious and those who fraternize should be careful. Times are changing. People are growing vengeful.' His smile widened. 'Even Hitler. Did you know he's appointed a new commander for Paris? It's the man who destroyed Rotterdam and Sevastopol, and his orders are to raze the city to the ground.'

After Lambrouille had left they sat in silence for a while, staring at the remains of the meal. Then Ludo, as if embarrassed by what had passed, excused himself and left the room.

Scully remained at the table, staring at it as Sidonie rose to clear away. As the door slammed and Ludo clattered down the stairs, he lifted his head.

'What did he mean by fraternizing?' he asked. 'He's always going on about it. *Did* you fraternize with the Germans?'

She shook her head but she didn't meet his eyes.

'Holzmeier can do you no harm if you're careful.'

'That isn't what he means.'

'What *does* he mean?'

She paused, standing at the table, with the crockery in her hands. Still she didn't meet Scully's eyes. 'There *was* a German,' she said. 'It was when I was still shocked after the death of my husband.'

Scully said nothing and she went on quietly.

'It occurred when I took Ludo to the house we had at that time at Trouville,' she said. 'It's gone now. I sold it. But we went there in 1941 to get away from Paris and the Germans. Nobody knew what happened. Only Pierre.'

'What *did* happen?'

'Ludo fell ill with diphtheria and I had to get help. The German – he was very correct and very kind, his name was von Leo – he helped me, and Pierre found out.'

'Were you in love with him?'

'No.'

'Was there an affair?'

'No.' She still avoided his eyes. 'I was too afraid. But he found a German doctor and obtained drugs. I was grateful and showed it. Some people would say I was wrong.'

'That's not collaboration.'

'It is.' Her voice was quiet with a sense of guilt. 'It's something we've all been guilty of in the last four years. Everybody collaborated a little just as everybody resisted a little. I'm no worse than anyone else, but the person who accepts a cigarette from a German, the person who directs them to where they wish to go, they are collaborating just as much as the ones who use German petrol and buy German food on the black market. It's impossible *not* to collaborate a little.'

2

It was impossible to tell where Lambrouille had obtained his information but the following day Scully had it confirmed by Hasler.

'Yes, it's right,' he said. 'The Germans have got the wind up. We landed in the South of France this morning.'

'Who did?'

'Matter of fact, it was the Yanks, and the order's come from Hitler to destroy Paris. We know a team of explosives experts has arrived and we've seen crates with black skulls and crossbones on them. You know what that means, sergeant, don't you? Explosives. There were pneumatic drills and a coil of air hose as well, and they aren't going to use that lot to bury SS prisoners. They're going to mine the city.'

'Where?'

'Trying to find that out now. Only know so far that they're going to. One of our people got a look at a map.'

'How the hell did he do that?'

Hasler shrugged. 'No trouble at all. He's a she – typist for the Germans. Map was covered with red crosses and they weren't there because they were first-aid posts or to mark lottery booths or pissoirs. They're sticking explosives in the sewers and hundreds of saws have been brought in to cut down the trees to block the roads. The Germans are being cut to pieces at Falaise, so they're going to hold Paris to give their troops a chance to recover on the west bank of the Seine.'

The stories were clearly common property and Scully was aware of a mounting excitement about him. Suddenly, the

Americans, who had seemed so hesitant in the Normandy bocage, had become emboldened to the point of recklessness and were sweeping towards the Seine. Even the infantry had picked up the spirit of the mechanized cavalry while the Germans, dependent now more than ever on the horse because of the shortage of petrol, had forgotten how fast a motorized army could move.

The whole city seemed to be listening, its head cocked, its ears trained to the west to catch the first sound of gunfire that would indicate the Americans were coming.

The holiday for the Feast of the Assumption started with cloudless blue skies and half Paris seemed to be on the move to do the one thing they could do these days without the Germans objecting – go fishing along the Seine or picnic in the Bois de Boulogne.

The increasing excitement had invaded the narrow confines of the Petite-Ville and even the courtyard of the Hôtel Bouboulis was affected. Madame Weinspach's German cook had not been for some time because the Germans were no longer allowed to wander far from barracks in case they were called on to move. Old Virec became a virtual telephone exchange between his ex-colleagues of the Opera House orchestra. On the second floor, there was an air of eagerness and hope, and they decided to celebrate by taking advantage of the weather with a visit the following day to the banks of the river.

That afternoon, however, an excited Virec met Scully in the Bar du Weekend. Resistance men he had previously quietly pointed out had disappeared and he was certain that something was in the air.

Scully went to bed that night thinking how things had changed between Sidonie and himself. She was ready to smile, was even faintly shy in front of him. Lying in bed, aware of her in the next room, quiet between the sheets, breathing, warm and feminine, made him wonder what he was waiting for, why he didn't march in and grab her, because he had a feeling that for the first time she would have raised no objection. After four years, she was desperate for warmth and affection and Scully knew he had established himself sufficiently as her ally for her to be willing to accept them from him.

As he lay thinking, he heard the tinkle of Madame Weinspach's bell in the courtyard. It was repeated several times before he heard her door open and caught the sound of her throwing the bolts of the great gate under the porte-cochère. After a while footsteps sounded on the stairs, then a quiet scratching started at the door of the apartment.

A few moments later, Sidonie appeared in Scully's tiny room, pale, sleepy, beautiful and a little frightened.

'It's you they want, Charley.'

He was already sitting up, alert and waiting. As he went to the door, he touched her hand and she clutched his fingers and squeezed them anxiously. A man was waiting outside on the landing, watched warily by Madame Weinspach, who stood at the curve of the stairs, an overcoat over her night clothes.

'He said he had to see you,' she announced. 'He insisted on being let in.'

The man was dressed in working clothes and a beret, no different from thousands of other Parisian working men.

'You're wanted outside in the street,' he said quietly.

For a moment Scully had an uneasy suspicion that Lambrouille had finally put the Germans on his track. But the Frenchman was tough-looking and looked more French than the Eiffel Tower, so that Scully couldn't believe he was a collaborator.

Dressing quickly, as he passed Sidonie once again she touched his hand. In reply, he pressed her shoulder. 'It'll be all right,' he said.

The Frenchman led Scully across the courtyard and into the street. There were two other men standing in the shadows of the archway and Scully noticed they both held pistols.

For a moment he thought it was a rubbing-out. He had heard of Hitler's *Nacht und Nebel* decree, by which offenders against the régime were no longer brought before the courts. Now they just disappeared. Doctors were called to false alarms and murdered down side streets. Priests were caught visiting the sick. Students were invited to late parties and quietly knocked on the head. Then one of the men in the shadows spoke his name.

'Sergeant Scullee,' he said. 'We have a job for you.'

'Who the hell are you?' Scully demanded.

'You will remember me, my friend. Yves Kehec, who shared a doorway with you on the night of July 20th, when they tried to blow up Hitler and, with good German inefficiency, managed to fail. The man to whom you sold four eggs.' There was a flash of teeth in the darkness as Kehec grinned. 'I'm an officer in the Free French Army, here by order of General de Gaulle to organize resistance in Paris. It didn't take long to find you because it seems everybody on this side of the river knows about the tall Englishman in the Petite-Ville who sticks out like a sore thumb.'

'Why do you need *me*?'

'Not just you, my friend,' Kehec said. 'The Germans are moving political prisoners to Germany. A trainload has already left the Fresnes prison. An attempt was made to stop it but it failed and they've gone beyond our reach. We've heard now that they're sending the next lot in a convoy of trucks for safety and we need you and everybody we can get to stop them.'

Half an hour later, Scully found himself in a big black Citroën of the type the Gestapo liked to use. Where it came from and where the petrol came from that fuelled it he had no idea. They had moved through the dark streets cautiously at a half-trot, keeping always to the shadows and hiding in doorways whenever there was a suspicion of German patrols being about. There seemed to be scouts and look-outs everywhere whom they picked up as they went so that they were trailed by small groups of armed men ready, if the Germans saw them, to protect their rear long enough for them to get away.

Pausing in a doorway, Scully was handed one of the short checked coats the French called *Canadiennes*. A rifle followed and he took it by the narrow part of the stock and weighed it in his hand. He was skilful with weapons and enjoyed using them, and it was good to have a rifle in his hands again.

'It's a Lee Enfield,' he said. 'Where did it come from?'

'Never mind where it came from,' Kehec said. 'It's a good weapon. I've heard you can use it.'

Somewhere one of the kids had been talking, Scully decided, because no one else knew of his military skills.

They climbed into the car and the engine roared. No one seemed to be worried that the Germans might hear and move patrols to intercept them. Kehec explained. 'Bribes,' he said shortly.

He paused. 'We are depending on you, Sergeant Scullee. The men we are hoping to save include many of our friends. One of them would have been me but for a bit of luck. I was captured four months ago and was being taken off in a bus with my cousin. But when someone rang the bell in defiance the driver stopped automatically and I had three seconds of grace. I jumped out and ran. My cousin tried to follow me but he was too slow and they stood him up against a wall and shot him there and then. He died singing the "Sambre et Meuse" which, in case you don't know, was the song of the French Revolutionary armies and has a special meaning for us. He was seventeen.'

Stopping in the shadow of a warehouse, they climbed out of the car to be greeted by a group of men. There were brief handshakes, then Scully recognized the tall figure of Hasler.

'What the hell are you doing here?' he demanded.

'I organized the bloody thing, old man. I gather you're a marksman, and shot at Bisley.'

Then Scully realized where Kehec had learned of his skill with a rifle. Doubtless Hasler was in contact with London and had checked that he was all he claimed to be.

As they climbed into the car again, Kehec looked round from the front seat.

'What is this Bisley?' he asked.

'Never mind what it is,' Hasler said. 'If he's shot there, he's the man we need.'

To arms

The car was moving quietly now, twisting and turning, keeping always to the dark narrow streets where the German patrols never dared go. The man at the wheel had been a Paris taxi driver before the war and knew every twist and turn of the city.

They were far out in the countryside when dawn came. As they had left the outskirts near Coeuilly, they had picked up a man smelling faintly of manure who directed them down lanes and under empty archways of dark trees. They were in a convoy of half a dozen cars by now, all going at full speed.

Soon afterwards, they stopped and climbed out. Hasler led the way across a field full of ripe corn until they found themselves at the top of a low hill, round which the road curved from west to east, skirting a river and a low line of bushes. Hasler gestured.

'That's Paris,' he said. 'In that direction.' His arm swung. 'That's Germany. In that direction. They're coming along this road. Seven lorries. Around thirty prisoners in each.'

'They include Resistance men we need,' Kehec added. 'Heroes who've given everything to the cause. Political workers. Women. People who helped your fliers escape to Spain. Men who've stirred up patriotism. We failed with the train. This time we *mustn't* fail.'

He gestured at the road curving round the bottom of the hill.

'Two hundred metres,' he said. 'It's up to you.'

Scully frowned. 'How me?'

'We're here to rescue these prisoners,' Hasler said. 'Not burn them with the Germans. We can't plant a mine to blow them up. We might injure the men we want to save. You're here to shoot the driver of the first lorry so that it blocks the road, and, in case it runs off the road, the driver of the second. When the road's blocked, you'll shoot the driver of the last lorry as well, so they can't turn tail and head back the way they came.'

Scully stared about him, weighing up the situation. 'You're not asking much,' he grumbled. 'And you haven't picked a very good spot.'

Live Free or Die!

'This is the only spot we know where the tail-end of the convoy will be within range at the same time as the head. We have a line of men down there among the bushes.'

'Downward shots is always bad. I'll measure it out.'

'You'd better hurry, *copain*.' Kehec turned to the others waiting behind. '*Les gars*, give him all the help he needs.'

'Can I shoot?' Scully asked. 'A trial shot, to see how the rifle pulls.'

'You'd better get it over and done with before the Germans are near enough to hear,' Hasler said. 'We don't want them scaring away.'

Flinging himself down, Scully cradled the Enfield against his cheek, staring along the barrel and adjusting the back sight for the range.

'Hurry, man,' Hasler snapped.

'Dry up,' Scully snapped back. 'Nobody can shoot without concentrating.'

He saw a piece of twig floating in the water, moving slowly to the west. He put his sights on it, behind him a low mutter of conversation that stopped dead as he squeezed the trigger and watched how the twig jumped in the water. The shot had missed by a fraction and, working the bolt, he fired again quickly, then stood up, satisfied.

'You're ready?' Hasler asked.

'No, I'm not. If you want a job doing, you'll want it doing properly.'

Moving down the slope of the hill to the road, Scully measured his footsteps. The guess of two hundred metres was a poor one, because it was almost three hundred. Finding a white stone, he placed it alongside the tarmacadam where he'd be able to see it from the hill, then trotted round the curve of the slope, checking distances. As he ran, heads popped up from among the undergrowth.

'You short of exercise, *copain*?' someone asked. 'We're here to kill Germans, not to train for the Tour de France.'

Scully ignored the gibes. He'd been a soldier long enough to know how much distance seven lorries would occupy and he guessed that the Germans, afraid of ambushes, would keep them well closed up. Finding a piece of rag, he tied it to a bush, then began to head up the slope again.

Halfway up he heard a shrill whistle and, looking round, saw Kehec waving frantically. Deliberately, he didn't hurry. Nobody could shoot when they were out of breath and panting. He needed to be in full control.

'For the love of God,' Kehec said when he reached the top. 'They've been seen!'

'Shut up,' Hasler growled. 'He knows what he's doing.'

Selecting his position, Scully lay down behind a slight rise in the turf that would hide him from the road, and began to scoop out a niche in the top of the little bank. Placing the rifle in it, he eyed the road along the sights, made himself comfortable, and settled down to wait.

'It requires all this nonsense to shoot a rifle?' Kehec asked.

'It does when *I* shoot it.'

'It must have been a very slow war you fought, *copain*.'

There was another long wait. The sun was over Scully's left shoulder and he realized it was warm enough for the drivers of the lorries to have their windows open. There was a faint reflection of the sun on the barrel of the rifle and he scraped up some of the dusty soil and rubbed it across the metal so that there would be no glinting to put him off his aim.

As he settled himself, there was another whistle and Kehec waved to the men in the valley. There was an answering wave, then all the bobbing heads vanished. Round them, there was a buzz of excited conversation.

'You ready?' Hasler asked.

Scully was wiping his hands on his trousers. 'I'm ready,' he said.

'There must be no mistake.'

'There won't be.'

'They must be stopped.'

'For Christ's sake, dry up! You're making me nervous. If people had talked all the time like that at Bisley, I'd never have won no prizes. I want quiet. So bloody well be quiet and keep those other buggers quiet!'

Hasler backed away, waving his hand, and immediately the talking stopped.

There was another whistle and Scully saw the lorries approaching down a long straight on his right, towards the hill, where the road curved and went off on another long straight to the east. They were led by a kübelwagen containing a machine-gun and three men. At the tail of the convoy there was another kübelwagen, and among the lorries were motor-cycles with sidecars. Not for the first time, Scully reckoned that the Resistance was showing more heroism than sense.

He could feel the tension behind him as he cradled the Enfield. The leading lorry was no more than 700 yards away now, just approaching the curve.

His rifle followed it. Because of the curious Continental habit of driving on the right side of the road, the driver was on the left of the cabin and he had his window down, his elbow on the ledge of the door. He wasn't wearing a steel helmet and he seemed relaxed, certain of the strength of the escort.

The rifle followed the lorry as it entered the curve, moving slowly as it turned. Out of the corner of his eye, Scully saw the white stone appear and took first pressure on the trigger. The white stone drew nearer. The German's head was in the sights quite clearly, his expression one of pleasure, as if he were enjoying the drive in the sunshine away from the growing tensions of Paris.

As the Enfield kicked, the German's cap flew off and a dark hole appeared in his temple. As the lorry slowed, the driver of the vehicle behind clapped on his brakes to avoid a collision and the following motor-cyclist was hit by the third lorry as he braked in turn. The crunch came clearly up the slope, and Scully heard the cry of an injured man. The first lorry had slewed broadside-on to the road, and the leading kübelwagen was reversing frantically, its gun swinging, the crew looking for their unseen attacker.

'The last lorry,' Hasler snapped. 'For God's sake, the last lorry!'

The lorries had concertinaed now and, as he swung the

rifle, Scully saw the driver of the last vehicle had his head out, trying to see what had happened. As the Enfield kicked again his body went slack and he lay sprawled half through the window.

'Excellent,' Hasler said. 'Now it's up to us!'

'Hang on,' Scully yelled. 'Hang on, you bloody heroes!'

The machine-gunner in the kübelwagen had swung his weapon and was spraying the slope wildly. As the Enfield cracked again, he threw up his arms and disappeared backwards out of the vehicle. The rear kübelwagen was struggling to turn, its machine-gun lifting. As Scully fired once more, the gunner fell out; then, as the vehicle continued to swing, he shot the driver. Swinging to the first kübelwagen, he picked off the driver, then the man who was reaching out to take the place of the machine-gunner, and used his last shot to knock over one of the motor-cyclists who was trying to bring his machine-gun to bear.

Kehec was staring in astonishment at the slaughter. Scully studied the scene below for a second, then he turned to Hasler.

'Okay,' he said quietly. 'It's all yours.'

Kehec continued to stare as though he couldn't believe his eyes.

'Well, go *on*!' Scully yelled.

Coming to life, Kehec waved a hand at the gaping Resistance men and they began to flood down the slope, shouting and waving their weapons. A few wild shots were loosed off that didn't appear to hit anything, and as the men from the undergrowth by the roadside swept out, the Germans flung their weapons away and threw up their hands. Only one small group tried to resist and they were blasted into extinction by the concentrated fire of every weapon within reach so that their bodies were flung down on the grass verge, torn and covered with blood.

Scully slung the Enfield over his shoulder and walked slowly down to where the surviving Germans were being rounded up and the tailgates of the lorries lowered. Staring round him, he gestured at the laughing, excited Resistance men.

'Don't know why you had to bring all this lot for a job like that,' he said.

Kehec grinned and clapped him on the shoulder.

'My friend,' he said. 'That was magnificent. Not a single Frenchman hurt. *Vive le Bisley!*'

That evening, Scully found himself sitting down to a meal in a large country house of a sort he had never seen before. It was old and shabby but it was magnificent and there was champagne. Scully had never seen so much champagne in his life.

An old woman, white-haired and frail, insisted on kissing him on both cheeks, talking all the time in a hurried whispered French that he couldn't understand.

'The Baronne de Moën,' Hasler announced. 'She owns this place. Her son was among those you saved from Dachau.'

Scully slept that night in the best room in the house. The others all slept on the floor, but Scully was given a bed to himself and a bottle of brandy. He drank none of it, however, didn't undress in case of alarms, and was up next morning before anyone else was awake. Only the sentry was about, yawning heavily in the morning sunshine.

'Farms,' Scully said. 'Are there any farms about?'

Turning into the Hôtel Bouboulis the following afternoon, Scully was met by Madame Weinspach.

'What happened?' she demanded.

He ignored her and mounted the stairs. Sidonie was sitting at the table with a sewing-machine endeavouring to patch Ludo's trousers, but as Scully entered, she rose slowly, her face pink with pleasure and relief.

'You are safe?'

'Don't I look safe?'

For a second longer she looked at him, then she ran to him and hugged him with a spontaneous warmth that made his heart thump with happiness.

'I can't believe it,' she said. 'What happened?'

'Bit of resistance,' Scully said. 'That's all.' He fished in his pocket and produced a packet of pork fillets which he put on the table. 'In the country, I was able to pick up something for supper.'

She stared at it, her eyes wide; then, looking at Scully, she hugged him again, shaking with laughter.

'Oh, Charley,' she said. '*Que tu es formidable!*'

3

For several days, the Germans were busy about the stations and streets, stopping home-going workers and shoppers to check their papers. Houses occupied by relatives of the men who had been rescued were visited, and the pavements rang with the tramp of steel-shod boots. But no one knew anything, and as the ambush had been carried out in an unpopulated area it was difficult to fasten the blame on anyone.

Slowly, life slipped back into what passed as normality, but the Germans remained edgy, looking for reasons to challenge people, not allowing them to gather in groups, moving them on even at the stations. The loss of their convoy of prisoners had shaken them; they were quick to make reprisals, and a notice appeared: 'Twenty Frenchmen from the district of Belleville were shot today at the fortress of Mont Valérien in return for the murdering of German soldiers near Meaux earlier this week. Their names appear below . . .'

It was Kehec, meeting Scully in one of the bars of the Petite-Ville, who made it clear that he wasn't to feel any guilt. 'We freed over two hundred,' he said. 'Twenty lives in return is a small payment. You've no need to be afraid. They know Hasler was behind it and it's him they're looking for.'

By this time the Germans had plenty to occupy them. With the railwaymen out, and the police threatening to follow suit, the air was full of talk of strikes. It was also noticed that the Rue des Saussaies now had a patina of powdered ash that indicated the Gestapo were burning their papers.

Then news came that the German front in the north had collapsed and that the Americans had broken out. Paris remained calm but there was a mounting excitement as shattered units passed through the city; a shabby lot, no longer the proud young men of 1940, but sweaty, exhausted and unshaven, their faces wearing a stunned look. By afternoon, the strings of lorries had become a flood and thousands of people were out on the boulevards to watch the retreat, their faces unsmiling. The German vehicles were painted in the black and green camouflage of Normandy and the noise of the engines filled the breathlessly hot streets.

Then the story spread that the Paris garrison was joining the march east and that the city was being emptied of Germans. 'It's over!' Old Virec yelled. 'They've thrown their hand in!'

This was something they couldn't miss and they left the apartment and headed for the Boulevard Saint-Michel.

A struggling mass of vehicles was converging on Saint-Germain-des-Près to cause one of the first traffic jams the city had seen since 1940. Generals, platinumed typists, naval cadets, fat sergeant-majors, liaison officers, interpreters and mistresses moving out of requisitioned hotels, were all helpless in the confusion.

The turmoil extended into the side streets and people hurried from swimming in the Seine and sunbathing on the grass to watch the bizarre procession of trucks, motorcycles, even horse-drawn carts, loaded with Germans and containing every imagineable kind of loot. There were refrigerators, cases of champagne, wine and brandy, clothes, rolled rugs and carpets, furniture, radios, bathtubs. One lorry carried pigs and chickens, another bidets, another was piled with safes topped by a soldier clutching a sewing-machine.

The British Réseau were standing among the crowd in a little excited group and when a German major asked the way, Auguste Woof solemnly directed him into a cul-de-sac so that a whole formation of trucks turned off and vanished from sight.

'All that lot stuck in a cul-de-sac ought to make a splendid traffic jam,' Auguste grinned as he slipped away.

'Pity we haven't got petrol bombs to drop on them,' George said sternly. 'That would make an even better one.'

As the last of the vehicles crawled by, a heavily-laden kübelwagen broke down and one of the officers in it, stopping a lorry, hoisted a suitcase out of the back. As he did so, it burst open and packets of silk stockings fell to the ground. There was an immediate cheer from the crowd and several women ran forward. By the time the German got his suitcase on to the lorry, he was minus a dozen pairs and the women had melted into the crowd, triumphantly clutching their prizes.

From the open windows of an upstairs flat, came the sound of Wagner's *Götterdämmerung*, played at full blast. The Germans heard it, too, and as the grins widened at their expressions, Sidonie turned to Scully, her eyes alight with excitement.

'Are they really going?' she asked. 'Are they really leaving Paris?'

She so wanted to be reassured it troubled Scully to deny her the pleasure.

'They're clerks,' he said flatly. 'Clerks and storekeepers. Look at them: old men, fat and pasty-faced. They're just getting rid of the useless mouths, that's all.'

'Does that mean they'll fight for Paris?'

It jerked at his heart to tell her the truth, but he suspected that what Hasler had told him had been genuine.

'God knows what it means,' he said. 'Still – ' her distress worried him and he felt the need to make a gesture – 'whatever it means, it's a sign they're being defeated and that eventually they'll be gone. Let's celebrate. With a meal. At a restaurant.'

'We can't afford the coupons.'

'Not one of *them* restaurants,' Scully said. 'A black market restaurant. I've still got money. We'll put on our best bibs and tuckers and eat with the collaborators for once.'

That evening, Scully found two more shirts on his bed, a

selection of ties and a different suit, and with Ludo walking between them, they made their way to the Boul' Mich'. The restaurant they chose was full of flashily dressed men and women and they took their seats warily, half ashamed to be there. The prices seemed astronomical and Sidonie gave Scully an apprehensive look.

'We can afford it,' he insisted. It would make a hole in what was left of the money he'd taken from the dead Germans but he had a feeling that it marked the beginning of a new relationship between them. Curiously, he expected nothing more. The ambition he'd cherished before he'd met her had vanished, and though other thoughts were beginning to play about in his mind, secret ambitions he barely dared think about, for the moment he was content to have only her friendship and to feel the warmth and trust she clearly now felt for him.

There was a nervous air about the people eating around them and they were able to enjoy the meal all the more for being immune from it. As they left they could feel the mood of the city. It was like a pot coming to the boil.

The following afternoon there was a heavy thunderstorm, the rain falling in torrents and bouncing high on the hot pavements, then stopping as suddenly as it came, to leave the roads steaming and pink-topped clouds in a transparent sky giving a rosy tint to the dusk. As soon as possible, Scully headed for Clichy and the Bar du Destin.

Hasler was there as usual, drinking with hard-faced workers whom Scully guessed were Resistants to a man. He was quite calm, quite undisturbed by the fact that he'd be shot if he were found. He didn't attempt to reassure Scully.

'Don't let anybody kid you, sergeant,' he said languidly. 'The Germans have orders to fight for the place, and they're already preparing to dynamite the telephone exchanges. Even the one under Napoleon's Tomb at the Invalides. The French'll enjoy that – seeing Napoleon go up in the air with the dome and the coffin and the Army Museum. And, although nobody's noticed it yet, they're also evacuating the buildings round the bridges over the river. They're going to blow the bridges.'

As he returned to the Rue Fantin, Scully saw Holzmeier's car down the road and almost immediately after he entered there was a knock on the door. Sidonie's eyes met his.

'It's him,' Scully hissed. 'Find out what you can.'

Holzmeier's face was worried. 'I have come to warn you,' he said. 'Things are being tightened up in Paris.'

'More than they are already?' Sidonie was unable to keep the outrage from her voice. 'Did you know that the newspapers are so aware how desperate people are they're telling them which leaves of which trees can be used in salads?'

'That's not my fault,' Holzmeier's voice was shaking with earnestness. 'I'm concerned for you. I owe you a great deal for your understanding.'

'You owe me nothing. I've done nothing.'

'Nevertheless, I could have got into trouble for the accident. I had taken the car without permission. Besides' – Holzmeier's face twisted – 'it doesn't grow less lonely in Paris.'

'Whose fault is that?'

Behind the door, Scully's elbow jabbed. '*Find out*,' he mouthed. '*For God's sake, find out!*'

Sidonie's eyes flickered. 'What are you intending to do with us now?' she asked, her voice harsh and unwilling. 'Blow up our city? We have heard so.'

'A few buildings,' Holzmeier admitted. 'But only *public* buildings. No homes. Please stay away from them.'

Sidonie's voice was unsteady. 'You'd better tell me which,' she said. 'If we're to have another Warsaw here, it will be nice to know where it will be safe.'

'Stay home! That's the best. Stay home.' Holzmeier pushed at the door. 'May I not come in?'

'No.'

'Just this once! Please!'

'No.'

'Listen' – Holzmeier's voice was agonized – 'I may be leaving. Make sure you have plenty of water. They're going to destroy the viaducts that bring the city's supply. They're going to blow up the power plants.'

She gave him a cold look. 'I don't normally visit the power plants. *Or* the viaducts.'

'Of course not. But stay away from the Luxembourg Palace, and the Chamber of Deputies and the Quai d'Orsay. They're being mined.'

'I don't normally visit those places either.'

'The telephone exchanges then, the stations, the bridges over the Seine, the factories. Stay here in the Petite-Ville. You're safe here. Laval and Pétain are leaving. You're losing your leaders.'

'They were *never* the leaders of France!' Sidonie spat. 'Only the caretakers of a graveyard.'

'No matter!' Holzmeier's voice was cracked with the urgency in it. 'We really are going to make a fight of it. The new governor has orders direct from Hitler himself. They're already mining the Panhard factory, Siemens-Westinghouse, Blériot and the tunnel at Saint-Cloud.'

Her eyes anxious, Sidonie nodded. 'I thank you for your consideration, Herr Leutnant,' she said. 'I cannot ask you in, but I'm grateful nevertheless for your help.'

'I'll come back,' Holzmeier said. 'When it's all over. Is there anything you need? I have money.'

She shook her head and Holzmeier's voice came again.

'For God's sake be careful! I know of the Englishman who came here'. Sidonie's eyes flew to Scully's, wide and terrified, but Holzmeier's words reassured her. 'Hasler. I know he was here and they're looking for him. They're determined to get him after that ambush at Meaux. You must take care. *Auf wiedersehen.*'

As his footsteps sounded on the stairs, she turned to Scully, her face concerned.

'He came to warn us,' she said slowly. 'Just to warn us.'

As she closed the door, the telephone rang and she snatched it up.

'It's Madeleine' – Scully could hear the words quite distinctly because the voice was high and excited – 'I rang to ask how you were.'

'I'm safe. And so is Ludo. So is the English soldier who brought him home.' There was a trace of tartness in Sidonie's voice but her sister seemed not to hear.

'I'm in Laval,' she said excitedly. 'A friend has taken me in. Tanks are coming through! Free French tanks! Thousands of them! They'll be in Paris before long! Everybody's gone mad here!'

'I think everybody has gone mad here, too,' Sidonie said.

Slamming down the telephone, she flung her arms round her son. 'Lulu,' she said. 'De Gaulle is coming home!'

As Scully reached for his coat and his twisted spectacles, she looked at him in alarm. 'Where are you going?'

'To find Hasler,' he pointed out. 'He and his friends will want to know what Holzmeier said.'

She stared at him, unhappy and uncertain. 'This time I felt sorry for him,' she said.

'Save your sorrow,' he snapped. 'He's still a German.'

Snatching up his cap, he went downstairs and dragged out the bicycle. There were still a few Germans moving about the streets, all heading east, and as he wheeled the machine out of the courtyard, he noticed that they kept lifting their heads. It was then he heard the first distant thud of gunfire.

Excited, he looked about him at the flat-fronted houses. Paris meant nothing to him. To him, this city of steeples and domes, with its centuries of life and architecture, was just a city like any other. The fact that it had been painted by Utrillo and Renoir and Manet, left him untouched. He'd never heard of Utrillo or Renoir or Manet and he knew no history beyond that of the British army. He knew by this time that the Gare de Lyon could take him to the South of France, something he was beginning to fancy, and that had far more moment for him than the fact that a king of France had been beheaded in the Place de la Concorde or that the overthrow of the monarchy had started in the Place de la Bastille.

He found Hasler in the Bar du Destin as usual, leaning against the zinc counter, his face brooding. The man Scully knew as Pusy was with him and they were both sipping at

152

cups of the loathsome *café national*. Scully leaned on the counter alongside them and ordered a coffee himself.

As Hasler nodded at him, Scully carried his coffee to an empty table and sat down. A few moments later, Hasler joined him with Pusy and started to play dominoes. Passing on what he'd learned, he saw Hasler frown.

'That bloody tunnel,' he said, 'is a Kriegsmarine factory and torpedo depot. There are enough torpedoes there to last two wars like this one. If that goes, so will half the west of Paris.' He glanced at Pusy and shuffled the dominoes, and over the clatter turned to whisper to Scully. 'Situation's bloody touchy,' he said. 'We've got all the ingredients for a rising.'

He clattered the dominoes again. 'Only wants one shot,' he went on, 'either ours or theirs – and there'll be fighting, and then the dynamiting will start. So far no orders have been given, but it'll grow worse. The food situation alone could bring everybody out on to the streets.'

'We don't want another Warsaw here,' Pusy growled.

'What about you?' Hasler asked Scully. 'Where do you stand if it comes to a fight?'

'I'll fight.'

'Communists, too, sergeant?' Hasler's lean intelligent face twisted into a smile. 'It might come to that. They're setting it up. That's why the Germans are clearing the prisons and why they're burning papers in the office of the Militärbefehlshaber. They're going to destroy the place as if it were Oradour. They know they can't win and so do the Vichyites. Take a look around. Do a recce. Even the collaborationist newspapers have gone from the streets and Germans who've never done anything for four years but push pens are rolling up their sleeves and setting up *stutzpunkts*. And if they're beaten it'll leave a nice political vacuum, so that whoever grabs what civil authority remains will be in power.'

Hasler lit a cigarette and blew a smoke ring. 'Roosevelt doesn't favour de Gaulle,' he went on. 'Neither does Churchill. But I suspect they'd favour the communists a damn sight less.' He frowned, his face angry. 'He'd better get here fast, though, or he'll miss his chance. The place's ripe for revolt. They've been humiliated, they're hungry and they've seen the Germans leaving. They feel the moment for revenge's come.'

4

When Scully returned to the Rue Fantin, Sidonie greeted him with a smile and bright eyes.

'The Americans are in Marseilles and Toulon,' she said. 'It was on the BBC. They're already driving towards Avignon and Lyons.'

Scully glanced round the apartment. There was no sign of the boy, which was unusual because he considered himself sufficiently adult not to have to go to bed early, and Scully knew that Sidonie would never have permitted him to be on the streets in the late evening.

'Where's Ludo?, he asked.

'He was tired. He cycled to Clichy this afternoon.' She gave Scully a smile. 'I think he was feeling energetic after last night's meal. George Presteigne telephoned and he went with Grand Charles. They're up to something. They've all heard so much talk of resistance. They all want to be part of it.'

Scully listened to her, puzzled. Ludo was a sobersides boy, without the gamin charm of Grand Charles, but he was also responsible, idealistic, intelligent, and, despite his claim to be British, intensely patriotic towards France. He nodded in the direction of the bedroom.

'Mind if I talk to him?' he asked.

The boy was sitting up in bed, reading a newspaper. Raising his eyes, he gave Scully a quick smile then, realizing something was wrong, the smile gave way to a nervous look.

'Come on,' Scully said, without hesitation. 'What are you up to?'

'Up to, sir?'

'Yes, up to. You and that réseau of yours. What have you been doing that you won't tell your mother about?'

'Nothing, sir.'

Scully glowered. 'Listen, flower,' he said. 'When I was your age, I was still in an orphanage. They were prepared to accept a lot from us. We could kick up a noise, pull the doors off the hinges, anything. But they wouldn't stand for lying. For lying we got a beating. You can't live with someone who doesn't tell the truth.'

The boy said nothing.

'Why do you think George Presteigne finds it so difficult?' Scully went on, talking like a Dutch uncle. 'Because he's lived with lying all his life. *You've* not been lied to. I've never lied to you and I bet your mum's never lied to you, has she?'

'No, sir.'

'Then, come on. What's going on?'

'Nothing. We only – '

Scully pushed his advantage. 'Only what?'

'We only have – ' the boy sat up straighter in bed. 'We have a petrol bomb, sir.'

Scully's eyebrows shot up. 'Give it to me!'

'I can't, sir. We paid for it. The réseau.'

'Who did you pay?'

'A boy in Passy. His father is making them for the Resistance. He watched how it was done and made one himself.'

'You bloody young fool!' Scully's face was only inches from the boy's. 'He probably doesn't know how to do it proper. He's probably doing a bit of guessing. You could burn yourself to death. Your mum too!'

'We only wanted to help. In the fight for France.'

'Where is it?'

'Behind the bicycles, sir. Downstairs.'

'Christ, you could set the building on fire. What's it made of?'

'Petrol, sulphuric acid and – '

Scully's great hand shot out and he yanked the boy from the bed. 'Do you know anything about sulphuric acid?'

'Not much, sir.'

'You could be scarred for life! And if you'd dropped it, you'd have been dead.'

'We thought everybody should accept their share of danger – '

'Danger's for adults! Not kids! Show me where it is!'

Followed by Scully, the boy headed for the dark little store room off the courtyard where they kept the bicycles and began to move a roll of old carpet. Thrusting his hand into the shadows he brought out a bottle filled with liquid, its neck stuffed with rag.

Scully took it from him and placed it in a corner. 'Go back to bed,' he said.

As the boy vanished, Scully dragged his bicycle out and, pushing the bottle into a haversack, began to wheel the machine to the street.

'Where are you going?' Sidonie was on the stairs, her face worried. 'What's happened?'

'Nothing. I'll be back.'

Madame Weinspach was just closing the courtyard gate. 'You can't go out,' she said. 'It's nearly curfew time.'

'I'll have to risk that.'

She was eyeing the haversack curiously. 'What have you got there, my friend?'

'None of your business, old woman.'

She gave him a sly look. 'I know you for what you are, *mon brave*. You're a soldier, an English soldier. And not an amateur either. I can tell an English soldier when I see one. They walk differently from the French. They are more upright because they're better clothed and have more pride. In the other war, I lived in Amiens and there were many there. And I learned to recognize the real soldiers from the ones who only wore uniform because there was a war on. You're on business, aren't you?'

'Yes.'

'Then go with God! When you come back, tap on my window. I'll let you in.'

Cycling down the street, Scully headed for Clichy. At the end of the Rue Paul-Lecours he passed Holzmeier waiting in his car. For a while he wondered if he were wise to leave Sidonie on her own, but what he had to do had to be done there and then, and she'd have to look after herself for a while. He was taking an enormous chance and if he were caught the Germans would show no mercy.

Hasler was in the Bar du Destin, with an open newspaper in front of him. As Scully appeared, he closed it and looked up.

'More Jewish businesses for sale,' he said. 'I had friends in the circus who were Jews. I expect they've all been made into cakes of soap by now for Hitler to wash his fat backside.'

Scully sat down alongside him without speaking, the haversack on his knees, and Hasler became aware of his expression.

'What have you got in the pack, sergeant?' he asked warily. 'Grenades? To join the fun? Because there's *going* to be fun when the Reds find we've diddled 'em. They were going to start an insurrection.' He carefully opened the newspaper again and laid it flat so that Scully could see a printed notice which he'd been concealing between the pages. 'Take a look at that.'

It was headed *République Française* and called for a general mobilization. 'The commissar appointed by the Provisional Government of the French Republic,' Scully read, 'in accordance with the Paris Committee of Liberation, reminds you that all organized formations of the Resistance movement are an integral part of the FFI, as also are the police force, etc. All such formations in the department of Seine, Seine-et-Oise, Seine-et-Marne, and Oise are placed under the orders of the regional commander, Colonel Rol.'

'It'll be all over the city tomorrow,' Hasler said. 'But this feller Rol's going to get a shock if he thinks *he*'s going to start an insurrection. Because we're starting it first.'

Scully leaned forward and folded the paper back over the notice. 'The trouble with you, flower,' he said slowly, 'is that, like a lot of officers, your mouth's too big. This seems to belong to you.'

Hasler was frowning at the haversack he pushed forward. 'What is it?'

'It's one of your bloody petrol bombs?'

'Where did you get it?'

'From a kid. From Sidonie's boy. He bought it from one of your bloody assassins.'

Hasler smiled. 'Shows the right spirit, don't you think?'

'Petrol bombs aren't playthings for kids.'

'They'll be playthings for everybody before next week is out, old man.' Hasler's face was suddenly hard and unrelenting. 'You can't expect Resistants to be choirboys.'

'You needn't expect 'em to be bloody fools either.'

Hasler stared at the haversack, unsmiling. 'What do you want me to do with it?'

'Give it to one of your pals to throw and tell whoever it is who's making 'em that if I find any of those kids with one again I'll come and shove it down his throat.'

Hasler smiled. 'Growing nervous, sergeant?'

Scully glared. 'Listen, flower, I've been a soldier twenty-six years and I've learned *not* to be nervous.'

'I was only thinking you ought to be. The Gestapo are after people like you. Escapers, agents, evaders, shot-down fly-boys who've gone underground. They're after *me*, too. My God, they're after me!'

Scully glanced round the bar. 'Then why the hell are you sitting in here?'

'Safer in a crowd. Know how to melt into the background. You're different. Better watch yourself. We might need you later.'

Scully left, not knowing whether to admire Hasler for his nerve or despise him for the way he used people. It had grown dark as he headed back towards Montparnasse and eventually he decided to leave the bicycle at another bar he frequented and finish the journey on foot.

The night was warm and stuffy but Scully walked with hunched shoulders, his collar up to hide his face. In the darkness, broken at rare intervals by unreflected patches of blue light, he felt the empty desolation of the boulevards. Alert to danger, avoiding the railway station where there might be police or German security patrols, he made his way along the deserted quais, keeping close to the walls. As he crossed the Ile de la Cité, however, he was surprised to see numerous shadowy figures moving near the Quai des Orfèvres and the Préfecture de Police. Retreating to a doorway, he watched for a while.

They all seemed to be men and gave him the impression of policemen out of uniform. There seemed to be hundreds of them, all heading silently towards the grey mass of the Préfecture. It was impossible to avoid them but they showed no interest in him when he eventually slipped past. As he headed along the Boulevard Saint-Michel, there were more of them, all converging on the river.

The summer night was already growing pale as he reached the courtyard gate of the Hôtel Bouboulis. No sooner had he tapped at the window of Madame Weinspach's apartment than he heard her call out, and a few moments later she appeared, an old coat over her night clothes, her face pale in the half-light.

'It is done?' she asked.

'It's done.'

He climbed the stairs quietly to the second floor and, when he knocked gently on the door, it was opened at once by Sidonie. She was wearing a pink housecoat and her eyes were dark and tired-looking, as though she'd been up all night waiting for him.

'Where have you been?'

'I've been seeing Hasler.'

'Lulu told me what it was he had.'

'He won't get another from that source.'

She glanced at the door, her manner agitated. 'Holzmeier came again. He tried to get in. I had to threaten to call the police. He's worried sick about the future. He thinks something's going to happen.'

'It is,' Scully said grimly.

'Oh, Charley – ' her eyes lifted to his ' – when will it be over?'

'Soon. The streets were full of men.'

'Germans?'

'Frenchmen.'

'Charley – ' she hesitated ' – you took the bomb from Lulu. What can I say?'

'Don't say nothing.'

She shook her head as if to try to reshuffle her thoughts. 'Pierre also turned up again. I think he's afraid too.' Her eyes filled with tears. 'He hammered on the door for ages. Eventually Monsieur Virec came, and he went away. I was terrified.'

He took her hands, noticing as he did so that they were trembling.

'Listen,' he said, 'what we have to do now is lie low and keep our heads down.'

Moving to the windows, he peered through the slats of the shutters. Outside, the air smelt damp and the first people were just beginning to emerge. Paris was stirring and soon the lines of housewives would head for the shops in their daily search for food.

For a while they stood motionless. Sidonie was watching him. His very maleness troubled her and, as he turned, she managed a weak smile and her fingers touched his and tightened on them.

Scully's eyes rested on her face but, as he took a step nearer to her, outside there was a sudden clatter of firing. It came from the Ile de la Cité area and seemed to crash into the Petite-Ville, even into the Rue Fantin and the Hôtel Bouboulis. The moment snapped and, dropping Sidonie's hand, Scully pushed at the shutters.

'It's coming from the Préfecture,' he said. 'That's where I saw all those men as I came home. That's what Hasler meant. The fighting's started.'

There was another burst of firing, louder and longer this time, beating along the Boulevard Saint-Michel towards them. Then they heard distant cheering and, peering from the window, Scully saw an enormous tricolour, dusty from non-use, fluttering down from a building along the street. Another appeared, then another.

161

As they watched, old Virec burst into the apartment, his face flushed with excitement. 'The allies are at Versailles,' he shouted. 'I've just heard! The *Milice* have bolted, but the Germans fired on a crowd in the Boul' Mich'. The tricolour's gone up above the Préfecture. You can see it quite clearly. There's another on Notre-Dame. The police have come out against the Germans.'

As he stopped, faintly, they heard the 'Marseillaise' being sung, in strong unfaltering voices. Ludo appeared. He was fully dressed, his face white and tense. Crossing to the window, he peered out. As Scully wrenched him back, the boy turned and gave him a bitter glance.

'It's the rising,' he said. 'It's started!' His angry eyes were on Scully's face, dark and accusing. 'You promised to help when it came! Yet you have taken our bomb! Frenchmen are fighting the Germans and we have nothing to help them with!'

5

By the time they had swallowed a piece of bread and a cup of coffee, they could hear firing coming from all over the city, increasing all the time in volume and duration.

'I'd better go and see if I can find out what it's all about,' Scully said.

As he headed towards the river, he noticed that few shops had opened but that there were tricolours everywhere. It was as if a message had been radioed throughout the city and the city had responded.

The streets were black with people, many of them carrying weapons. A man wearing an armband inscribed *Vivre Libre ou Mourir* was standing on the quai cheering and people were having their photographs taken in front of the commandeered cars of collaborators. A few civilians were being pushed past, hands above their heads, pale-faced and nervous as the crowd booed. One of them tried to protest. 'By whose authority are you taking my car?' he demanded.

A boy with a revolver brandished it at him. 'This is all the authority I need,' he said.

'Look!' The man with the armband was pointing across the river. In the windows of the Préfecture it was possible to see armed men, and they could hear the sound of the 'Marseillaise', sung by dozens of strong male voices. Then Scully realized that all round him posters with blood-red lettering had been stuck on walls – communist calls to arms, the paste and printer's ink still wet.

A green-camouflaged car appeared on the Quai du Louvre, moving swiftly past the tall grey buildings; then, crossing the Pont-Neuf, it swung into the Quai des Orfèvres.

Scully found he was holding his breath. Somewhere behind the trees in the Place du Parvis-Notre-Dame, he could see a column of smoke rising into the sky.

'Look,' the man with the armband said again.

As he spoke there was a burst of firing from the Préfecture. There were four Germans in the car and, as the firing smashed the windscreen, one of the men in the rear seat slowly buckled forward. A second man was trying to bring his machine-pistol round but the firing caught him as he rose. As he fell against the door, it burst open and he rolled out, sending the weapon flying. One of its front tyres punctured, the car was swinging wildly, then vanished from sight near where the column of smoke was rising. At once, men started to run from doorways round the Préfecture and there was a clatter of firing across the water, a scream, then silence.

'Three,' the man with the armband yelled triumphantly. 'That's the third car they've caught. One got away.' He held up a machine-pistol. 'I got this at Passy. They told us to surrender and we shot the lot of them.'

Scully was about to move away when he heard a commotion behind him. A radio was playing music somewhere up above, soft with the whining of accordions, then there was a sudden scream, terrifying and harsh, of a woman in terror. It was followed by a clattering of footsteps on stairs and a German, his jacket unfastened, still trying to buckle the belt that held his pistol, burst into the street. A workman carrying a spade, who had been watching with the man with the armband, turned and saw him; almost as if he hadn't even thought about it, he swung the spade with all his strength.

The blade caught the German in the base of the neck and, without even a cry of pain, he fell against the peeling, painted wall beneath one of the communist posters, the paper flecked with his blood. A woman who appeared, to fling herself across his body, was immediately grabbed and dragged upright. Other women appeared at windows, spitting at her and shrieking abuse, while the man with the armband wrenched at the neck of her dress, dragging it open to her waist. She screamed and staggered against the wall, tripped over the dead German and began to cower, her hands across her breasts.

'*Putain!*' The cries were coming from all round now. 'Whore! German whore!'

'Brand her,' someone yelled. 'Let everybody see what she was!'

'Paint a swastika on her tits! That's what they're doing!'

'They're shaving their heads! Shave hers!'

Hands grabbed and the woman was forced on to a chair. While she wept, her heaving breasts were savagely marked with swastikas in blue pencil. A pair of scissors appeared and her long dark curls fell round her feet.

'More! More! That's not enough! That's just fashionable!'

The scissors clicked again until the woman's head was covered with nothing but uneven tufts of hair. Still the crowd wasn't satisfied. Clippers were brought out to shave her bald and her forehead was marked with another swastika.

It was harsh and brutal and it occured to Scully that some of the French, who hadn't always resisted as much as they might, were working off a little of their own guilt.

'Strip her!'

The tormented woman was sobbing. 'No, no,' she pleaded.

It made no difference and soon she was cowering naked against the wall.

'How fat she is,' one of the watching women observed conversationally. 'I knew her, of course. It always did take seven or eight men to satisfy her.'

'If they did that to me,' her friend commented, her voice totally without compassion, as if she were watching nothing more than a chicken being plucked, 'I think I'd die.'

Among the crowd round the wretched woman, Scully noticed George Presteigne, his face thin and ugly with hatred. With him was Tom Cléry-Kidder, who looked faintly shocked and sickened. He gave them a shove. 'Go on,' he said. 'Get off 'ome. This is no place for kids.'

'I'm not a kid,' George snapped. 'And she deserves it. She has betrayed France. I would do it to them all.'

As the sobbing woman was shoved from hand to hand, Scully remembered Sidonie. For Christ's sake, he thought in sudden panic, some fool might have seen Holzmeier outside her door and might try to inflict this monstrosity on her!

His heart was pounding as he turned to run. Hasler had been right. After four years of sullen silence, the city had finally turned on her oppressors and all those associated with them. Paris had come to life with a vengeance.

6

It was harder work getting back to the Petite-Ville than it had been leaving it. Flags had sprouted everywhere and people were standing in groups reading the posters calling for a rising, but German lorries were now out, the soldiers shooting from them as they passed, so that several times Scully had to shelter in doorways. The streets were also full of boys wearing tricolour armbands who were heading for strategic points, their weapons concealed in briefcases, violin cases and parcels. Outside a bar, a group of earnest-looking men were handing out leaflets, one eye open for collaborators who might give them away. The crowd round them spilled over the pavement to block the roadway, and Scully had to stop again. A distraught waitress was beseeching customers to hurry.

'We're closing,' she kept saying. 'And I have to get home. My little boy will be out playing and it's no day for him to be doing that.'

Her pleas went unheeded as a youth came running up with the news that the newspaper *Paris Soir* had been taken over by the FFI.

'Tonight we shall be getting a *French* newspaper with *French* news!' he yelled.

His voice was drowned by another boy shouting that the Préfecture was under siege. 'They've got every weapon under the sun in there. Some English, some French, some German. They need reinforcements. Are you coming?'

As the two youths tore off together, fresh shooting broke out somewhere nearby. The men handing out leaflets vanished into doorways, and, as the café shutters came down

167

with a roar, Scully elbowed his way inside the bar where other men were taking advantage of the confusion to sink a few drinks.

The waitress was weeping openly now, sitting at one of the tables and dabbing at her eyes as a procession of German lorries and cars came past at full speed. They were heading in the direction of the barracks and had bunched together for safety. The men in them looked hunted and were firing at anything that moved. A star-shaped hole appeared in the door, and a bottle on the shelves collapsed into splinters.

The waitress set up another wail of misery but, as the Germans vanished, the proprietor began to tear down the barricade of chairs the barman had been building at the door, announcing that he was going to join the rising himself.

'I didn't even know there *was* a Resistance,' he yelled. 'If I had, I'd have joined it long since!'

As he hustled everybody outside, Scully headed back to the Petite-Ville. Two young Germans passed him on foot, each with a revolver. They looked desperate and dangerous, and no one jeered or molested them. Near the end of the Rue Lescaut, however, a German lorry was blazing, sending up a coil of black smoke between the houses. Several dead Germans lay in the gutter, divested already of their weapons. A woman wearing a German helmet was waving a tricolour from a second floor window but, even as Scully hurried past, he heard another clatter of firing and the woman disappeared abruptly and the tricolour fluttered in a spiral of coloured cloth to the pavement where it was immediately snatched up by a youth who ran from a door-way and vanished again at once.

Turning into the courtyard of the Hôtel Bouboulis, Scully pounded up the stairs. Sidonie was pulling at Ludo who was standing at the window, determined to see everything that was going on. Scully swept her aside and, wrenching the boy away, flung him into the room. Almost as he did so, there was another burst of firing and they heard bullets chinking on the stonework outside.

The boy was wildly excited and scrambled to his feet, his

face flushed, his eyes wide. 'They shot five of them,' he yelled at Scully. 'They shot five! They hit the driver and the lorry hit a tree. They killed the others as they jumped out!'

As Scully reached out to close the shutters, a hidden German fired two more shots. One hit the woodwork, sending splinters flying, and he fell back into the apartment, the shutter slamming against the frame as he did so. Somewhere below them a man was screaming. Picking himself up, Scully saw a German run across the street. He was fat and his pasty face was sweating, and Scully recognized him as Madame Weinspach's cook friend, unfamiliarly garbed in belts and straps, wearing a steel helmet and carrying a rifle. He had just reached the opposite pavement in an ungainly run when a bullet hit him in the chest. He took two staggering steps to one side, then sat down and flopped over on to his back. There was a long silence, followed by a cry of anguish that floated up to them from the hall. It was Madame Weinspach.

'Oh, the fools!' she moaned. 'They've shot the only decent one among them!'

The German was lying across the gutter, his feet on the sidewalk, his head in the roadway, his fat stomach sticking up in the air, his rifle alongside him. A boy ran out to snatch up the weapon but was caught by a bullet. As he screamed and rolled on his side, a second boy appeared, grabbed the weapon and began to drag his friend to shelter. The wounded boy's cries mingled with those of Madame Weinspach. 'Don't! Don't! Mother of God, my back!'

As he secured the shutters, Scully saw a German-driven Peugeot come round the corner near the burning lorry and stop, as if uncertain which way to go. As it halted, a bottle came from a balcony above, spinning over and over before crashing on the pavement alongside the car. As the vehicle was engulfed in a huge flower of flame, the Germans dived from it, yelling, their uniforms ablaze, and fell into an archway opposite, one of them with his face streaming blood.

'*We* could have killed them with my petrol bomb,' Ludo said sullenly from behind Scully. 'We could have done it easily from here.'

'Don't talk like that, Lulu,' Sidonie begged, her eyes tragic.

The boy turned and stared at her coldly. 'And don't call me Lulu,' he said slowly. 'My name's Ludovic. Lulu's a baby's name and I'm almost a man.'

There was no going out on the streets, so they made a meal from a carefully hoarded tin of meat, with stale bread and the dreadful coffee. Ludo was still distinctly rebellious, his eyes angry and bitter as they rested on Scully's face. Sidonie was nervous, worried for her son and shy with Scully, whose thoughts were far more on her than on any attempt to liberate the city.

By this time the Germans had escaped from the archway opposite. A scouting lorry had stopped long enough to pick them up and they had loosed off a final barrage of bullets at the houses around, breaking windows and splintering shutters, before disappearing.

'They'll come back,' Sidonie said. 'They always come back. Whenever there were murders they always came back and shot people in the street.'

Old Virec, who had been caught taking his breakfast at the Bar du Weekend, looked in to report that the proprietor had been in touch with other bars in other districts and had culled a great deal of news for his customers. The Préfecture, it seemed, had been completely taken over by the police who were now prepared to withstand anything the Germans could throw against them. The communists, who had hoped to lead the Resistance themselves, had found themselves outsmarted and, in a fury, were stirring things up all over the city. The Rue Fantin was already plastered with their notices, they had destroyed the Germans' wire-tapping equipment in the telephone exchanges, and were busily arming themselves with the weapons of the men they had killed.

By nine o'clock shooting was going on throughout Paris, and few other people ventured out. Those who did went only to protect their businesses or in search of food, and they moved stealthily from door to door, their eyes everywhere. Cyclists kept to the pavements and only an occasional car, with the letters FFI painted on its side to indicate it had been taken over by the Resistance, shot past with screeching tyres, driven at full speed in case of ambush. The rate at which the insurrection had spread had startled everybody. With people keeping their secrets, no one had known just how eager the spirit to resist had been and now the men who had started the fighting were trying less to intensify it than to control it.

'They're taking over public buildings,' old Virec shouted from the doorway. 'They're taking over the *mairies*, the police stations, the post offices, the slaughterhouse, the mortuary, even the Comédie Française. Flags are going up everywhere. Bed sheets and old dresses, most of them, but they're going up. Look from the window; you can see them.'

'But the tanks are out now,' he went on, still panting after his dash up the stairs. 'If you listen you can hear the gunfire.'

As they stood near the closed shutters, they could hear a sporadic thudding coming across the city roofs. Then the telephone rang, a harsh sound in the silent apartment. Ludo turned.

'I'll answer it,' he said.

The call was evidently for him, and they barely noticed what he was saying.

'Yes,' he said, 'yes, of course I will. Have no fear, I know what to do.'

The sound of rifle fire continued to be interspersed with the occasional heavier thump of artillery. Through the window they could see the Rue Fantin was empty, and Scully slipped from door to door to bring back bread and fruit and a few slices of sausage from the Rue Noyelle. The woman in the shop gave him snatches of news.

'The Préfecture's still holding out,' she said, 'but tanks have appeared in front of the *mairie* at Neuilly. I heard it on the telephone.'

Hurrying back, certain some hidden German sniper would pick him off as he slipped along, Scully fell into the Hôtel

Bouboulis and ran up the stairs to find old Virec had picked up more news. He was dancing a jig on the landing.

'My daughter-in-law called from Chartres.' The words tumbled out. 'The telephone was cut off in the middle of it but she managed to say that troops are pouring through in an unending stream – trucks and tanks and armoured cars! She said she had never seen so many vehicles or such big ones! They all have the white American star on their sides and they are all wearing American uniforms! They are coming here! They *must* be coming here!'

PART THREE

To the barricades

1

The scattered shooting went on all day.

Madame Weinspach's wails had died down and Scully found her realistically trying to put the dead German cook out of her mind.

'He only brought me food,' she said coolly. 'Now he's dead and there'll be no more. It's a pity, because he wasn't a bad man.'

As Scully returned to the apartment the firing from the river grew louder and through the window they could see men moving along the street. They were all young and swaggered a little, showing off with red handkerchiefs at their throats and their shirts open to the waist.

'They have been looking at the pictures of Delacroix,' Sidonie observed dryly.

Then came the phenomenon of the singing. Someone somewhere started the 'Marseillaise'. They heard it drifting in from the street, sung by dozens of voices, both male and female, and coming from open windows of houses and apartments where the occupants were watching the street for signs of fighting. It seemed quite spontaneous and they opened the shutters to hear it better. Across the Rue Fantin, a stout woman stood in the shadows behind the pots of geranium that filled her window sill. Behind her stood an old man and they were both singing, their faces lit with fierce pride and exaltation.

Virec arrived with his violin. 'If they can,' he said, 'so can we.'

As he laid the bow across the strings, Madame Weinspach appeared and joined in, then Sidonie and the boy. Scully watched them, bewildered, unable to imagine the British, even in so emotional a moment, standing together to sing 'God Save The King'. But the sweeping tune finally caught him up too, invigorating, triumphant, compelling, its clarion call making his blood beat faster.

As they stopped, Virec's telephone sounded.

'I have established the information bureau the most effective,' he called as he bolted for his apartment.

When he came back, however, his voice was subdued. 'The Americans are still a hundred miles away. My daughter-in-law must have been wrong when she said they were passing through Chartres.'

'Perhaps it was the Free French,' Scully said.

'Can it be?' Sidonie asked.

'It must be!' Old Virec did his little dance, eager to be convinced. 'Of course it must! My son went to fight with them. Perhaps she saw *him* passing and was cut off before she could announce it. I must telephone Louis Thoumas. He used to play next to me in the first violins. He lives at Sèvres, and Sèvres is on the road from Chartres.'

He returned again a few minutes later. 'There *are* troops at Chartres,' he said. 'He confirmed it. He has a neighbour whose son is with the Free French forces and he telephoned his father. They are trying to reach Paris. But he also told me that there are *no* Americans. *They* are going to bypass us and let the city fall of its own accord.' He stared at Scully in bewilderment. 'They must be the only people in the world who do *not* want to be in Paris!'

The blue sky was full of columns of brown smoke that lifted into the clear air and drifted over the roof tops. The lorry and the car in the Rue Lescaut were still smouldering, filling the nostrils with the acrid smell of burning rubber.

Old Virec appeared yet again, his face long. 'The *mairie* at Neuilly has fallen,' he said. 'And the Germans have brought up tanks at the Préfecture.'

Late in the afternoon, they heard the Germans had blown in the main gate of the Préfecture but there were men behind barricades of sandbags and abandoned lorries with bottles full of petrol, and the Germans were paying a high price. Even as dead soldiers were being carried away, however, their comrades were spraying the building with mortar fire and trying to get in through the roofs, and the surrounding streets were full of glass and wreckage.

Old Virec's news service continued to keep them informed. 'The Préfecture's still holding,' he announced late in the evening as the light was going. 'But they're in need of help. They've issued an appeal to all old soldiers to rally round and attack the Germans' rear.'

Scully hitched at his trousers. This seemed to mean him.

'You haven't got a gun,' Sidonie said.

'Hasler'll find me one.'

Her expression indicated that her wish for him to stay was struggling with the knowledge that he ought to go. 'We have a gun,' she said. 'A small one. It was my husband's. It's in the bottom of my wardrobe.'

'No – ' there was an expression of triumph on Ludo's face ' – it's in the bottom of *mine*. I took it and put it there.'

Sidonie stared at him, shocked, but Scully gestured.

'Get it.'

The boy returned with a pistol and a small box of cartridges.

'Belgian,' Scully commented, holding the weapon in his great fist. 'Only big enough to kill a cat. All the same – ' he slipped it with the ammunition into his pocket ' – it'll be better than nothing.'

As he reached for his jacket, there was a burst of firing outside. Hurrying to the window, they were just in time to see a German car hurtle round the corner from the direction of the Boul' Mich'. Even at that distance, they could see the terror on the driver's face. As he saw the vehicles in the Rue Lescaut and the sprawled bodies of German soldiers, he clapped on the brakes and made a complete turn, the tyres screeching as he swung round in a desperate attempt to escape the blocked street.

Bouncing over the pavement with twanging springs, the car began to head back the way it had come. Then there was another burst of firing and, as the driver slumped over the wheel, the car leapt on to the pavement again and hit a tree. The doors flew open and the dead man fell out, sprawling head down, his feet caught by the pedals. An officer in the rear seat looked about him frantically; then, grabbing a small canvas bag, he crawled out and hid behind the vehicle. As the rattle of firing sent chips of plaster from the walls behind him, he rose and started to run.

'It's Holzmeier!' Scully said.

Madame Weinspach's bell jangled wildly. As she opened the wicket gate, it was flung back, throwing her aside, and they heard footsteps clatter across the courtyard and up the stairs.

Even as Sidonie turned the key, the door handle jerked and there was a heavy pounding on the panels.

'Let me in! Madame, I beg you, let me in!' Holzmeier's voice was harsh with fear.

Sidonie stood by the locked door, her back to the wall, her hands at her throat, her terrified eyes on Scully's face.

'Keep away,' Scully advised. 'He may try to shoot the lock off.'

He slipped the Belgian pistol from his pocket and stood alongside the door as the pounding began again.

'Madame – ' Holzmeier's voice came once more, broken and agonized ' – they want to kill me! I've done them no harm! You must save me! I have civilian clothes with me! They'll never know! I beseech you!'

Sidonie's eyes were still on Scully's face, begging him to show mercy. 'We can't let him be killed,' she whispered.

Scully glanced at the pathetic little pistol he held and thought of the weapon he'd seen on Holzmeier's belt. 'Let him in,' he said.

But, even as Sidonie wrenched at the key, Holzmeier's feet sounded on the stairs again. Then there was a shout, followed by several shots, and they heard the thump and clatter of a body rolling down the steps.

Sidonie gazed at Scully in horror. 'I killed him,' she said. 'It was my fault!'

Scully stared back at her for a second; then, turning the key, he wrenched the door open and glanced over the banister into the hall. Holzmeier was lying across the bottom steps, a spreading pool of blood under his body. Poor little bastard, Scully thought. He'd hated the war and, despite what he was always saying, had hated France and the French too. The only thing he'd really wanted was to be in Germany. He should have married a nice German girl instead of lusting after a French widow who loathed him simply because of what he stood for.

As he stared, Ludo appeared alongside him, craning his head to see round him. Scully pushed him back.

'Get him inside,' he snapped at Sidonie. 'This is no place for kids!'

'He's a German!' the boy yelled furiously. 'He's a dead German! We shot him! Why shouldn't I see him?'

Scully turned and gave him a violent angry shove into the apartment. Sidonie disappeared after him and slammed the door. With the boy's shrill cries of rage in his ears, Scully went down the stairs. Two men appeared in the hall from the courtyard.

'Got him,' one of them said with satisfaction. 'Rou said we'd find him here.'

It was clear the death sentence had come from Hasler.

As they stood staring down at the body, Madame Weinspach descended on them like an avenging angel.

'Get him out of here!' she screamed. 'I don't want his blood all over my clean hall! The Germans will come and raze the place! Take him away!'

As the two men backed away before her, Scully bent down and wrenched Holzmeier's pistol from his holster. At least, he thought, he now had something worthwhile to fight with.

The two Frenchmen seemed loathe to touch the body, and Scully turned it on to its face with his foot. Then, reaching down to the collar of Holzmeier's tunic, he began to drag him out of the hall and across the courtyard. The two Frenchmen made no attempt to help. As he opened the gate and dragged Holzmeier into the street, people began to crowd into the courtyard to see what had happened, staring at the blood, questioning Madame Weinspach, and gazing up at Sidonie who had come out on to the stairs. Inside the apartment the boy was screaming to be let out.

The two dead Germans, looking like broken dolls, were already surrounded by a group of men and women, standing in a half-circle staring blankly down at them. The man who had shot Holzmeier began to tug at his field boots.

'My size,' he said cheerfully and, as he spoke, the other man grabbed for the boots of the driver.

The car appeared to be little damaged and Scully climbed into the driver's seat to see if the engine still worked. Several men leaned over him, peering under the seats.

'Any more weapons? Any booze?'

The man with Holzmeier's boots sat down to change into them. 'Where was he heading?' he asked. 'He was going *somewhere*.' He lifted Holzmeier's canvas bag. 'He's got a civilian suit in here.'

A woman with a face like a witch whom Scully had often seen in the Rue Noyelle, irritably poking at vegetables with her fingers, raised her voice. 'He was going to *her*,' she said. 'He's been before. I've seen him often.'

Sidonie was still on the stairs and, as the crowd turned and stared at her, she gazed back at them, petrified. Then a yell went up and they streamed into the hall. Terrified, she turned and bolted for the second floor. The witch-like woman, foam at the corner of her mouth, her face ugly with hatred, was screaming at the top of her voice. 'Bring her down! Brand her! Let the whole world see what she's been!'

Seeing the two men who had killed Holzmeier drop the boots they were holding and rush after Sidonie, Scully flung the men around him aside in a fury and scrambled from the car just as she was being dragged to the courtyard, sobbing and calling Scully's name. Old Virec was jumping up and down on the fringe of the crowd while Madame Weinspach pounded on the backs of the men in front of her.

'She's not his woman,' she was screaming but, in the din and the excitement, nobody could hear her.

A grinning lecherous-eyed youth snatched at the front of Sidonie's blouse just as Scully reached her. Sending him flying with a blow at the side of the head, he grabbed one of the men holding Sidonie and, wrenching his arm behind him, thrust Holzmeier's pistol in his face.

'Move,' he yelled, 'and you're a dead man!'

Though he spoke in English, the meaning was clear and the man froze.

'Kill him,' someone yelled from the back of the crowd. 'He's probably another German!'

The pistol jabbed. 'Tell them to get back!' Scully snapped. 'Tell them or I'll let you have it!'

The motionless man staring into the muzzle of the pistol, lifted his hands carefully, and waved the crowd back. They moved slowly, unwilling to be cheated of their prey.

'Further!'

The wavering hands moved again and they edged back again towards the archway.

The man Scully was holding rolled his eyes towards Scully's face.

'Who are you, my friend?' he asked quietly.

'No friend of the Germans,' Scully said.

Old Virec began to yell. 'You fools!' he raved. 'It's her Uncle Charles from Normandy. He came here to bring the boy home!'

'Fool yourself,' Madame Weinspach yelled at him. 'If you believe that, you'll believe anything! He's an English soldier. I know who he is!'

The tension slackened visibly and Scully lowered the pistol.

'Thank you, my friend,' the Frenchman said. 'I was just afraid it might go off. I think you'd better tell us who you are.'

'I brought him here!' Freed as the door of the apartment was flung open, Ludo had appeared now, his anger at Scully forgotten in his eagerness to claim some part in the rising. 'I brought him because I knew my mother would hide him! He killed a German. I saw him!'

There was a lot of muttering but the story was accepted.

'And I thought she'd taken a lover,' one of the women said. 'I wondered what she was coming to because she was never that sort.' She nodded approvingly at Scully. 'You

181

look better without those spectacles, Monsieur. I scarcely recognized you.'

Scully felt Sidonie's hand touch his and he put an arm round her and was about to shepherd her back to the apartment when a boy on a bicycle came hurtling into the courtyard, his eyes bulging with excitement.

'It's over!' he shouted. 'The fighting's over! The Germans have agreed to a truce!'

There was a disbelieving silence.

'Already?' The man who had killed Holzmeier looked blankly at the crowd. 'It's a trick to make us lay down our weapons!'

'No, it's true! It's true! I heard it on the radio! The Paris radio!'

There was a wild yell and, as the crowd began to pour through the archway into the street, Ludo dived for the gate that led to the Passage du Chien-Nomade to tell Grand Charles what had happened. Scully put his arm round Sidonie's shoulders.

'I will come with you,' Virec announced. 'I have a bottle of brandy I have been keeping for a day such as this.'

As he set off after them, Madame Weinspach grabbed his jacket. 'Stay here, you old fool,' she snorted. 'I have a bottle of brandy too.'

The door of the apartment was wide open and Scully pushed Sidonie through and slammed it shut with a movement of his heel. As he laid the German pistol on the table, she was standing opposite him, her hands over her breasts, holding the torn remnants of her blouse in place. She was still shaking with shock and fear, and when he stepped across to put his arms round her, her hands went out to him and she clung to him, shivering and sobbing.

'What will happen to our children?' she whispered. 'What will happen when they see all this? We are teaching them to become gangsters.'

She was clutching his sleeve, her fingers working on the rough material of what had once been her husband's jacket.

He released her gently but, as she stared at him, her eyes

filled with tears; then she flung herself into his arms again and, before they were aware of what they were doing, they were kissing wildly.

2

When Scully woke the following morning it was barely day-light, but the day was humid and through the half-opened shutters he could see grey ridges of cloud moving over the city from the north.

There was a stuffy stillness in the air, a curious silence after the racket of the previous day's fighting. The unex-pected truce was evidently holding. It was still not clear how it had been brought about but at least the killing had stopped.

For a long time Scully lay quietly, puzzled by his own behaviour. He had moved into the Hôtel Bouboulis with every intention of finding his way into Sidonie's bed. But something, he didn't know quite what, had kept him from taking advantage of her loneliness and need. Even the pre-vious night, the situation ready-made for a big seduction scene, he had quietly released her and left the room. She had been more than willing. They had been alone until the boy returned home. Yet when they had come face to face again, she had not been able to look him in the eye, and he had done no more than compliment her on the dress she had put on.

Chalky White, he realized, would have laughed like a drain. But Scully had a feeling that he was very different now from the man who had been Chalky White's friend. That Scully had been a rough diamond like most old sol-diers, tough in manner and tough in thought, knowing ex-actly how many beans made five, keeping one eye always open for the main chance, whether it concerned food, money or women.

The present Scully was entirely different. His head was full of dreams, and for the first time in his adult life he was looking at a woman without a trace of the old soldier's feeling of well-being at having got his feet under the table. Perhaps, he thought, it was because for the first time in his life Charley Scully was serious about a woman.

She had introduced him to a new world and taught him to live like a gentleman. Even when there had been little to eat, she had always insisted on serving it properly. With her, he had listened to good music for the first time and had found himself afraid to speak in case he spoiled the fragile moment of pleasure she was sharing with him.

It was clear she was starved of love. She needed a man's arms about her. For four years she'd been struggling with her determination in a remorseless world, and the attack on her had broken down the last barriers of her courage. But Scully wanted to do it honestly. He wanted to marry her and his one concern was how to go about it. In his long career as a womanizer he had never experienced such feelings before and their intensity surprised him. If this were being in love, it was easier than he'd thought and he couldn't imagine why he'd backed away from it for so long. He knew she was his for the taking, and foreigners had married Frenchwomen before. The late McCosh had married this one.

What was more, she had a home. She even had a family. It was too bloody easy. It made him feel guilty.

As he went to the kitchen to make coffee for himself, Sidonie appeared, wearing the pink housecoat over her nightdress. Her eyes were dark-ringed and tired-looking and he guessed she'd spent as much of the night awake, thinking, as he had. While he prepared the coffee, she moved about, silently opening drawers and quietly placing cups and saucers and knives on the table, saying nothing, avoiding his eyes. They were both deeply aware of the other's presence, yet neither of them had sufficient courage to start a conversation.

'The boy still asleep?' Scully managed at last.

'Yes.' She answered with a whisper. 'He came home late from Grand Charles'.'

She left the kitchen and he heard her moving about in her room. Making the coffee, he knocked on the door.

'It's ready,' he said.

There was silence and he put his head round the door. She was still wearing the pink housecoat and was kneeling in front of the little crucifix that hung over her dressing table. He could just make out the murmured words.

'*Saint Père, sois compatissant pour la plus malheureuse de tes servantes. . . .*'

As she heard him, she rose, her eyes full of tears.

'What's up, flower?'

She drew a deep breath that seemed to hurt her.

'You don't have to talk about it,' he said.

'But I do. I am so guilty.'

He was about to turn back to the kitchen when she stopped him. 'Don't go. Please listen. I thought about it all night. I must say what's in my mind.'

He stood just inside the room, waiting, as she continued, fully aware what she was trying to say to him.

'We have often been told in France that the English are hypocrites. George Presteigne's father leads one to believe that it's true. 1940 didn't help. We were in despair and seeking scapegoats, and for that position the English were high on the list. We were almost hoping the British would surrender. It would have been a sop to our pride.'

'I told you. You don't have to talk about it.'

'I must.' She pressed the hair back off her face, overwhelmed by the heat. 'We were suffering from shock then. It was like finding yourself alive after a motor accident. Everything was unreal and you asked yourself "What happened?" I was the worst shocked of all. I had just lost my husband, and I hated the English because I felt, like so many others, that the English had dragged us into a war we didn't want.'

Scully was silent, aware that he was gaining more by saying nothing than by trying to pursue his advantage.

'*You* are not a hypocrite, Charley. You are a good and true man.'

Scully had been called many things in his life, but never that before.

'I've done as much that's bad as any man,' he said.

'You have behaved with nobility. You have been a good example for Ludo. He needs a man.'

'He can have me any time,' Scully said. He tried to make it sound jocular but underneath there was no jesting. He meant every word. He wanted her. He wanted to marry her but he hadn't the courage to say so.

She seemed about to reply, then she changed her mind. For a long time she was silent, staring at him, almost beseeching him to relieve her of the responsibility of doing the talking. Finally, she started to speak again.

'When you first came,' she said, 'I didn't trust you. I was afraid. But you have done nothing – nothing – with which I could reproach you. You have kept us fed when there was no food. You have protected us when there was no protection. You have advised me when there was no advice from anywhere else. You have – ' she stopped and her eyes brimmed over with tears ' – I – ' she stopped again, at a loss, unable to go on any more.

As Scully stepped towards her, she flung herself into his arms. Through the thin material of the housecoat he could feel her body, slim and warm and soft, and instinctively, Scully – the old Scully, the old-soldier Scully who knew exactly what to do in any given set of circumstances where women were concerned – kicked the door to with his foot.

When Scully woke, he was dazzled and humbled and he lay straight-limbed and silent, staring at the ceiling. Sidonie was sitting up, resting on one slim naked arm. She looked bewildered.

'What's wrong?' he asked.

She gave a sad puzzled shrug. 'I was looking at you.'

'What was I doing?'

'Just sleeping. It's four years since I looked at a man sleeping. For nine years I watched my husband. He was always slow to wake and I always woke first. I always watched him. I longed to see his eyes open. I was terrified they might not.'

She gave a little shiver and he pulled her to him, holding her close so that he felt her breathing somewhere in the angle of his neck.

'Oh God,' she whispered, 'I so needed affection! It became unbearable to think of you sleeping in the next room. I loved my husband, but sometimes now I find it hard to remember even what he looked like. Is that wrong?'

'You can't live on your own for ever.'

'No.' She paused. 'But there has been a restriction on love in France. You always had to beware that someone to whom you wished to give your affection might not think as you did, and would store up what you said to tell the Germans.' Her eyes met his, worried and anxious. 'I discovered in 1941 how much we need affection. I lied to you. Constantin von Leo *was* my lover.'

He was faintly disappointed, but somehow it didn't really matter.

'Two days,' she went on in a whisper. 'Just two days. Then he left for the Eastern Front. Perhaps he was just being a German, because in those days it was German policy to be kind. There were notices everywhere, telling us to trust them, and it was hard not to. When I learned that Ludo was going to live, I was so grateful, I . . .'

Her voice died away and she became silent for a while. 'I needed a man,' she went on slowly. 'Not just his body, but his presence, his strength, his courage. I failed France. We were both aware he was not going to stay, and after those two days he just disappeared. I had a letter later from somewhere outside Stalingrad and then nothing more. I – ' she made a small fluttering movement with her hand and Scully took it in his own.

'Forget it,' he said. 'It's over.'

'There have been no others. I swear. This is why I was so frightened of Holzmeier. He, too, was kind. I'm sure of it. When he knocked me off my bicycle he was so concerned. But I was terrified of it happening again. I daren't take chances. I felt too guilty already. Not just because people who collaborated and fraternized with the Germans were hated. But because of *me*. Ever since 1941 I had felt ashamed. Do you feel I'm a traitor?'

Scully smiled. 'Why should I? It's over and done with.'

She managed a smile back at him. 'It's so wonderful to be able to talk. It was like a weight in my chest. Soon afterwards I sold the house in Trouville and returned to Paris, so that nobody knew but Pierre. I never dared tell anyone. Now I can.'

'What about this Armande of yours?'

There was a fleeting expression of distress in her face but it went as quickly as it came.

'I don't even know where he is.'

'You were in love with him?'

'Yes. He was a friend of my husband's. He was a lecturer at the university, too, and if I hadn't married my husband I might well have married him. But he just vanished one night, leaving nothing more than a note to say he was going to join de Gaulle. I couldn't believe it. He had told me he loved me and wanted to marry me, but then he simply disappeared. I hated him for it. I've realized since it was the only safe way to go without incriminating anyone.' Her shoulders lifted in a shrug. 'We heard on the radio that he was with the Route Regiment de Tchad and then nothing.'

'Are you still in love with him?'

'After two years of silence?'

'Suppose he turned up? Suppose he was with the first troops to enter Paris?'

'It wouldn't matter now,' she said firmly.

'Are you sure?'

'Yes – ' she paused ' – I'm sure.'

'What about when it's all over?'

'Not even then.'

Again there was a faint hesitation and he wondered how much of what she was saying stemmed from gratitude towards him. He was prepared to have her on any terms, however. For the first time in his life he saw security, and he was as much in need of roots as she was.

She still seemed uncertain as she went on. 'Are *you* married, Charley?'

'Was.'

'What happened?'

'Left me.'

'Why?'

'Soldier. Posted abroad. Had to leave her behind. She couldn't take being alone. Went off with a sailor off a battleship.' He didn't attempt to accuse.

'Perhaps this is why you understand. Have you ever thought of remarrying, Charley?'

'If I found the right person.' He was looking hard at her as he spoke, wondering if she realized what he was thinking.

'I, too,' she said slowly.

Scully took a deep breath, and then came straight to the point.

'You could always marry *me*,' he said.

She stared at him for a moment without speaking. Then she kissed him gently, her face enigmatic. What she was thinking he had no idea but he chose to believe that she was in agreement.

3

By the time Scully had shaved and dressed, Sidonie was in the kitchen making fresh coffee. Crossing to her, he put his arms round her, his hands on her breasts, and she became still, as if petrified by his touch. But as he bent to kiss the back of her neck, he heard the click of a door and moved hurriedly to the window. He was staring out as Ludo appeared, his hair tousled, his face flushed with sleep.

'The truce's still on,' Scully said, withdrawing his head. 'There's no shooting.'

'Do you think the Germans will leave?' Sidonie asked, in a matter-of-fact voice that would have fooled no one but a boy.

'It's probably just a trick to give them the chance to bring up more troops. Best stay indoors until we're certain.'

Sidonie turned to Ludo. 'You heard what Charley said.'

The boy gave Scully an uncertain look, as if he still hadn't forgiven him for taking the petrol bomb.

Soon afterwards Old Virec appeared beaming, to tell them the truce was holding.

'I've been down to the Place Saint-Michel,' he said. 'There were Germans and Frenchmen alongside each other and posters on the wall saying that, since the Germans asked for the truce, it's no disgrace to agree to it. The Germans made no attempt to tear them down.'

Sunday morning remained calm and people began to appear on the street to view the damage, and Sidonie decided it was safe to attend mass. Holzmeier's car and the bodies had disappeared though there were still stains on the pavement where they had lain.

While Sidonie dressed for church, Scully sat on the balcony smoking a cigarette. The snapshot Ludo had taken of him had found itself a frame, he noticed, and now stood on the table by the window with a photograph of Sidonie and the boy, while the crêpe-hung picture of the late McCosh had vanished. When she appeared beside him she was impeccably turned out, the boy alongside her, his hair plastered down in spikes.

'I shall pray for us, Charley,' she whispered. 'I shall pray for many things.'

After they had left, Scully set off to find food. As he turned into the Boul' Mich', George Presteigne passed him on his flashy racing machine. His head didn't lift and, though Scully knew he had seen him, he gave no sign of recognition.

He had not seen the British Réseau for several days until the previous afternoon when they had been hovering outside the bar in the Rue Noyelle, looking preoccupied and doubtless mourning the fact that they had not managed to become involved in the rising. They hadn't changed much – George still noisy and self-assertive, Grand Charles waving and friendly, his spectacles smeared to the point of blindness.

Unearthing a lettuce, a swede and half a sausage from a shop near the Bar du Destin at Clichy, Scully had just turned for home when he saw Hasler outside on the *terrasse* drinking a coffee. He seemed satisfied with the way things had gone the previous day.

'We gave the Germans a bloody nose, didn't we, sergeant?' he said. 'La McCosh won't be troubled any more by the baby lieutenant. I put the boys on to him.'

'Your stupid bloody boys,' Scully snarled, 'thought Sidonie was his woman! You bloody nearly got her stripped to the buff!'

Hasler seemed unperturbed. '*That* would have been a sight for sore eyes,' he observed cheerfully. 'Ah, well, it was all in a good cause. You come to warn me again?'

'No, I haven't.'

'You could save your breath, anyway, because I know they're still after me. The bastards never let up, do they? They know they'll never get the leaders of the FFI so they're rounding up every other dissenter they can find. Jews, socialists, even professors from the lycées who dare tell their pupils that France'll soon be free again. They haven't forgotten people like me just because they're a bit tied up at the moment. Quite the reverse, in fact. They're scared now and they're lashing out blindly. But we've got 'em to recognize Resistance fighters as regular troops. It means they'll be treated as normal prisoners of war now if they're captured.'

Scully was unimpressed. 'Who're you kidding?' he said. 'If the Germans win and take Paris over again they'll shoot every poor bastard who stuck his fingers to his nose and shouted "Boo!" You trying to say Hitler won't want vengeance?'

Hasler shrugged, dodging the question, and his self-satisfied smile came again. 'When a few people like us can force the great German army to sign a truce at all, it's surely the sign of the beginning of the end. It's been quite a battle.'

Scully gave him a contemptuous look. 'You call this a bloody battle?' he said. 'I've seen bigger battles than you ever dreamed about. I started in battles when I was a kid in 1918 and you were still in knee breeches. You haven't worried the bastards one jot. They could finish you off like that, if they wanted to.' As he snapped his fingers Hasler frowned. 'They aren't trying. Perhaps someone *wants* Paris to fall. Perhaps this new commander they've got's looking to his future. Remission of sentence for good behaviour. The Americans haven't changed their plans. They still aren't coming here.'

As Scully returned along the Quai Saint-Michel, having at last managed to collect his bicycle from the bar where he had left it two nights before, the banks of the river were crowded with people out to stare at the battered Préfecture. There was a burnt-out German tank near the Parvis-Notre-Dame, and wrecked vehicles that had been caught in the crossfire. Some of the bridges were guarded by Germans and some by ragged boys of the FFI, but facing the Ile de la Cité was a whole row of fishermen, sitting in the sunshine over their rods, their eyes shaded by sunhats made of folded newspapers.

'Caught anything?' Scully asked one of them.

'Harder than you think, my friend,' the man grinned. 'These fish are the cleverest in the world.'

The summer day was still, the city breathless in the heat, but Scully's mind was still on Hasler's words. The bloody politicians would probably make a balls-up of the truce, he reckoned. As they did of everything. It wasn't in American interests to send soldiers into Paris, the British no longer had any say in the matter, and the French were unable to stop squabbling among themselves. They were all only concerned with political power and it didn't matter a damn how many good men were killed to achieve it. Numbers of dead never meant much to politicians; while Scully had watched his friends dying at Amiens in 1918, the politicians in London had still been concerned less with winning the war than with who was going to be in control when it was all over.

His mind full of plans, he began to wonder what he would do when the war ended because clearly it was coming to an end. He had no doubts that, with his record, he could reach the rank of sergeant-major which had once seemed so utterly beyond his reach. But that would be only for a short time, and after that, what? Civilian employee on an army camp? Sitting in the stores filling in forms? He couldn't see himself doing it. But what else? He had to find something. He couldn't offer himself to Sidonie with nothing.

He was totally absorbed with his thoughts when a burst of firing brought him back to the present. It seemed to come from somewhere well to the north of the river, but almost immediately, as if it had been a signal, more firing broke out along the bank of the river and there was a fusillade of shots from the Préfecture. Ricochets and overs were crossing the water, whining and striking the stone embankment; as women and children screamed, men grabbed them and thrust them down on the pavements, and tricolours hanging from windows were quickly snatched inside as they attracted German fire.

In no time the quai had emptied of people. It was impossible to abandon the bicycle and Scully, with an old soldier's concern for food, had no intention of giving up what he'd found. Diving into the tangle of twisting streets between the Seine and Saint-Germain-des-Prés, he headed towards the Boulevard Saint-Michel, his heart thumping, his feet driving at the pedals, only to find he had run into a miniature battle.

An open truck went past, full of bareheaded German soldiers. As it was caught in the blast of fire, it careered into a wall and burst into flames. The driver, trapped in the cabin, died, but the others scrambled free and surrendered at once.

Suddenly all the quiet strolling men and women he'd seen were shouting with triumph again, snatching up dropped weapons and stripping the Germans of their boots. Then a hidden machine-gun somewhere along the street opened up and a woman fell to the ground, screaming. A man grabbed her by the ankles and pulled her into a doorway, her dress riding up over her thighs, and a young man in a white smock and an old-fashioned French steel helmet bent over her.

Pounding up the hill, feeling his heart would burst, Scully turned thankfully out of the long straight thoroughfare, which could be dominated by one strategically placed rifleman, into the Petite-Ville. As he reached the Hôtel Bouboulis, Madame Weinspach was just closing the gate. Dropping the bicycle, Scully turned to help her, just as old Virec also fell in from the street, his eyes excited.

'The communists started firing on German patrols,' he gasped. 'It's started all over again.'

He leaned on the gates with Scully, still breathing heavily and, as they secured them, he mopped his brow and fished out a handbill. 'Look what someone shoved into my hand,' he said. 'Instructions on how to make a petrol bomb.'

As Scully snatched it from him, the old man's eyebrows shot up. '*You're* going to make them, Monsieur?'

'No, I'm not,' Scully snapped. 'I'm going to keep the boy from making them.'

4

When Scully reached the flat, Sidonie was by the window, the dark circles under her eyes more pronounced than ever. He crossed the room in half a dozen strides and pulled her aside.

'Come away from there!' he said. 'If the Germans see anyone at a window, they'll expect them to have a gun.'

Through the day she remained close to him, so that their hands could touch – surreptitiously for the most part, however, because Ludo was usually near too. Nevertheless, when the opportunity arose, their fingers curled round each other and she did not move away when he came up behind her, his hand round her waist, to kiss her.

The meal that evening was a quiet affair behind shutters, with Ludo sitting silently, his face brooding, his eyes never leaving his plate. He was well aware of the meaning of the glances that passed between Scully and his mother and, though Sidonie tried to make conversation with him, he answered only in monosyllables and, as soon as he had finished, excused himself and vanished to his room.

Because they were concerned for the boy, both Sidonie and Scully were careful how they behaved towards each other, especially with old Virec constantly at the door with fresh news culled on his old-colleagues information service.

'The communists have taken to the sewers,' he announced. 'They have headquarters under the Lion of Belfort and sewer workers to act as guides. This, of course, is an old trick. They took to the sewers after the rising of 1871. They are also bringing out newspapers with names that sound like bugle calls of freedom – *Le Parisien Libéré*,

Libération, *Defense de la France* – and they've given their detachments the sort of names that will rouse the nation – *Bir Hakeim*, *Marseillaise*, *Jeanne D'Arc*, *Gallienne*, *1918*. There are some good left-wing ones too – *Stalingrad*, *Victor Hugo*, *Marceau*, and a few more.'

The sound of scattered shooting came at intervals throughout the night. Mostly it was nothing more than odd shots but every shot pushed the truce further into the background. Occasionally, also, there was a rattle of firing from the Ile de la Cité where the Germans were trying once more to get into the Préfecture. When daylight came, Scully knew he must become a part of the battle.

Sidonie's eyes sought his, momentarily alarmed, then her head bowed and she nodded. 'Very well,' she said. 'I'll make you a sandwich so you don't go hungry.'

She spoke almost as if she were his wife sending him out for his day-to-day tasks about the city. It gave him a comfortable feeling and he resolved that when this little lot was over, he must make the arrangement permanent as fast as he could. He had already made a few discreet inquiries and gathered he only had to get her in front of the maire and the deed was done. Unfortunately, at that moment, with the *mairies* occupied by the Resistance, weddings were unlikely to be solemnized until the Germans were flung out of Paris.

As he headed for the Rue Paul-Lecours, he saw that a poster had gone up on the walls giving orders about baking bread, providing milk for children and the suppression of looting. In the Bar du Weekend a man was yelling into the telephone. 'Yes, we've equipped most of them,' he was saying. 'With German weapons! But we need reinforcements! We can't hold without them!' Just outside, a group of men were reading newspapers. It didn't require a French scholar to understand the meaning of the headlines. '*Aux Barricades*!' they screamed. '*Français! A La Defence De Paris*!'

The response had been immediate and in the Rue Lescaut, which led directly into the Boulevard Saint-Michel, setts and paving stones were being prised up with pickaxes and manhandled into position as the basis of a barricade. To this a steady stream of enthusiastic helpers were adding an extraordinary mass of material collected from every conceivable source. Sandbags from public buildings were packed in with sewer gratings and railings. Old armchairs perched precariously on mattresses and upturned handcarts. Shopkeepers cheerfully contributed the pictures of Hitler and Pétain they had been obliged to display. German signs proclaiming *Achtung Minen* and *Zür Normandie Front* had been torn down and thrust into the pile. There was even part of an iron pissoir and the remains of a burnt-out staff car, destroyed in the previous day's fighting.

Auguste Woof staggered past, balancing a painted board lettered 'Fashion' on his narrow shoulders, followed by Xavier Lipski pushing a barrowload of bricks. A priest, wearing a pistol in the belt of his tucked up soutane, was helping to direct operations. The whole of the Petite-Ville seemed to be out, with those not actually working standing to watch and admire. Never mind what others were doing across the city. This was *their* barricade.

'It's better than the one they have in the Rue Aristide-Brune,' the proprietor of the nearby bakery said proudly, clasping a bundle of the wood women and children were sawing to heat his ovens.

Two armed men, both holding glasses of beer, were grinning at each other over the growing heap of debris.

'I thought you were a collaborator,' one was saying.

'I thought *you* were just yellow.'

There was handshaking and back slapping as the masks they had been forced to wear for four years were dropped.

'I wouldn't have thought our chances when it started were worth the money you'd put on a tired horse.' The first man lifted his beer, making a noise like a fire hydrant as he drank. 'But it's different now. The *haricots verts* don't know what's hit them.'

A horse and cart drew up, loaded with still more material for the barrier, its owner a little drunk on celebratory glasses of wine and too much excitement.

'They're going up all over Paris!' he cried. 'It's a huge

spider's web to force the Germans off the boulevards into the side streets where they can be tackled with safety.'

'They'll not come here,' someone retorted. 'We've got nothing *but* side streets.'

One man was complaining bitterly that he had been trying for three days to get to the Hôtel de Ville to register the birth of a daughter, but hadn't been able to get past the burnt-out lorries.

'Three days,' he said. 'And because of all this nonsense, I can't do anything about it.'

The men who had shot Holzmeier were now working with the priest, and one of them shouted down at Scully. 'Are you coming to help us, English sergeant? The tanks have been called out so we shall need every man we can get.'

Hurrying back to the apartment in the Hôtel Bouboulis, Scully snatched up Holzmeier's pistol.

'Trouble,' he said. 'They've called out the tanks.'

'Can I come?' Ludo begged.

'No, flower, you can't. Fighting tanks is no job for kids. Besides, your mother needs you here.'

Instead of heading straight back to the Rue Lescaut, Scully went the other way in the hope of seeing what was going on, but as he reached the corner of the street, firing broke out and he fell into the entrance of the Bar du Weekend where men were crouching down trying to spot the marksmen.

A German lorry appeared. The men at the barricade promptly started to fire and, caught in the open, the Germans stopped the lorry and dived for the bar. The men inside didn't attempt to stop them but, as they stood in the doorway, their helmeted heads peering out nervously, someone sniggered.

'Having trouble, *copains*?' he asked and, as laughter started, Scully saw the Germans whisper together.

Not wishing to be found with a German pistol on him, he headed for the lavatories. As the door closed behind him, he heard one of the Frenchmen give a derisory shout and the laughter grew louder, to be silenced by a burst of firing, through which he heard a bottle fall and break and a low moan of pain. Standing on a lavatory seat, he knocked out the window with his elbow and scrambled through into the alley outside.

Standing there, he saw people in an open doorway across the street shaking their fists and shouting curses at the Germans in the bar. In front of them was a girl in a yellow dress.

'Go,' she was shouting. 'Boche murderers! Go!'

When she reached behind her and straightened up holding a bottle, Scully decided it was a petrol bomb and looked for somewhere to shelter in case it dropped near him. As it sailed through the air, firing started from the bar. The bottle landed with a crash on the pavement, shards of broken glass skidding down the alley about Scully's feet, and he realized it had been nothing more than an empty bottle the girl had hurled in her frustrated rage and hatred. But the Germans in the bar, their nerves on edge, had also been expecting a petrol bomb, and their bullets had slashed across the girl's chest. The yellow dress blotched with red, she was leaning on the wall of the building opposite, crucified against it, her arms outspread, a look of bewilderment on her face. As her legs slowly buckled under her, she sank to the pavement, the yellow dress floating out about her knees, her head drooping forward, her dark hair falling over her face. Everybody else in the doorway had vanished, wiped away as if they were chalk figures rubbed off a blackboard.

His face grim, Scully looked about him.

Exploring the alleyway, he found it led to a yard and, standing on a low concrete shelf that covered a row of dustbins, he reached up and dragged himself over the wall. Landing in a courtyard that looked like the one belonging to the Hôtel Bouboulis, he made his way into the Passage du Chien-Nomade and was emerging into the Rue Lescaut when he was stopped by the man he had threatened with Holzmeier's pistol.

'What was the shooting?' he asked.

'Germans,' Scully said. 'In the Bar du Weekend.'

To the barricades

The man frowned. 'Can you shoot, *monsieur le sergent*?' he asked. 'Because, if you can, you'd better have this.'

Reaching behind him, he snatched a rifle from the hands of a plump bespectacled man in a butcher's smock. 'André here fancied himself as a hunter and bought it years ago to slaughter the rabbits and pigeons in his native Normandy. But he never hit much and now his eyes have gone and he couldn't hit a bull in a passage.' As the butcher grinned sheepishly, he fished in his pocket and drew out a tricolour armband bearing the letters, FFI. 'You'd better have this, too. *Forces Françaises de l'Intérior*. You have become a member of the Resistance. Now let's go and attend to your Germans.'

Slipping through the courtyard of the Hôtel Barrac into the Passage du Chien-Nomade, Scully led half a dozen men into the alley next to the Bar du Weekend. They were armed with machine-pistols, revolvers and rifles snatched from the Germans they'd killed, and as they pushed each other over the wall into the yard at the back of the bar, they could hear the snapping of rifles from the Rue Commandant-Sardier.

Climbing through the window of the lavatories, Scully waited until they were all inside before cautiously opening the outer door. The Germans were crowded in the street entrance, watching for hidden marksmen. Turning, he exchanged the rifle for a German sub-machine-gun, then, crawling behind the counter, he waited for the others to gather behind him before rising silently to his feet.

The careless banging of the door as the last man slipped through alerted the Germans and, as they swung round, Scully fired. Tables went over as the Germans fell against each other, and the glass from the door sprayed into the street. Two wounded men writhed on the floor and one of the Frenchmen lifted his machine-pistol to finish them off, but Scully's hand flashed out and knocked the weapon upwards. As the bullets flayed the ceiling, plaster dropped on their heads and bottles and glasses rolled to the floor.

'They are Boches!' the infuriated Frenchman stormed.

'They're prisoners of war!' Scully snapped back. 'They can be used as hostages to bargain with.'

He couldn't find the words to explain in French but he saw old Virec standing in the doorway, his eyes wide and scared.

'Tell him,' Scully shouted at him. 'Tell the bloody fool!'

The old man gaped, then nodded vigorously and launched into a lengthy explanation. The Frenchman with the machine-pistol stared at Scully, scowling, but he seemed to see reason and lowered the gun.

The German weapons were picked up by grinning Frenchmen who appeared from the street and the two wounded Germans, grey-faced with pain, were made to sit on the floor with their backs to the wall, guarded by a boy with a gun and a glass of brandy alongside him. The terrified landlord was crossing himself behind the bar and a crowd began to gather, staring as the bodies were taken away in a captured German truck and the dead girl across the street was lifted on to a stretcher.

When the last body had been removed, there was a strange sense of anti-climax, and they were standing in a group, noisily debating what to do next, when a youth on a bicycle came hurtling round the corner.

As he reached the crowd outside the bar, he skidded to a stop, lost control and crashed to the ground. Leaping to his feet, he began to heave his machine upright.

'Tanks!' he screamed. 'Tanks! They're coming! They're coming this way!'

5

The cyclist, still dizzy from his fall, shot away in an uncertain line down the street to warn other pockets of resistance, and the crowd began to flood into the Rue Noyelle where the barricade in the Rue Lescaut would provide them with protection. Then it dawned on them that the tanks might not head directly into the Rue Paul-Lecours but might well circle the Petite-Ville and come at the barricade from the rear, and there was momentary consternation until it occurred to someone that the answer was to build more barricades to make the Petite-Ville a small fortress.

The FFI man now in command of the barricade despatched a squad to start the new fortifications and the rest of them sprinted back to take cover behind the old bedsteads, paving stones, mattresses and handcarts in the Rue Lescaut. There was no panic, but the men, women and children struggling to find the wherewithal to build a new barricade, when they had already produced what they had thought was everything possible, looked like the inhabitants of a stirred ant hill. A man was using the telephone in the Bar des Martyrs, shouting to make himself heard to his wife above the din.

'Just don't worry, *chérie*,' he was bawling. 'I've already got three Fritzes! Just don't go out and don't let the kids go out! Not even for food!'

They were all still shouting at each other when the tanks appeared – two of them, nosing their way round from the Rue Paul-Lecours. The first sight of them was the long pole of a gun, seeming to go on forever, easing out from behind the buildings. Then the snout of the tank to which it was attached appeared, and finally the turret.

The two machines halted at the end of the Rue Fantin, swung into position and halted again. They were PzKpfw IVs, 25 ton square-built monsters with a 75 millimetre gun and an automatic weapon mounted on the turret for the use of the commander, old machines brought out of hibernation to release the heavier Tigers and Panthers for Normandy. After a moment they clanked round to face the barricade, reversed and lurched out of sight again. The man who owned the horse and cart, let out a plaintive wail.

'My cart! My cart!'

But it was on the wrong side of the barricade, and as he had no intention of risking himself beyond its shelter, he could only watch in anguish as his horse happily tugged at the leaves of torn-down trees.

It was clear immediately that the barricade had been badly sited and protected nothing. It had been thrown up too quickly and too enthusiastically and with little thought for what it was intended to protect.

Then the telephone in the Bar des Martyrs started to shrill. The proprietor answered it, listened briefly and ran out waving frantically at the men with the tricolour armbands.

'It's them,' he gasped.

'Who?'

'The tank commander. He's telephoning from the Bar Petite Montparnassaise in Paul-Lecours. He says you've got to dismantle the barricade or the tanks will blow it apart.'

The FFI men exchanged grim looks. They all knew what the threat meant but giving up the barricade meant defeat and humiliation and no one was prepared for that.

As they debated what to do, a man appeared wheeling a barrow full of bottles. His wife, still wearing a frilly apron, was alongside him carrying a basket filled with more bottles.

'Bombs,' she said. 'Petrol bombs! You can stop them with these!'

A captured kübelwagen hurtled up and stopped with a screech of brakes. Behind it were two lorries, both containing fully armed men. A man in a khaki uniform and wearing a beret climbed from the kübelwagen and started to direct the men to the barricade. It was Kehec, and as he turned and saw Scully he grinned and slapped him on the shoulder.

'My friend Scullee,' he said. 'I'd recognize that upright figure anywhere. I've brought you the Austerlitz detachment to help. I'm finally a fully fledged, fully dressed officer in the Free French army!'

He glanced at the rifle Scully carried, snatched it from him and, reaching into the rear of the kübelwagen, tossed him the Enfield rifle he had used near Meaux.

'Take this, my friend. It'll be more use in your hands.'

Suddenly the wavering direction of the defence seemed to have stiffened, and Kehec turned to the barrowload of bombs.

'You have a problem with tanks, I believe,' he said calmly. 'Can we use these?'

'They're on the corner of Lescaut and Paul-Lecours. We can't throw the things that far, for the love of God!' The man in command of the barricade was growing edgy with worry.

'You don't have to,' Kehec said. 'This is the Petite-Ville. In this area you can get from anywhere to anywhere else without going on the streets.'

Scully found himself diving with Kehec and his men and the man and the woman with the bottles down the Passage du Chien-Nomade. At the end, entering another alley, they picked their way up a flight of stone steps green with moss, dragging the barrow after them. Reaching a cobbled court-yard, Kehec began to pound on a door.

As it was opened by a protesting concierge, Kehec brushed her aside and, their arms full of bottles, they climbed the stairs to a landing where there were three doors in an exact replica of the Hôtel Bouboulis. Kehec hammered on the nearest and, as it opened, Scully saw a frightened face. Immediately, the door was swung to in their faces again but he shoved the butt of the Enfield forward and the door bounded back into the face of the man trying to shut it. Without arguing, Kehec pushed past. The apartment was well furnished and spotless and the man and his wife who owned it were clearly well-to-do.

'You can't come in here!' the husband protested. 'This is a private apartment.'

'This isn't a private war, though,' Kehec said. 'We need your windows.'

The husband beat his forehead with the flat of his hand and his wife went into screaming hysterics. Kehec promptly silenced her with a slap on the face.

'Dry up,' he snapped. 'You'll have the Germans on to us!'

Opening the windows cautiously, they saw the tanks below them, just poking round the corner from the Rue Fantin. Behind them was a lorryload of infantry waiting by the entrance of the Bar du Nord on the opposite side of the street.

'We can't reach them,' one of Kehec's men said.

'Wait until they move forward.'

'Suppose they don't?'

As they argued, a burst of firing came from the direction of the barricade and they heard the ricochets chinking against the outside wall and whining away.

'They're moving!'

There was a crash as one of the tanks fired its gun and, peering round the curtains, Scully saw the barricade start to disintegrate. The bodies of men and women sprawled on the pavement, a child screamed with terror, and the horse, still standing in the shafts of the cart near by, suddenly sagged like a stuffed toy. There was another spattering of fire and the tanks began to move forward again to smash down the rest of the barricade, the infantry fanning out behind them to take possession of the Petite-Ville.

'Now!'

Kehec swung his arm and a bottle sailed out of the window, the neck wavering like the stick of a descending rocket. It landed near the snout of the first tank, close to the driver's slot, and a sheet of flame leapt up. Screams came to their ears and the tank stopped dead. The turret hatch opened and an officer appeared clutching a pistol. Leaning against the window frame, Scully worked the bolt of the Enfield. As he fired, the officer's body buckled and slumped across the hatch. Another man, fighting to get out, pushed the body aside and struggled free, his clothes on fire. Again the Enfield cracked.

As the second man disappeared, the other tank edged backwards and Scully saw the turret hatch open. A head appeared and the tank commander reached out and swung the machine-gun. A burst of firing shattered the windows, showering Scully with splinters of glass and wood. The shutters leapt and danced and the bullets traced a line across the ceiling. A chandelier tinkled and plaster showered down. The owner of the apartment flung himself down and his wife began to scream again, her voice rasping in her throat, the muscles of her neck rigid as she threw her head back.

As the machine-gun fired again, one of the shutters, its louvres shattered, its hinges broken, lurched over to hang sideways, half obscuring the window, and the bullets began to gouge out more plaster at the top of the wall facing the window. A vase of flowers fell over, then a bookcase. The woman who had brought the bombs was lying on the floor alongside the whimpering owner, blood on her face, her skirt above her knees, showing fat thighs and rolled stocking tops.

'Another bomb,' Scully panted. 'For Christ's sake!'

One of Kehec's men leaned out to throw it but the machine-gun caught him and he fell back. The bomb crashed on the pavement outside, sending a sheet of flame up the wall, charring shutters and doors and setting fire to the awning of the Bar du Nord.

Darting from the room, Scully pounded on the door of the next apartment. It was opened at once by an old man.

'Come in, *mon brave*,' he yelled enthusiastically. 'You can hit them from here!'

The commander of the second tank was still firing at the window Scully had just left. As Scully leaned out, working the bolt of the Enfield, the German wrenched the gun

207

round, the bullets spraying the wall. Even as Scully pulled the trigger, the shutter alongside his head jumped and the window fell in. But as he picked himself up from the floor, the firing stopped and the old man yelled with delight.

'You have killed him, my friend! You have killed him! I was a sniper at Verdun and that's the way to do it! I know!'

Running back to the other apartment, Scully saw Kehec firing and one of his men struggling to his feet, blood pouring down his face, a bottle in his hand. Snatching the bottle from him, Scully leaned out to see a second head appearing through the tank's hatchway. The bottle crashed almost alongside it and, as the flames leapt up, there was a shout from outside and men and women poured from the barricade and ran down the street. One man had escaped from the tanks and was backed up against the wall, his hands in the air, screaming for mercy. Somebody hit him at the side of the head with a rifle and he crashed down, only to be dragged to his feet again and beaten half senseless with fists and weapons.

By the time Scully reached the street below, the German tanks were sending up twin pyres of smoke and people were hanging out of windows, cheering. But the awning outside the Bar du Nord was blazing furiously and, as the flames penetrated the building, men ran out, risking their lives in the firing to try to put them out. Two of the Germans had climbed on to a roof to shoot down into the barricade, but Scully saw them as they slipped behind a chimney. Resting the Enfield against the angle of a doorway he fired twice. One of the Germans slid down the roof to fall five storeys and land with a crash of equipment on the pavement. The other clung desperately to the chimney stack, the blood bright red on his face.

The firing died as the Germans, deciding the Petite-Ville was a stronger proposition than they had imagined, retreated towards the Boul' Mich', from where they kept up sporadic shooting.

As the flames in the Bar du Nord gradually died down, the owner of the cart climbed over the barrier to where his horse sprawled lumpishly between the shafts, its eyes glazed, its thick tongue protruding, and stood staring at it, tears streaming down his face. A small girl, her dress smudged with blood, stood alongside the body of a young woman, tugging at her arm. 'She won't wake up,' she kept saying. 'She won't wake up.' As a man picked her up, she began to cry, then a boy wearing a white coat and a French helmet with a red cross painted on the front came running down the street, followed by two girls pushing a stretcher on wheels.

'I'm a medical student,' he called out. 'Anybody hurt?'

Scully gestured at the shattered windows on the second floor and they disappeared. The dead Germans, their arms and ammunition already snatched up, were carried away, two to a stretcher, head to foot. Photographs fell from the pocket of one of the men and were trampled indifferently underfoot. One of Kehec's men offered a drink to the captured man who was now lying on the pavement moaning with pain, and one of the onlookers jeered.

'The bastards wouldn't have given *our* lads a drink,' he said.

The Bar du Nord was almost gutted and the Bar des Martyrs behind the barricade was a wreck. Bullets and blast had shattered glasses and mirrors and there were sandbags and guns on the counter. But the owner, exhilarated by the fighting, seemed indifferent and slightly hysterical, grinning and backslapping the unshaven, dusty Resistance men as they squelched around in a wet mash of rubble, water, broken glass and empty cartridge cases, pushing bottles at them as if he had no care for the cost. A car appeared, bringing cigarettes for the men at the barricade, and the bar owner produced hot coffee. Every kind of weapon imaginable was visible – grenades, rifles, pistols, revolvers – and there was an air of celebration about the men who carried them. One of them was wearing his tricolour armband round his hat and, with two grenades in his belt, his trousers tucked into red woollen socks, looked as if he'd stepped out of an American Wild West film.

As they drew breath, swallowing coffee or wine, the boy in the white coat and his helpers reappeared with a wounded woman on the stretcher. They were followed by Kehec, who looked at Scully and lifted his hand in salute.

Kehec grinned. 'I shan't forget you, Scullee,' he said. 'I think there will be more work for you before we've finished.'

6

With the destruction of the two tanks and the German retreat, the fighting in the area seemed to have come to a stop. But the feeling of triumph was marred by the news that the Germans were still planting dynamite about the city. They had mined the Eiffel Tower, the Pont Sully and the Pont d'Arcole leading to Notre-Dame, and intended to destroy the cathedral itself.

Despite their very real concern for the city, however, the thing that bothered most Parisians was the lack of food. Trucks weren't getting through and there was a shortage of everything except the hateful swedes. The main fight still seemed to be going on round the Préfecture but isolated little struggles were also taking place all over the city, and as people slipped out between the shooting to try to obtain food, accidents happened and more than one unwary old lady was carried home, a bundle of black clothing stained with blood.

The evening brought a short rainstorm but it also brought news over the telephone of the Bar des Martyrs from the rest of Paris. Barricades had sprung up all over the city now – four of them securing the Petite-Ville – and the Germans were paying a heavy price in burned-out tanks, while in the narrow streets of the Left Bank the Resistance were absolute masters and were even sniping across the river at the Germans trying to manoeuvre against the Préfecture. The wreckage of thin-skinned German vehicles lay everywhere.

There was an acrid smell of burning in the air as Sidonie prepared the evening meal alone in the apartment at the Hôtel Bouboulis. Scully was still at the barricade and she had permitted the boy to go through the Passage du Chien-Nomade to Grand Charles's home to see what was happening. She was in low spirits because the victory had brought about the deaths of people she knew. Already a small wreath wound about with red, white and blue ribbons had been placed on the spot where the girl had been killed opposite the Bar du Weekend. Above it someone had scrawled in chalk, *Geneviève Perry. 19 ans. Tuée par les Nazis. 22 Août 1944.*

As she worked, the door opened and Lambrouille appeared. He looked as immaculate as ever.

'Don't bother to apologize,' he said. 'I don't expect to be offered a drink. Not even a cup of coffee.'

'There *is* no coffee,' Sidonie said wearily.

Lambrouille smiled. 'I saw Uncle Charlot on the corner,' he said. 'I notice he's abandoned his spectacles. I'm surprised he finds things so easy with such bad eyes. Doubtless, it's looking at you, Sidonie, that has improved them.'

She gave him an unhappy look. 'What do you want?'

'I've brought news. I hear the Germans have called in an SS Panzer division and that it's already hurrying south to join the fight. They'd just heard at the barricades, too, and I thought I detected a bleaker, more thoughtful look on their faces. Personally it would suit me if the last German killed the last American and the last Russian killed the last Englishman. Then there would be only the French left.'

'Is this why you've come?' Sidonie demanded bitterly. 'To bring bad news?'

'Oh, no,' he smiled. 'I came to bring congratulations. I heard you'd joined me and been accused of taking a German. I couldn't believe my ears. Again! You! Of all people! I heard he was shot on the stairs trying to get into your apartment. Who was it, the child lieutenant I used to see watching the place.'

'I never asked him to come!'

'Nevertheless, beware that his death isn't held against you. The Germans haven't gone yet and they're taking note of where their casualties occur.' Lambrouille's face grew hard. 'And certainly don't expect the Americans to bail

ARCHITECTURAL DIGEST

2014

JANUARY

S	M	T	W	T	F	S
			1	2	3	4
5	6	7	8	9	10	11
12	13	14	15	16	17	18
19	20	21	22	23	24	25
26	27	28	29	30	31	

FEBRUARY

S	M	T	W	T	F	S
						1
2	3	4	5	6	7	8
9	10	11	12	13	14	15
16	17	18	19	20	21	22
23	24	25	26	27	28	

Rachel Davis · ○ Lynn

MARCH

S	M	T	W	T	F	S
						1
2	3	4	5	6	7	8
9	10	(11)	12	13	14	15
16	17	18	19	20	21	(22)
23	24	(25)	26	27	28	29
30	31					

APRIL

S	M	T	W	T	F	S
		1	2	3	4	5
6	7	(8)	9	10	11	12
13	14	(15)	16	17	18	19
20	21	22	23	24	25	26
27	28	(29)	30			

MAY

S	M	T	W	T	F	S
				1	2	3
4	5	6	7	8	9	10
11	12	(13)	14	15	16	17
18	19	20	21	22	23	24
25	26	(27)	28	29	30	31

JUNE

S	M	T	W	T	F	S
1	2	3	4	5	6	7
8	9	10	11	12	13	14
15	16	17	18	19	20	21
22	23	24	25	26	27	28
29	30					

ARCHITECTURAL DIGEST

2014

JULY

S	M	T	W	T	F	S
		1	2	3	4	5
6	7	8	9	10	11	12
13	14	15	16	17	18	19
20	21	22	23	24	25	26
27	28	29	30	31		

AUGUST

S	M	T	W	T	F	S
					1	2
3	4	5	6	7	8	9
10	11	12	13	14	15	16
17	18	19	20	21	22	23
24	25	26	27	28	29	30
31						

SEPTEMBER

S	M	T	W	T	F	S
	1	2	3	4	5	6
7	8	9	10	11	12	13
14	15	16	17	18	19	20
21	22	23	24	25	26	27
28	29	30				

OCTOBER

S	M	T	W	T	F	S
			1	2	3	4
5	6	7	8	9	10	11
12	13	14	15	16	17	18
19	20	21	22	23	24	25
26	27	28	29	30	31	

NOVEMBER

S	M	T	W	T	F	S
						1
2	3	4	5	6	7	8
9	10	11	12	13	14	15
16	17	18	19	20	21	22
23	24	25	26	27	28	29
30						

DECEMBER

S	M	T	W	T	F	S
	1	2	3	4	5	6
7	8	9	10	11	12	13
14	15	16	17	18	19	20
21	22	23	24	25	26	27
28	29	30	31			

Paris out. The Jew Roosevelt isn't going to get involved in Paris's affairs, you can be sure, and he won't have de Gaulle riding back on a white horse. He knows that if Paris is destroyed, money to rebuild her will have to come from American banks – at a good interest rate – no doubt.'

Goaded, Sidonie turned on him. 'Is this why you're here? To sneer at de Gaulle?'

Lambrouille shrugged and for a moment his expression was hunted and uneasy. 'I'm here because it seems safer than in my own apartment. I'm beginning to suspect that the Germans have lost the war and it seems wiser to go to ground for the time being. De Gaulle has a lot to answer for.'

'De Gaulle's not responsible, you've brooded over that so long it's become a mania! Where are you going?'

'Never mind where I'm going,' Lambrouille snapped. 'And don't imagine I shall be so far away I shan't be able to keep an eye on you. You could be my salvation. Think how easily I could destroy you. Indirectly, I even control the money you were left – even the money your half-witted Scot left you. I could beggar you with a word. I haven't forgotten the German I found at Trouville and now I have Holzmeier too.'

'Holzmeier has never entered my apartment!'

'So you say. It may not be believed when the day of reckoning comes.' Lambrouille's smile was cold. 'You could marry me, of course. That would certainly ensure my silence, as your presence might protect me. Why not try it?'

Her face showed her disgust. 'I despise you. I despise you for your German mistress in her flat in the Rue Saint-Florentin. They're stripping and branding women who've slept with German soldiers. I can't think why they don't strip and brand you too.'

'Perhaps they will.' Lambrouille gave a nervous gesture. 'Perhaps that's why we should disappear together. I heard that the baby lieutenant stayed overnight.'

'That's a lie!'

'It's what I heard,' he snapped. 'How do I know it's not true? I only have your word. When it's all over, there'll be a period of vengeance, with no questions asked, and many who'll have to answer in court for what they did to the communists. I doubt if they'll be called to account for the Jews, but there are plenty of others besides *them*. The rich and powerful will find themselves having to explain how they became so.'

'And so will you!'

'And so, my dear, might you! Mud sticks and you're too attractive not to arouse suspicions. The Germans don't sleep with ugly women. A man has been seen regularly in this apartment, and it *could* have been Holzmeier. And what would your precious Armande think then? He might *not* react as you expect and I might tell him the story differently.'

Lambrouille was still in the apartment when Scully returned.

'What do *you* want?' Scully demanded.

Lambrouille's smile widened. 'Do I notice a protective – even a possessive sound – in your voice, Englishman?'

'Never mind what you hear. What do you want?'

'Could it be you, Englishman? I have to confess that I've thought of it.' Lambrouille glanced at Sidonie. 'But, you know, I don't regard you as much of an opposition. Sidonie is an educated woman and highly intelligent. She's not your type at all. Hasler's different. I could regard *him* as a threat.'

'He means nothing to me, you fool!' Sidonie snapped, her eyes blazing. 'Your twisted mind's making you think things that don't even exist!'

Lambrouille ignored the interruption and went on smoothly. 'On the other hand, if the invasion fails and the day of reckoning doesn't come after all, I'll need *German* allies. Our good friend, Hasler, might provide them. They want him, of course. They always did. They know he organized that rescue near Meaux. And now they know where he hides. I told them.'

As he opened the door, Ludo was standing outside with his hand lifted, about to turn the handle. Lambrouille stepped back and bowed as he entered.

'Voilà,' he said. 'The young innocent. How many good German throats have you slit today?'

As the boy stared blankly at him, he turned in the entrance and looked at Scully. 'I may be wrong, of course,' he said, 'and de Gaulle *may* finally make it to Paris. But, if he does, then you can be sure *I* shall be here to meet him.'

Sidonie's eyes widened. 'What are you intending?'

'His presence is a challenge.' Lambrouille's eyes were cold and far away and for a moment he didn't seem sane. 'It would strike a blow that would set the whole city roaring with the intoxication of a successful riot.'

Sidonie's voice rose. 'What do you intend?'

'It's for the soul of France. She'll understand.'

The meal was eaten in silence. Scully was tired and Sidonie depressed by Lambrouille's visit. Ludo's eyes flickered between them. He felt he had missed all the excitement and he was restless and fidgety and unable to understand his mother's fears and Scully's reticence.

'Can I go into the Rue Lescaut to see the two German tanks that were destroyed, maman?' His words cut the quiet harshly and Scully realized his voice was breaking, as if the last few days were making him grow up faster than normal.

'Later.' Sidonie's reply was sharp.

'Why later? Other boys are there. Grand Charles has been there.'

'There could be more shooting, flower,' Scully said. 'The Germans aren't going to let people get away with killing their men.'

'How many were killed?'

'Too many!'

The boy shot him a bewildered glance. For him victory meant only triumph, devoid of tragedy or shock.

'Why can't I go and see the tanks?' he asked. 'Grand Charles climbed on one. I only saw them from his window.'

'Later,' Sidonie said.

The boy looked at Scully. Some of the lost respect had returned. 'Grand Charles said he saw you shoot four of them yourself.'

'Yes.' Scully had laid the Enfield on the floor by the door alongside the German machine-pistol he'd acquired.

'Is that what you shot them with?'

'Yes.'

'One after the other?'

'Yes.'

The boy was silent for a moment, gazing at the weapons, clearly longing to know more about what had happened. Scully showed no interest and he tried again.

'Monsieur Virec says you also shot three Germans in the Bar du Weekend.'

Sidonie made a face at him. 'Charley doesn't want to talk about it,' she said quietly.

'Why not?' The boy was indignant at their refusal to talk. 'We defeated them, didn't we? If everybody fights them as well as we fought them here, they'll not be able to stay.'

There was no reply, and he became silent again. Sidonie cleared the table, her eyes sad, and as Scully smoked the boy studied him.

'Are you going to marry maman?' he asked suddenly.

Scully was startled but he forced himself to appear calm. The boy was clearly no fool and had long since become aware of the different atmosphere that existed now.

'Would you mind if I did?'

The boy frowned. 'I thought she wished to marry Armande,' he said. There was a trace of disappointment in his voice, as if he felt betrayed.

'She doesn't know where he is or if he'll ever come back.' Scully pushed his advantage. 'He might even have married someone else by now. He's been away a long time.'

'Yes.' The boy frowned. 'That's possible, of course.' He considered Scully's suggestion for a moment. 'No,' he admitted. 'I wouldn't mind. It would be pleasant to have a father like the other boys.'

7

Stubbing out his cigarette, Scully rose to his feet and picked up the weapons.

'I'll be going back,' he said.

Sidonie watched him, searching his face for some indication of affection behind the bleakness. When he didn't respond, she nodded dumbly, then flung herself into his arms.

'It'll be over soon,' he said in a flat voice.

He opened the door and began to walk slowly down the stairs. As she stood on the landing, watching him over the banister, Ludo joined her, his expression puzzled.

Scully spent the night in a chair in Bar des Martyrs, but there was no further sign of the Germans. Kehec had appeared with more reinforcements and every now and again, fresh supplies of Molotov cocktails were delivered in clothes baskets and beer crates, so that Scully wondered what in God's name they'd do with them all if there were no more fighting. He was just dropping off to sleep when he became aware of a small figure in front of him, its twisted spectacles as opaque with fingerprints as ever.

'I saw you shoot the Germans,' Grand Charles said proudly. His hand moved. 'I was up there in that window. On the fourth floor.'

'You should keep away from windows, flower,' Scully said. 'They're dangerous.'

'Oh, no, I'll be all right. They won't kill me.' Grand Charles grinned. 'I think we're winning, sir, don't you? I think we know round here how many beans make five, don't you?'

Scully managed a tired smile. 'It's a bit early yet to say,' he said. 'But keep counting.'

During the night – he didn't know which night it was – it started to rain, and the drizzle went on through the next day. For most of it, he waited in the bar with the other men from the barricade, drinking wine and eating sandwiches, aware only of the absence of firing and once the presence of George Presteigne, his face twisted in a bitter grin.

'Rain's stopped play,' he said.

The following morning arrived muggy and damp. Someone passed a bottle of brandy round and they were drinking when there was a shattering explosion in the distance that jerked heads up.

The vibration had set the glasses in the bar tinkling and windows were opening above their heads as people leaned out to see what had happened.

'Somewhere near the Place de la Concorde,' someone called down. 'You can see the smoke rising.'

There was a pause in which they heard the sound of fire engines, and then another voice rang out. 'It's the Grand Palais! The Germans have blown it up!'

They had barely taken this in when Kehec's kübelwagen drew up with a screech of tyres, closely followed by a lorry containing two or three youths.

'As many men as you can spare!' he shouted. He gestured at Scully. 'You, too, my friend! We have need for good shots just now!'

Because of the isolated battles going on all over the city, it was impossible to go direct and when they arrived the fighting was over. The police who had been holding the Grand Palais had been marched off into captivity, and there was a group of German trucks and a burning car under the trees of the Champs-Elysées. In the smoke-laden atmosphere a line of German soldiers were passing round bottles of champagne from the buffet, getting in the way of the firemen trying to put out the flames with punctured hoses. They could hear the shrieks of frightened women, and the terrified cries of circus animals coming from inside.

As they watched, Kehec was called to the telephone and

came dashing back to order them to another fight near Clichy. There they found the local réseau had its headquarters in a school where a few German prisoners were squatting in front of a blackboard, across which had been chalked in bold letters: A CHACUN SON BOCHE – to each man his own German. Round the walls were drawn a procession of rabbits, dogs, ducks and cats, and the place smelt of chalk, ink, sweat, blood and fear.

'For you the war is over,' Kehec said to one of the prisoners. 'You a Nazi?'

'I've never been one.'

Kehec turned to Scully. 'That's what they all say,' he observed dryly. 'It's amazing where all the Nazis have gone to.'

A heavy clash had taken place just beyond the school, but in the comparative safety of the next street a queue of women was patiently waiting for bread. As a wounded German, his face covered with blood, was carried past they blanched with horror.

'Haven't you seen blood before?' Kehec asked bitterly. He turned to the stretcher-bearers, a fighting man aware of a fighting man's suffering. 'Concentrate on what you're doing and keep in step. It'll shake him less.'

A German ambulance appeared in the distance and an officer with a white flag climbed out. He was waved forward and allowed to collect his casualties from beneath the trees of a little square. Near them, in a pool of petrol, blood and dirty rainwater, lay a wounded Frenchman, refusing to move because he held his pistol to the head of a German sergeant and had no intention of letting him go.

The fighting went on until darkness and Scully slept the night in the school. The following morning they found the Germans had retreated through nearby houses and were now on the roofs. Posted in the window of an attic apartment opposite, Scully was joined by a student and his girlfriend, who kept them supplied with coffee and ammunition.

During the afternoon, the student was shot through the head and carried away– his girlfriend followed behind, her face ugly with grief. As Scully watched them emerge into the street below, a black man carrying a Sten gun moved forward to help, but a shot rang out and he stumbled to a wall and slid down it on to his face. A young German appeared in a doorway opposite, running towards him with a grin of triumph on his face, but the black man was far from dead and, rolling over, he fired with the Sten gun. The German took the bullets full in the chest and staggered back, clawing with crooked fingers at his uniform. Immediately a group of Red Cross workers rushed out and carried him to the trees. The minute he was alone, a woman darted at him, a knitting needle in her hand. He screamed, and as the woman was dragged away Scully saw that the German boy's eye was streaming blood.

Eventually a white flag went up and a German appeared in a doorway, waving a towel, followed by another, then a whole group, all holding their hands in the air.

There was nothing more for them to do and they were driven back to the Petite-Ville. There a strange lull persisted, though they could hear firing from La Villette and Montmartre, and the Germans were said to be still planting dynamite. Already several telephone exchanges had gone up in a shower of debris. All it now needed was the final command for half Paris to collapse in a pile of rubble.

By this time they were all growing hungry and their faces were grey with fatigue and the dust of the streets. A plateful of the sodden cooked swede appeared in front of Scully and he gulped it down, drinking from a bottle of cheap wine. Then he slept in an armchair for an hour or two, and when he woke it was daylight again and the men and women all round him were yelling crazily.

'They're coming! The Free French are coming! They telephoned from Rambouillet, telling us to hang on! They're coming via Trappes, Saint-Cyr and Longjumeau. They'll come straight down the Boul' Mich'.'

Bottles appeared and there was a sudden rush beyond the barricade to the end of the Rue Lescaut. The Boul' Mich' was only a few hundred yards away and everybody wanted to be on hand to greet their saviours. Clutching his violin to his chin, its throat tied with red, white and blue ribbon, old

Virec was playing the 'Marseillaise' again, leading the others like an ancient Pied Piper as they flooded towards the Rue Paul-Lecours. Tricolours had appeared once more and everybody was cheering, waving or weeping. As he reached the corner, the old man paused for the others to catch up, doing a little dance as he played.

The rattle of firing from the direction of the Boul' Mich' stopped everyone dead in their tracks and Scully saw Virec stagger. The violin dropped from his nerveless fingers and a stumbling foot caught it so that it went slithering away, the red, white and blue ribbons trailing. Without thinking, a youth ran to help but he fell, too, and the bullets nudged at the violin, spinning it along the asphalt.

The street had emptied as the crowd bolted back towards the Rue Lescaut. Scully waited for them, his heart pounding; then, pushing through the courtyard of the Hôtel Barrac to the Passage du Chien-Nomade, he climbed the staircase to where the old man who had let him in before was waiting.

'Is it the Germans?' he asked. 'Have they come back?'

Scully nodded and pushed past him into the apartment. As he turned, he was surprised to find that half a dozen men had followed him, sensing that he knew what to do.

The old man opened his arms wide. 'Take what you want, *mon brave*,' he said. 'You'll need something to hide behind. I have many books, and books stop bullets.'

The bookshelves were stuffed with expensive gilt-covered volumes, many of them enormous, and they flung them out, moved the bookcase into the window, then stuffed them all back so that they had a solid barricade with nothing but mere slits to shoot through.

When they looked round, the old man held two bottles of champagne. 'I was saving these until Paris was liberated,' he said. 'But what better than to die drinking it?'

As they swallowed the wine and turned again to the window a German armoured car appeared. It carried a 20 millimetre cannon and a machine-gun, and it remained tucked well back almost out of sight. Behind it was an armoured half-track filled with troops and behind the half-track another vehicle and possibly yet another. This time

221

the Germans had brought a large number of infantry and, judging by their movements, they were experienced soldiers. Only by pressing his head close to the wall could Scully see them at all.

The German carriers were keeping well clear of the buildings, and as the soldiers dismounted they huddled in the shelter of their vehicles. They seemed strangely unwilling to move forward and, cocking his head, Scully realized why. Over the distant sound of musketry from the Préfecture and the Place de la République, he could hear the low thump of shelling. It was too far away to be in the city, but it seemed to be growing closer.

'It's gunfire,' the old man hissed behind him. 'It's true! They're coming! This time they're really coming!'

The Germans were still trying to make up their minds when one of the men with Scully pointed. A small spotter aircraft was roaring along the line of the river, just above the roofs of the building.

They all saw the white American star on its wings and the stripes that designated it as part of the allied invasion force. It dropped no bombs and fired no guns, but it was the first real sign that help was at hand and a tremendous cheer went up. As the Germans pointed at it, one of them moved forward for a better view and, as he did so, he allowed his head to appear just over the bonnet of the armoured carrier. As Scully fired, the German's helmet spun off and he dropped from sight. Immediately the walls outside were spattered with machine-gun bullets. The long barrel of the cannon swung round and a shell gouged out bricks and mortar. The woman in the next apartment was screaming hysterically again, but the old man who had let them in was grinning as he lay on his face under the window.

'That made them think, my friend,' he said.

Scully had one eye on the door, wondering how long it would take him to reach it and bolt down the stairs if the Germans made an attempt to rush the place. Could he be downstairs and into the Passage du Chien-Nomade and the Hôtel Bouboulis before they reached the stairs to cut him off?

The telephone rang, harsh in the tension, and the old man crawled across to answer it.

'*Oui*,' he shouted as it crackled in his ear. '*Oui! Mais certainement!*' He turned his head. 'It's a friend of mine. They've passed through Fresnes. They're on the doorstep of Paris.' He listened again. 'What's that? They're at Sceaux and Bagneaux? But that's only half an hour away. Less, if there's no traffic.' He rang off and beamed at Scully. 'The first French tanks will soon be crossing the Seine. We are saved, *mes enfants!*'

As he spoke, the machine-gun outside rattled again and pieces of splintered shutter, glass and stonework spattered into the room, covering everything with dust. The old man, far from being upset, seemed delighted to be part of the fight.

Then, from outside, they heard yells and saw German soldiers edging round the corner into the Rue Paul-Lecours. There was an immediate roar of fire from the barricade. Two Germans fell and another, his leg smashed, dragged himself into the shelter of a doorway. As he did so, a dim figure inside stepped out of the shadows, put a revolver to his head and fired.

More Germans were trying to edge round the corner into the gale of fire and Scully picked off one of them. A sergeant rose to his feet and began to run, sweeping the others along with him. Scully's shot hit him in the neck, and he spun round and subsided against a wall. The other Germans decided it was wiser to dive for cover.

Once again the fighting stopped. The Germans seemed to be debating what to do and Scully saw an officer pointing towards the south. The gunfire they had heard seemed closer and they could now hear the thump of heavy machine-guns. The telephone shrilled again and the old man answered it.

As Scully turned to watch him, he saw himself in the mirror. His eyes were puffed and red with lack of sleep, his beard showed thick and dark and he was covered with sweat, and the dust from walls and shattered ceilings. The firing to the south was growing louder and more insistent and the old man had clapped one finger in his ear to drown the sound as he tried to listen to the telephone.

'*Oui*?' he yelled. '*Porte-d'Italie? Je te remercie, mon ami! Je les dis!*' He turned to Scully. 'The Free French have reached Paris! They're passing through the Porte-d'Italie at this very moment!'

Moving to the window, Scully saw that the German vehicles had disappeared. A youth came running from the direction of the Boul' Mich', shouting and waving his arms.

'We've won! It's a victory!'

His face bleak, Scully shouldered the Enfield. It wasn't a victory, he knew. The Germans had also heard of the arrival of the Free French.

8

Grim-faced, longing for sleep, Scully watched the crowd as it began to move from the Rue Paul-Lecours and the Rue Commandant-Sardier, swelling in number as it streamed into the Boul' Mich' to welcome the arrival of the liberators. Bottles were moving from hand to hand, and cigarettes, many of them German, were being exchanged when suddenly they heard tank treads, and the crowd scattered into doorways and alleys.

A tank loomed up through the rays of the setting sun and for a moment there was silence as everybody held their breath. Then someone cried out, '*Les Américains!*'

Immediately, a great flood of ecstatic human beings poured back into the boulevard. The pavements were lined with cheering people, tricolours waving frantically, and men and women watched with tears streaming down their cheeks.

The streets were full of dust and warm yellow sunshine. To the delighted Parisians the newcomers looked like giants, inches taller and more handsome than they were themselves, while their tanks seemed bigger and more powerful than anything the Germans possessed. As they halted, women and girls clambered on to them, offering flowers snatched from vases, fruit snatched from bowls, kisses, bottles of wine, tears of happiness. Tomatoes, sprigs of greenery, whatever food was available, were all thrust up to the figures in the tanks.

'*Non, madame –* ' Scully heard the yell ' *– nous sommes Français,*' and another yell of delight went up as the Cross of Lorraine was noticed for the first time.

The women were going mad to reach the man in the

turret of the leading vehicle, kissing him, clutching his hand, slapping his shoulders. A jeep that was following seemed to have disappeared under a sea of screaming, frenzied girls. It was only with difficulty that the column managed to get going again. Small boys climbing into a Bren-gun carrier were yanked out like puppies and deposited on the pavement, only for them to come back for more. Men with accents from all over France were shouting questions, asking for relatives, or giving their names and asking that their parents should be telephoned.

Tank after tank passed, their names white on their sides – *Valmy*, *Résistance*, *D'Artagnan*, *Le Mort-Homme*, *Libération* – then the half-tracks with their 76 millimetre guns – *La Méthodique*, *L'Entreprenant*, *L'Adroit* – and finally the little jeeps, sarcastically called *Criquet* and *Puce*.

Scully watched them pass, then, suddenly weary, he turned back towards the Rue Fantin. Old Virec's body had been pulled on to the pavement from the centre of the road and left beneath a tree. Scully stopped alongside it in silence. Someone had placed the old man's beret over his face and there was a long smear of red where his feet had dragged through his own blood. The youth lay beside him, his face now covered with a handkerchief, a small bunch of flowers at his feet.

A boy with an intelligent, sensitive face and wearing a uniform hastily slipped on over his civilian clothes, stopped alongside Scully. He was carrying an old shotgun.

'Even victory can be sad,' he commented.

Scully nodded, then, unslinging the German machine-pistol, he handed it to the boy. 'Here, kid,' he said. 'You'd do better with this. If you're going to war, you might as well go properly armed.'

Whether the boy understood him or not, he took the machine-pistol gratefully, weighing it in his hands as if it were made of gold. Scully fished the spare magazines from his pocket and watched the boy tuck them in his jacket. Then, impulsively, the boy held out his hand. Scully took it and watched him stride away, full of pride and determination, willing to die if necessary for a free France.

Scully sighed and, picking up old Virec in his arms, began to walk back to the Hôtel Bouboulis. His feet dragged with weariness and the Enfield thumped against his hip. The old man's door was open, as if he'd left in a rush and forgotten to close it. Scully pushed it with his shoulder and went inside.

The apartment was bare but neat. On the walls were pictures of Virec holding his violin, and groups of the orchestras in which he'd played. The bedroom door was ajar and he went in and, laying the old man down on the polished lino alongside the bed, dragged off the bedding. Then, lifting the body to the mattress, he covered it with a sheet.

As he left the apartment, he could hear the cheering from the street. The crowds were watching a column of trucks go by, and he could see them silhouetted with their flags against the headlights of the vehicles. Walking slowly back to the barricade, he searched in the shadows until he found the wreckage of the old man's violin. The bow seemed to have disappeared, kicked aside by running feet. As he turned away, he noticed two weeping women by the body of the youth and paper flags, tricolour cockades, and Crosses of Lorraine stuck into the tree trunk round a sheet of cheap, lined paper. On it someone had written: 'A young patriot fell here. Noble Parisians, leave a flower and observe a moment of silence.' As he passed, the women crossed themselves but didn't lift their heads and he heard their muttered words – 'Holy Mary, Mother of God, pray for us sinners, now and at the hour of our deaths.'

Walking slowly back to the Hôtel Bouboulis, he laid the violin on the old man's breast, wondering whom he should inform and where Sidonie was. The apartment was empty, however, and he went down to the courtyard again. Madame Weinspach was just leaving, dressed in her best and carrying a small tricolour flag.

She gave him an arch look. 'She is in the street with the boy,' she said. 'Monsieur is frantic. I can see it beneath the British phlegm.'

'Virec's dead,' he growled. 'I've just put him in his apartment.'

She crossed herself hurriedly and hestitated, as if wondering if she could help. But the wish to be part of the liberation was stronger than the desire to mourn old Virec and, crossing herself again, she pushed her hat straight and hurried away into the crowds.

Sidonie was with Ludo near the corner of the Rue Paul-Lecours. She was talking to a soldier sitting in a jeep.

'Do you know Armande Démange?' she was asking. 'Route Regiment de Tchad.'

'We're the Tchad Regiment,' the soldier said. 'But I don't know him. I think he must have been killed.'

Her face grew pale, then her back stiffened and she held her head up. As she turned away, she saw Scully and hurried to him as if, her last hopes dashed, he represented the only security she possessed. The boy, his eyes bright with excitement, grabbed Scully's dirty fist and started to pump it.

'Grand Charles told me what you did,' he said. 'On the telephone. He says they're going to give you a medal.' Then he realized that some of the blood on Scully's hand had been transferred to his, and he stopped to stare at it, before slowly wiping it off on his trousers.

'Old Virec's dead,' Scully said flatly. 'The Germans shot him. He was playing the 'Marseillaise' on his violin.'

The following morning, Scully came surging up from a deep well of sleep, aware of shooting still going on in sporadic bursts of rifle and machine-gun fire and the occasional thump of a bigger gun.

He tried to cling to sleep, to hold on to the fragrance of Sidonie on the pillow alongside him, to recapture the warmth of her body beside his. As he fought to avoid waking, the events of the previous night came rushing back: old Virec's death; the excited announcements on the radio that the Leclerc Division of the Free French Army was in the heart of Paris; the noise outside the window; the radio playing the 'Marseillaise' for the umpteenth time; and the crowds in the street yelling the words as though they were some mystic chant so that the city seemed to be floating on a wave of sound that had drowned even the clamour of church bells coming over the roofs. Then the whole horizon had lit up as a German dump was blown up, tracer bullets had shot across the dark sky, and as the firing from down by the river had swelled up again, the radio had changed its tune abruptly. 'It isn't over yet! Go home! Stay off the streets! The Germans are still here and we want no more deaths!'

As if starting from a nightmare, feeling he was needed, he sat up abruptly, aware of someone tugging at his arm. Sidonie was standing by the bed.

'Ludo's disappeared,' she said in a shaking voice.

Sitting up, Scully passed his hand over his face. The bristles of his beard rasped. 'He'll have gone to Grand Charles's,' he said. 'To swop stories.'

'No. I rang his mother. He's not there. Neither is Grand Charles. Besides – ' Sidonie's face was ashen and her eyes were frightened ' – the pistol's gone again! The little Belgian automatic. I locked it in a drawer but he must have had a key.'

'Telephone Tom Cléry-Kidder's mother. Ask her.'

'He's not there. I rang every one of his friends. The answer was the same every time. They've all slipped out. Every one of them. And Tom's mother says Tom's taken her husband's shotgun. She'd kept it hidden all through the Occupation.'

Scully frowned. 'Think he knows about us? Could he have seen us in here? Think that's why he's gone?'

She shook her head, not knowing, then she grabbed angrily at his arm. 'What are we going to do? My child's disappeared.'

The unexpected anger startled him. As he reached for her to calm her, she dodged away.

'Leave me alone,' she shouted. 'My son's gone and there's shooting on the streets!'

'All right.' He held up his hands. 'I'll go and look for him.'

His offer took the fire out of her. 'Then *you* will

disappear!' she said, her voice desperate. 'And I shall have nobody. We'll go together.'

He pushed her aside and started to dress. 'The streets are no place for a woman. Stay here. I know what to do.'

He stuffed his pockets with ammunition and shouldered the Enfield. She watched him in silence then, as he reached the door, she touched his hand. As he turned towards her, she flung herself into his arms, kissing him, touching his face with her fingers, as if she were blind and needed to imprint on her mind its shape, its angles, its warmth, the fact that he was alive when everybody else she'd known was dead or had disappeared.

'You don't know where to start,' she pointed out frantically.

He thought of Hasler and the boy whose father made Molotov cocktails. 'I've got a good idea,' he said.

Near the Luxembourg, people were still taking cover. A burnt-out lorry stood in the middle of the street and medical students and girls in gay dresses crouched on the pavement bandaging wounded. The Place Saint-Michel sported a huge American flag and there seemed to be dead Germans everywhere.

A heavy German machine-gun started firing, and Scully found himself jammed in a doorway with a crowd of terrified people. The ones at the back were trying to see out while those at the front were trying to push themselves deeper into the crowd. Then a man came running down the street and flung himself in with them. Under his weight, Scully tripped over someone's feet and fell, and a girl sprawled on top of him.

The chatter of the machine-gun came again, and Scully saw plaster showering down as the bullets chinked on the walls and whined away. There was a crash of glass as a window fell in somewhere above his head.

The Germans seemed to be getting the better of the fighting just here and the crowd began to crumble and slip away until there were only a few left in the doorway with Scully. Somebody at the back was pounding on the door, yelling for it to be opened, but whoever was on the other side was taking no chances, and a youth holding a big old-fashioned revolver suddenly broke free and started to run. As he did so a German car appeared. There was a burst of automatic firing and the youth sprawled on the pavement. The girl who had fallen over Scully gave a whimper of anguish and flung herself across him, sobbing.

Two of the Germans scrambled from the car, brandishing their weapons, and the people in the doorway slowly raised their hands. There was no alternative but to join them and, leaving the Enfield propped behind the entrance pillar out of sight, Scully rose. One of the Germans, moving warily towards the fallen youth, kicked out and sent the revolver he had dropped skidding away. The girl scrambled to her feet and began to attack him with her small fists and the sergeant at the wheel of the car put his head through the window, laughing at his attempts to restrain her.

For a moment his attention was distracted. It was a chance that would not occur again and with all his strength Scully brought both fists down from above his head on top of the sergeant's helmet, driving his face against the edge of the car window. As he screamed with pain, Scully wrenched open the door and plucked him from his seat. Someone immediately kicked him in the face and snatched at the weapon slung over his shoulder.

Grabbing the Enfield from the doorway, Scully dived aboard the car as another boy who had jumped behind the wheel began to rev the engine. For a second, the wheels spun wildly, then the car plunged forward, the doors shutting under its momentum. The soldiers by the fallen boy pressed themselves against the wall but one of them was caught by the fender and began to scream; then with a clang and a screech of metal on stone, the car swerved away down the road. A machine-gun opened up, the rear windows scattered fragments of glass over them and the front tyre wrapped itself noisily round the axle. The boy behind the wheel fought desperately with the steering as the car took control. Rounding a corner to safety, it hit an empty newspaper kiosk, knocked over a seat, and crashed into a wall, the doors forced open and swinging on their hinges, a headlamp bouncing off and rolling ahead of them into the gutter.

As the city slipped from the Germans' grasp, on one street crowds were singing and cheering round the vehicles of their liberators, while on the next the liberating troops struggled painfully forward.

Bullets were still spraying the arcades of the Rue de Rivoli, and in the Place de la Concorde a tank battle was going on between the Germans and the Free French. Smoke was curling up from a burnt-out Panther and all the windows in the buildings around had fallen in from the blast.

Near the river, a few captured German soldiers had been backed up against a wall and a doctor and a German orderly wearing a Red Cross badge were attending a wounded man stretched on the pavement. The crowd filled the street, excited to the point of hysteria, and three or four wretched women, their heads shaved, stood in a group, while a man, once fat and pompous but now afraid, stumbled along stripped to his underpants, his bowed legs incongruous in sock suspenders.

As Scully reached Hasler's territory he found there were twice as many barricades as in the rest of the city, and they were well sited to force traffic into the dangerous side streets. Hasler was in the Bar du Destin. He was wearing uniform – not battledress but full service dress complete with Sam Browne belt and polished holster, his buttons the uncompromising black of the Rifle Brigade. His hand was bandaged and he seemed a little drunk.

When he saw Scully he gave a twisted smile. 'What did *you* do in the war, daddy?' he said. 'The Americans are coming, sergeant. You know that? We forced them to change their minds. They're on their way now with all they've got. We're expecting 'em any moment.'

'Never mind the Yanks,' Scully said. 'Did you know that Lambrouille's told the Germans where you hide?'

Hasler smiled. 'The trouble with Lambrouille,' he said, 'is that he talks too much. He told someone else, too, and they told me.'

'What about the kids? It's their hideout they'll search.'

Hasler shrugged. 'What about them? They want to be in the fighting so they can say when the war's over that they did their bit, don't they? You'd be surprised how many there are like that. Two days ago, there were only two thousand Resistants in this bloody city. Now the fighting's almost over there are twenty thousand.'

9

As Scully turned into the Boulevard de Clichy, the first
Americans arrived. The barricade at the end seemed to
vomit people and within minutes, the lorries were covered
with human beings who stuck to them like flies to flypaper.
Bottles, food, flags and flowers appeared once more and as
the men worked to clear the barricade, women flooded over
the trucks and jeeps, kissing the soldiers, handing them
anything they could think of to show their joy at being free.

Champagne – in a city which a few days before had
seemed empty of champagne – appeared miraculously.
Glasses, even whole bottles, were handed to the Americans.
Women appeared with babies, lifting them up so they could
say in years to come they'd been kissed by the liberators.
An old woman sitting in a chair, ancient, wrinkled and at
death's door, was carried out by four men and held up so
she could see what was happening.

'We're free! We're free!'

The words were chanted again and again as people kissed
each other, shook hands, danced and exchanged glasses of
wine.

The Presteigne house was shuttered. Slipping through the
gate, Scully tried the door but nobody was answering. The
old greenhouse was deserted, the door ajar, the faded notices the British Réseau had hung up, the rules they had
made, still on the walls. But he noticed that their souvenir
shelf was empty and guessed they had the souvenirs in their
pockets for luck and were out on the streets, still hoping to
be part of the liberation of the city.

There had been no fighting in this area and the windows

were full of watching faces. Just down the road more people, both men and women, stood in the sandbagged doorway of the Hôtel Saint-Breille.

Just where George had promised, a barricade had been built. It contained an old car, several barrows, and the contents of every back room in the district. As the firing started again, Scully dived behind it, to find himself surrounded by teenage boys and a few girls. All the boys were armed with some kind of weapon and he saw ancient muzzle-loaders, pistols and rifles. They were all excited to the point of hysteria.

Crouched among them, he found himself staring into the eyes of Ludo. Beyond him were George Presteigne, Grand Charles and Tom Cléry-Kidder. Ludo clutched the Belgian automatic, George held a petrol bomb, Tom Cléry-Kidder nursed a shotgun and Grand Charles held the rusty revolver his father had found on the battlefields of the First War.

'For God's sake,' Scully snapped. 'What the hell do you lot think you're up to?'

'Paris is being liberated,' Ludo said stiffly. 'We're helping. We've joined the Rue Mortmain Réseau for the time being.'

'You're coming home with me.'

As Scully reached out a large hand, Ludo shrank back. 'Leave me alone!'

Reaching out again, Scully found himself facing the muzzle of the little automatic. Tom Cléry-Kidder glanced at Ludo; then he swung the muzzle of the shotgun. Grand Charles looked bewildered but he also faithfully pointed his rusty revolver.

Scully tensed and became still.

'Look, flower,' he said quietly. 'You should never turn a loaded weapon towards anybody.'

'Unless he's an enemy,' Ludo said. 'At the moment, you're an enemy.'

Grand Charles nodded.

'Look – ' Scully lifted his hands ' – I'll not touch you. I promise. Just turn them guns the other way.'

For a moment, they stared at him, their eyes hostile; then the weapons were lowered.

'You promised,' Ludo warned.

'Okay, flower, I promised. What are you intending to do?'

'We're waiting for the Germans. They have to come this way to return to their barracks and the barricades are forcing them down the side streets.'

Scully was just about to protest when Tom Cléry-Kidder sprang up.

'They're coming,' he shouted. '*Sicherheitsdienst* – German police! A motor-bike and sidecar, followed by a lorry!'

Scully knew exactly why they were there. They had finally come to collect Hasler and they expected to find him in the old greenhouse at the bottom of the Presteignes' garden.

'Get ready!'

Scully tried to grab Ludo but the boy fought him off, pushing his hands away and dodging under his arms, while the other boys on the barricade began to yell abuse at him.

'*A chacun son Boche*! He wants to kill a German like everybody else!'

The motor-bike and sidecar combination had slowed down at the end of the street, moving warily. As it swung into the Rue Mortmain, a spatter of firing broke out from the barricade and the driver, realizing they'd been ambushed, tried to turn. But he was going too fast and the machine hit the wall opposite and fell on its side, its wheels spinning. The crew consisted of two other men besides the driver, an officer in the sidecar and a corporal sitting on the pillion, and the crash flung them all into the road. Scrambling to their feet, scared and looking for some way to escape, they saw Scully's rifle and flung down their weapons at once.

As they lifted their hands, Scully was just about to step forward to take them prisoner when George Presteigne slipped out from behind him. The bottle he'd been holding crashed against the wall and, engulfed by flames, the Germans screamed and began to run, beating at their clothing. There was a yell of triumph and as the little Belgian automatic went off, Scully heard the shot whine away. Then Tom Cléry-Kidder fired the shotgun, almost blowing Scully's head off as he swung. Lifting his arms, Scully knocked the weapons aside.

'You bloody young fools!' he roared. 'They were going to surrender!'

Heavy firing had started in the boulevard and the lorry which had been following the motor-cycle swung into the Rue Mortmain for shelter. Faced with the motor-cycle against the wall, however, the driver also tried to turn round. But bullets were flying in all directions now and the sergeant in the driver's cabin started yelling instructions. Everybody seemed to be firing as fast as they could, mostly without much sense of direction, and the Frenchmen pursuing the lorry from the barricade in the boulevard below began to duck back out of sight while the people in the courtyard of the Hôtel Saint-Breille opposite hurriedly dived for cover.

The lorry stopped, its crew in a panic, and started to reverse into the courtyard. Immediately, the firing was directed into the open gateway and, as the bullets started to flail the walls, windows fell in and the sandbags round the door began to leak little streams of dry soil on to the cobbles.

The air was filled with shouts of defiance as the gates partly swung to, almost hiding the lorry from sight.

'We have them! They're trapped!'

The sobbing Germans from the motor-bike and sidecar had been running towards the lorry but the firing now swung back in their direction, and, caught in the fusillade, the driver seemed to hop along on one leg, leaning further and further over until he finally fell on his side and lay motionless, the bullets pecking at his body. The officer was hit in full stride and went sliding across the road on his face. The corporal lifted his hands, backed against the wall and started begging for mercy. But the shooting didn't stop and he spun round, still upright, nudged along by bullets until his knees gave way and he fell in a crumpled heap on the pavement.

Immediately there was a yell of triumph and Scully saw men running from the boulevard towards them. The gates of the Hôtel Saint-Breille had slammed shut.

The boys alongside Scully behind the barricade were staring, awed by what they'd done. The motor-cycle combination lay on its side undamaged, the flames from the Molotov cocktail stretching up the wall nearby and licking at the shutters.

'They're not moving!' Ludo said slowly.

'Of course they're not,' Scully said furiously. 'This is for real, you stupid little bastards! Them fellers is dead! It's not like cowboys and Indians! They won't get up and go home for supper!'

The boys were still gaping at the dead Germans when the men from the barricade in the boulevard arrived, snatching up the weapons the Germans had dropped and donning their steel helmets. One of them shook Scully's hand.

'Thanks, *copain*,' he said. 'That was brilliant.'

Scully pushed him away angrily, but more men grasped his hand, thinking he'd been responsible for the victory. Then a woman, smelling of brandy and garlic, kissed him and someone shoved a bottle into his hand and told him to drink.

Warily, the youngsters came out from behind their barricade and stood in the street, over-bold and boastful now, their weapons pointed towards the gate of the Hôtel Saint-Breille, certain they were going to have the pleasure of killing more Germans.

'We've got them!' George Presteigne said loudly. 'Like rats in a trap! Let them just try to get out, and we'll mow them down!'

Angry and disgusted, Scully pushed through the crowd and reached for Ludo.

The boy dodged his clutching hands again. 'I'm staying here,' he said.

'Let the kid go, *copain*,' one of the men laughed. 'Let him enjoy the fun. It isn't every day he gets to see Germans killed.'

Ludo's face was bleak and stubborn and Scully decided it would be best to take things cautiously.

'Look, flower,' he said. 'Just for Christ's sake, keep your head down! Don't take risks.'

The boy glared at him. 'Don't keep telling me to keep my head down,' he snapped. 'Other boys have been in the fighting, too. They took risks. And stop calling me "flower".'

It was growing dusk now and Scully realized he was tired, hungry and thirsty and conscious of the sweat and dirt on his body.

'You should be home,' he said. 'Where it's safe.'

'We've done nothing yet,' George Presteigne sneered.

'For Christ's sake, you did for three men on a motor-bike! Isn't that enough?'

As they talked they heard the scrape of gears behind the gates of the Hôtel Saint-Breille and there was a rush back to the shelter of the barricade.

'They're coming out!' George shouted. 'Get ready!'

Grand Charles looked up at Scully. His spectacles were crooked and so dirty it seemed impossible that he could see through them.

'Will there be more fighting, sir?' he asked unhappily.

'This is war,' George snapped over his shoulder. 'We must take risks. Even you!'

Grand Charles swallowed noisily and clutched the rusty revolver. 'Yes, sir,' he said. 'Of course! I'm ready!'

'As soon as they open the gates,' George said. 'Everything we've got. Get the driver and stop the lorry; then they're trapped.'

But when the gates opposite opened, the lorry was not facing forwards. Despite the confined space, the driver had managed to turn it round and its rear had been filled with sandbags from the doorway, and through them the machine-gun poked.

'For God's sake – !'

George's half-broken voice skated up and down the scale, drowning Grand Charles's excited squeaking. As he swung himself up on to the barricade, clutching his petrol bomb, Scully saw Ludo also rising to his feet and, diving forward, he tried to scoop him and the other boys into his arms. Grabbing as many as he could, he flung them down just as the machine-gun in the lorry began to fire.

The crash of the bottle breaking and the whooff of the petrol going up mingled with the shouts of triumph. Sprawling on the ground, his big body over the squirming furious boys, Scully heard moans and cries for mercy. The bedlam of noise was still going on as he scrambled to his feet. Men with rifles were leaping the barricade and running across the street to where the Germans were scrambling from the lorry, their hands in the air. Snatching weapons and helmets, the Frenchmen pushed them into a line with blows and kicks.

One of the Germans was lying on the pavement, blood on his chest, his eyes those of a hurt calf. One of the boys from the barricade eyed him and, walking boastfully across to him, lifted his rifle and calmly shot him in the head.

'*A chacun son Boche*,' he said. 'That one's mine.'

Sickened by the coldbloodedness, Scully became aware of screaming and saw that where the machine-gun had swept along the barricade, several youngsters lay behind it on the pavement, one of them a girl, blood welling from her breast to stain the pink dress she wore. A boy knelt beside her, his eyes bewildered as he looked up at Scully. 'I think she's dead,' he said.

Beyond them, George Presteigne sprawled among the debris, almost unnoticed as the excited crowd swirled round the burning lorry. His right leg was bloody and lacerated, the foot almost torn off, his features twisted as he tried to bite back his cries of pain. Then, when he could contain it no longer, the agony burst from him and he began to howl like a wounded animal, beating at the pavement with his fists.

Almost hidden beneath him, huddled in a little ball against the angle of the wall, still clutching the rusty revolver, was Grand Charles, quite dead, a bullet hole where his right eye had been, the bent spectacles driven deep into his head. Like George, he had finally found out how many beans really did make five.

10

As a woman with tears in her eyes knelt by the body of Grand Charles, one of the medical students bent over George and, pulling out a syringe, jabbed it into his arm and shoved in the plunger. Gradually the writhing stopped; the harsh screams faded to a whimper and the student fished out a penknife and hacked through the last few strands of flesh, muscle and tendon that still held the foot to the ankle.

The tragedy seemed to have gone unnoticed among the other youngsters by the barricade. Several boys were posturing on top, waving tricolours and shouting '*Vive la France! A bas les Boches*!' Then one of them jumped down, righted the motor-cycle combination and, wheeling it out of the Rue Mortmain, turned it round on the corner of the boulevard. Immediately, four more boys clambered aboard, clinging on wherever they could. As the engine roared, the machine jerked, faltered, jerked again, lost one of its passengers, and finally set off, followed by a string of other youngsters, all yelling in triumph and indifferent to the butchery they had brought about.

Christ almighty, Scully thought savagely, what have we made of these bloody kids? Savages? Bloodthirsty hooligans screaming for more deaths?

Turning, he saw Ludo, his face deathly white, watching him. Tom Cléry-Kidder was leaning with one hand against the wall, vomiting into the gutter. Xavier Lipski and Auguste Woof stood as if petrified, their faces shocked. Savagely, Scully dragged down one of the tricolours that had been mounted on the barricade and spread it over Grand Charles's body. As he straightened up, he stepped forward and wrenched the Belgian automatic from Ludo's nerveless fingers and, swinging his arm, flung it as far down the street as he could. As it skidded into the gutter, he snatched up the shotgun Tom Cléry-Kidder had held and, raising it, brought it down on the edge of the gutter so that the stock broke.

Spent, he turned round. Tom Cléry-Kidder pushed himself from the wall. His eyes were red and streaming and a long string of bile was dangling from his chin.

'I'm going home,' he said, and as he looked at Ludo his expression was full of hatred.

'I'll see you on your way,' Scully said harshly.

He set off down the street, followed by the four boys. As they left, a woman was placing flowers round Grand Charles's body.

Scully sighed. There'd be another sign on the wall tomorrow. *Charles Rohan, agé 11 ans, fusilé par les Nazis. Mort pour la patrie.* Mort pour la patrie be buggered, he thought. Grand Charles had thought he was playing cowboys and Indians. There had been a lot of people playing cowboys and Indians in the last week.

The shooting seemed to stop everywhere. The Germans, clinging to their strongpoints, had been refusing to surrender to the mob for fear of being torn apart, waiting until they could see Americans or regular Free French forces. Only then did they begin to straggle out, throwing down their weapons, some of them nervously clutching suitcases or haversacks. Immediately the suitcases were snatched from their hands and their contents – underclothes, shirts, shoes, bottles of brandy – distributed; and as they passed between the lines of jeering people, they were made to raise their hands in an abjectness of defeat. Liberation was at last a fact.

As Scully reached the Rue Paul-Lecours, Tom Cléry-Kidder turned.

'I must go now,' he said.

Auguste Woof and Xavier Lipski joined him, halting in front of Scully.

'Thank you, sir,' Cléry-Kidder said. 'I'm sorry for what happened.'

He thrust out his arm to shake hands. Scully glared at him.

'Go home,' he said. His voice rose to a roar. 'Go home! Go home!'

Cléry-Kidder's face went pink and, turning meekly with the other two, he set off down the street.

Scully remained grim and unspeaking throughout the evening. With Ludo deep in an exhausted sleep, he listened unhearing to the radio, his mind black with guilt.

Troops were pouring into Paris by this time and excited Resistance fighters – a bottle in one hand, a gun in the other – were seeking out the last few Germans still trying to fight back. The battle round the Préfecture had finally died away and the place now stood in silence, pockmarked with bullets, the tricolour still flying, the courtyard filled with captured Wehrmacht vehicles.

The radio announcer was ecstatic. Between bursts of music, there was a constant running commentary.

'All major buildings have been occupied by Frenchmen,' he proclaimed. 'A representative of General de Gaulle is now in the prime minister's apartment. The fighting in the centre has finished and there are no longer Germans in control in any part of Paris.'

There was another burst of music then the announcer spoke again. 'Come out in the streets,' he urged, his voice hoarse. 'Come out and celebrate! Old acquaintances from four years ago are meeting each other again. They have fought the Germans back from the very windows of the city and the tricolour flies again from the top of the Eiffel Tower. Of the demolitions that were to have been carried out not one has been put into operation.'

Scully shifted uneasily. He was beginning to doubt now whether the German commandant had ever had any intention of destroying anything. Nevertheless, the excitement was understandable. Four years of shame and humiliation had been wiped out as de Gaulle arrived to find Paris in the hands of the Parisians.

'Almost twenty thousand Germans have surrendered,' the announcer was saying now. 'But the Free French have suffered too, so let us not forget those who died.'

Scully frowned. While Xavier Lipski's father had appeared, Auguste Woof had discovered that *his* never would, because he had been killed in Normandy.

The bloody world, he thought bitterly, was full of sorrow.

'Let us not forget the little islands of unhappiness amid the joy of freedom.' The radio announcer was talking for the sake of talking, indifferent to the killing. 'I am at the Hôtel de Ville, in the middle of an excited throng waiting to see de Gaulle. He's in there at this moment, meeting the men who were responsible for the liberation of the city. He's going to come out soon. I've just heard. He's – there he is! He's at the window now! I can see him! The square's black with people! You can hear them now!'

Wave after wave of cheering shuddered the radio, the name, 'De Gaulle, de Gaulle, de Gaulle,' coming in a chant like a litany. 'He's tall, that one,' the announcer went on. 'Head and shoulders above his aides. What a man! What a leader! What a Frenchman! The whole of France will be able to see him tomorrow as he leads the victory parade down the Champs-Elysées!'

Scully switched off the set. For a moment he sat in silence, then Sidonie moved restlessly.

'We were all so much to blame,' she whispered.

'Not you. Lambrouille. If he hadn't sent those bloody Germans after Hasler, it would never have happened.'

'It was still my fault. I should have been more aware.'

Scully sighed and shook his head. If anybody could be blamed, it was Hitler for starting the war. And Charles Walter Scully, for talking about comradeship and the spirit of the regiment to a set of immature boys whose eyes were dazzled by the idea of patriotism. He wondered what would become of them, now that Paris was free and they could all go where they wished. Would the Lipskis reopen their restaurant? What would the Rohans do? They were no longer young and Grand Charles had been a child of their middle age. Would Auguste Woof's mother go to his father's

Belgium or to her own America? Would Cléry-Kidder's
mother stay in Paris or would she go back to England? And
what would the Presteignes do? Would George's mutilation
stir them to some effort to make life easier for him. Would
George grow bitter at what had happened? It was hard to
be content with part of your body missing.

Scully woke slowly the following morning, stiff from the
exertions of the previous day. The sun was beating down,
gilding the roofs of houses scarred by shrapnel. Pulverized
glass swept into heaps near barricades was being kicked into
showers by the indifferent feet of thousands of people as
they flowed towards the Champs-Elysées, all eager to see
de Gaulle.

The cafés had reopened and hotels still marked *Nür für
Wehrmacht* were full of French and American soldiers who
hadn't slept in a bed for weeks. In the prisons the Germans'
captives had been replaced by their guards, collaborators
and *Milice*, while outside on the walls thousands of posters,
printed during the hours of darkness, plastered every available inch of space, giving de Gaulle's route and intentions.

Carrying the Enfield, Scully headed for the river with the
crowd. He had a job to do. Somewhere down there beyond
Notre-Dame, he was sure, was Pierre Lambrouille. With
him at liberty, Sidonie would never be able to live at peace.
He could still destroy her, and Scully was quite certain he
was capable of trying.

Police vans were everywhere, together with little Renault
police cars loaded with uniformed men. Everybody was
cheering them for their defence of the Préfecture and they
were making the most of it, knowing it wouldn't last long.
People stood on benches, packing cases, improvised plat-
forms built from dismantled German sentry boxes, and
crowded every window. Posters were on the trees, and
French, American, British and Belgian flags fluttered in the
breeze. There was every kind of uniform, even a Scottish
kilt.

At the bottom of the Champs-Elysées the crowd was
pulsating with excitement. 'He's coming, he's coming,'

Scully kept hearing as he prowled through the yelling people. 'The inspection's finished. He laid a wreath on the tomb of the Unknown Warrior. He's on his way now.'

All the way from the Place de la Concorde, the pavements were thick with people, and Scully could hear the cheering moving down the slope with the man they were greeting. Flags, streamers and summer dresses glowed in the sunshine. Then a police car appeared, its loudhailer going at full blast. On each curb, two rows of police and firemen linked hands and moved slowly along, holding back the crowds, and a detachment of the FFI took up their positions, uniformed in khaki shirts and trousers but as often as not wearing German boots and carrying German weapons.

A hurricane of shouting started with the thump-thump of a police band.

The procession down the Champs-Elysées was preceded by four French tanks; a mixed human chain of police, FFI men, stretcher-bearers, scouts and Equipes Nationales struggled to hold back a crush of journalists and cameramen. Then came an assortment of motor-cycles and sidecars and overloaded jeeps, and finally a military képi that towered above all the other heads.

Women who had made periscopes with mirrors and sticks began to scream ecstatically. An FFI lieutenant waved a captured German general's cloak. In front of de Gaulle walked a man in a black coat, with a white breastplate and silver chain, then the man himself, wearing a simple khaki uniform, devoid of decoration. He looked a little bored with the fuss, and, as if he was made of wood, showed his thanks with stiff little gestures of the hands.

'Is that him?' a woman near Scully asked. 'I didn't know he looked like that.'

Behind de Gaulle came the generals who had led his troops to Paris, among them Leclerc, who had brought his men all the way from Tchad, slim, brisk, with a red complexion and a small moustache. Along with a medley of Resistance leaders and politicians, they followed the tall figure in the most haphazard parade Scully had ever seen.

Amidst the roar of the crowd surging about them, the

marchers moved in a shapeless mass down the slope of the Champs-Elysées; the whole vast dense throng made its way towards Notre-Dame. The tall, austere figure kept bending to allow women and girls to kiss his cheek. Even men ran forward to grasp his hand, and children offered him bouquets of flowers which he passed expressionlessly to his aides.

Eventually the artificial barriers gave way and the people flooded through the lines of FFI men and police, but always they kept their distance from that tall forbidding figure, as though, despite their excitement and exaltation at being free, they felt he towered above them, not only physically but also in spirit.

Scully ignored them all. Somewhere among this crowd he kept reminding himself, was Lambrouille, nursing his ancient grievance. De Gaulle had played into his hands with this haphazard parade and if Lambrouille succeeded in what he was attempting, the repercussions of an assassination could destroy the whole of Lambrouille's family. The French were in no mood to ask questions or be merciful. There had been too many beatings the day before, too much collaboration and too much treachery in the past four years.

Moving along with the marchers, he threaded a route behind the jubilant crowds. Worried police officials, well aware of the danger, were sweeping the buildings around them with field glasses, eyeing the people on the balconies, splashes of colour against the grey stone. Then suddenly, Scully remembered Lambrouille's German mistress who had a flat somewhere in one of these buildings. He tried to recall the name. Florence? Florentin! Saint-Florentin! She had had a top-floor flat on the corner of the Rue de Rivoli and Lambrouille had had a key.

Forcing his way through the crowds, Scully began to run. There were still plenty of armed men about and nobody seemed to consider it odd that he still had the Enfield over his shoulder.

In the Rue de Rivoli, a fire was still burning, lifting its smoke to the sky. As he reached the corner of the Place de la Concorde, he saw the end of the Rue Saint-Florentin.

The grey buildings were tall and imposing, with the heavy mass of the Ministry of Marine on one side of the street. Outside it, naval gunners were grouped on tanks, behind them a burnt-out German vehicle and windows splintered by bullets. On the opposite corner the topmost window was open, the shutters thrown back, and there was a man standing on the balcony, holding a rifle with a telescopic sight.

Scully swung round. Behind him, the band of the Garde Republicaine in the Place de la Concorde was playing the 'Marseillaise' for what seemed the thousandth time. The roaring for de Gaulle increased as the crowd flooded into the great square. For a moment Scully hesitated, then he saw Kehec standing with a group of armed men wearing FFI armbands. Transformed by a clean khaki uniform and a képi, he was studying the buildings around him with field glasses.

Scully touched his shoulder and he swung round. Immediately, his face lit up.

'*Le sergent anglais*,' he smiled. 'I have not forgotten what you have done for the Resistance, my friend. I have written to de Gaulle recommending you for an honour. I have also written to Eisenhower and your General Montgomery.' He grinned. 'Perhaps they will give you the VC.'

'Never mind the VC,' Scully growled. 'I've got business for your boys.'

As he explained what he'd seen, Kehec's eyebrows shot up. He turned and levelled the glasses on the window Scully indicated.

'He has a rifle,' he snapped. 'Get the police!'

A uniformed man some distance away caught their gestures and began to run. Almost immediately an inspector arrived.

'We'll go in,' he said. 'Can you keep him covered from here?'

'*I* can't,' Kehec said, 'but our friend here can shoot off a sparrow's eyebrows without grazing the skin. *He* can.'

As the inspector and his men disappeared, Scully stood with the Enfield resting against the iron wreath decorating a lamp-post. He could see Lambrouille quite clearly now.

He was wearing his red bow tie as usual and held the rifle across his chest. For years he had borne his hatred against the man just beginning to cross the square, and now, with a rifle in his hands, he was only a few hundred yards from him. As de Gaulle marched ahead of his followers, he made a magnificent target. Lambrouille lifted the rifle. ·

'*Tirez!*' Kehec snapped. 'Shoot! Shoot, for God's sake!'

Scully ignored him, lining up the sights of the Enfield. Allow for firing upwards, he thought coldly. First pressure. Draw a deep breath and hold it. Then squeeze.

The shot cut across the cheering like a knife. Immediately there were screams. The figure in the window had fallen back out of sight, but the shot had started a fusillade. All round Scully as he lowered his rifle people had flung themselves to the ground. In a moment, every figure in the square seemed to be flat on its stomach, huddled on all fours or trying to scramble under vehicles as the bullets sent chips of granite flying. Turning, Scully saw officers trying to stop the shooting and Leclerc swiping with his gloves at an excited policeman brandishing a revolver. With almost everybody about him face down in the roadway, de Gaulle stood out, imperturbable and magnificently erect, his step quite unhurried and totally indifferent. Then, as someone pushed him into a car, a man pointed at Scully's rifle and shouted.

'*Assassin!*'

Kehec looked alarmed. 'You had better stay with us, my friend,' he said sharply. 'They probably think *you* were shooting at the general.'

Several more policemen joined them as he gestured and, as they moved into the Rue Saint-Florentin, the crowd swarmed round them. Pushing his way through to the doorway, Kehec gestured to his men to follow him and began to pound up the stairs to the top floor where the police had already forced their way into one of the apartments.

Staring past them, Scully saw Lambrouille lying on his back on the carpet near the window. The bullet had hit him in the middle of the forehead and blood was soaking the carpet round his head. He would never trouble Sidonie again.

Kehec said something quietly to the inspector, who turned. 'My friend,' he said, 'that was some shot.'

Kehec put his hand on Scully's shoulder and gestured towards the square outside where the shooting was changing back to cheering. 'This time the letter will come from *him*.' He grinned. 'They will make you a Chevalier of the Légion d'Honneur and your VC may become two VCs. You saved de Gaulle, my friend.'

'Bugger de Gaulle,' Scully growled. 'It was nothing to do with de Gaulle.'

11

By the time Scully reached the street again, the shooting
had stopped completely and the crowds were back on their
feet. Carrying the Enfield by the barrel, Scully walked
slowly between the dispersing people and, crossing the
bridge over the river, he stopped in the middle. Men and
women were still hurrying past to see what had happened
and, for a moment, he stood motionless, letting them flow
by. Then he drew a deep breath and taking the rifle by the
muzzle, he swung it with all his strength and let go. It
described an arc and dropped with a splash into the water.

The streets of the Left Bank were full of rejoicing people
as he headed towards the Petite-Ville.

Those who had not gone to the Champs-Elysées or
Notre-Dame were all out on the pavement, as if, now they
were free, they didn't know what to do with their freedom.
Nobody seemed interested in the usual daytime chores of
finding food, cleaning their homes or going to work. It was
as if Paris had stopped everything to savour the liberation.

There seemed to be Americans everywhere – all accompanied by girls. They were sitting in jeeps, on the pavement,
at café tables, standing in doorways, some of them stripped
to the waist in the sunshine, talking to women in courtyards
who were washing their filthy shirts. Everybody seemed to
be shouting. *Vive l'Amérique! Vive la France! Vive l'amour*!

The 'Marseillaise' seemed to be coming from every window. The radio played it. Gramophones played it. Men
played it on trumpets and children played it on flutes and
violins. Everybody seemed to be drinking, too, and empty

bottles stood in doorways and on windowsills and lay in the gutter. Long-hidden delicacies had appeared with dusty bottles of brandy laid down for no other occasion but this. Laughter seemed to be everywhere.

As he neared the end of the Rue Commandant-Sardier, Scully saw there were French trucks and armoured cars parked against the curb. His heart thumped at the thought of Sidonie. She had given him a pride in himself – as a man, as distinct from as a soldier. She had made him realize there was life outside the army, that a home meant more than just a barrack room, more than merely the noise and the pornographic wit of the sergeants' mess. For the first time in his life, he looked forward to having a home that contained his own possessions, with his own woman in it and eventually his own children.

For the first time in his life, he felt he had a future. He had a suspicion that neither Sidonie nor Ludo would wish to live in England but he felt he knew Paris well enough by this time to be able to make a life there. He felt no regrets at the thought of leaving England behind. His memories of it were of orphanages, boys' service in the army and finally the army itself, crude, not unkind in its own rough way, but always impermanent, always giving the impression that eventually, as age caught up, it would come to an end and he would have to start again in a new life he wasn't used to and of which he had always been just a little afraid.

As he turned into the Rue Fantin, Scully saw two or three jeeps drawn up outside the Hôtel Bouboulis. At first he thought the men in them were Americans, because they wore American helmets; then he saw that in addition to the white invasion star the vehicles also carried the Cross of Lorraine.

Men, women and children were crowding the entrance and as he saw Madame Weinspach smiling all over her face, he wondered what had happened to bring such good cheer when old Virec still lay dead in his apartment. Then, to his surprise, he saw Sidonie, watched by a laughing Ludo, in the arms of a French officer. He wore a khaki képi, a stained uniform and a neat beard, and she was clinging to him as if her life depended on it.

As Scully's steps slowed, Ludo saw him and ran towards him.

'It's Armande!' he yelled. 'Monsieur Scully, it's Armande Démange!'

Scully had stopped dead. Suddenly, with clarity, he realized he'd been building his hopes on faulty foundations. Sidonie had accepted him only through loneliness and need, but now, clasped in the arms of the French officer, she had forgotten him in a moment.

Ludo was beaming at him. He seemed to have recovered from the shock of the battle in the Rue Mortmain and Grand Charles's death.

'It's Armande,' he said again. 'He's come back.'

'Yes, flower,' Scully agreed stiffly. 'He's come back. I can see.'

As the boy turned and ran back, Scully swallowed noisily. He saw it clearly now. Sidonie was French and had been brought up to a way of life that Scully had never known and couldn't emulate. And in spite of everything he pretended, the boy had also always been more French than English. He knew no other country but France, spoke French with greater facility than English, and stood for the 'Marseillaise' instead of 'God Save the King'. The bearded Frenchman holding Sidonie, an academic like the dead McCosh, could provide just what they'd always been used to, could bring them back to life in a way Scully never could. Lambrouille had hit the nail on the head. She wasn't Scully's type at all. It was obvious in the boy's delighted announcement. Until Scully had arrived, it was what he had always expected and had always wanted.

Scully drew a deep breath. It seemed to be time to leave. Just when he was coming to understand this magnificent city of stony history, the home of France's great, the residence of its kings; just when he was beginning to realize why the Parisians had fought so bitterly to preserve it. But there was no alternative, he knew, no swerving. There was only one way to go, only one time.

Turning on his heel, he started to walk. Putting the sun behind him, he headed north. Somewhere up there he could get a lift from the generous Americans. He'd been mad to imagine he could create a home here. There was only one home for an old soldier and that was in the ranks of his regiment – the North Staffs Fusileers. Spelt with two *e*s.

Pity Chalky White wasn't still around, he thought. They'd have gone in for a shattering booze-up to celebrate his return.

For a moment he thought of the photograph Ludo had taken of him, which had been set alongside that of Sidonie and her son. It would disappear into a drawer now and be forgotten and, perhaps in years to come, someone would find it and ask 'Who the devil's this?'

His jaw was rock hard as he began to step out. The sun was catching his cheek and lighting up the planes and angles of a face that had become brown and battered through long-forgotten seasons of sun and wind. But his head was high and his back was straight and his boots went down firmly on the paving. Scully had never been a man for regrets. There was always Edna.

The regiment was what mattered. The regiment had been father and mother to Scully from the age of fifteen. He'd spent all his life with it, and in return had given everything he'd got to it, from the first day he'd begun to realize it was more than just a few snarling sergeants chasing him to be clean and tidy. It was a living thing and it also had given him pride. It would look after him, with no questions asked. Lieutenant Vaughan was the colonel now, and *he'd* not forget what they'd always said.

Cetera Desunt.

The others are wanting.

ARMY OF SHADOWS

John Harris

France – Winter 1944. The long-awaited liberation is at hand.

The bombing mission had gone well. The crew of the Lancaster bomber began to relax. Then the Messerschmitt came out of the darkness, its guns blazing.

Of the nine-man crew only Neville and Urquhart survived, parachuting into the heart of occupied France. Now, for both of them, the testing time had begun: a time of peril as the fliers joined forces with the Army of Shadows – the men of the French Resistance – and entered a deadly game of cat and mouse with a ruthless and desperate enemy.

'John Harris writes about war as few men can. . . . With gathering speed, the story moves to a thundering climax – and a cracking good read it makes' *Daily Mail*

£1.50

BESTSELLING WAR BOOKS FROM ARROW

All these books are available from your bookshop or newsagent or you can order them direct. Just tick the titles you want and complete the form below.

☐	PROUD WATERS	Ewart Brookes	£1.25
☐	A RUMOR OF WAR	Philip Caputo	£1.95
☐	ARMY OF SHADOWS	John Harris	£1.50
☐	NORTH STRIKE	John Harris	£1.50
☐	TOLL FOR THE BRAVE	Jack Higgins	£1.25
☐	THE PHOENIX ASSAULT	John Kerrigan	95p
☐	BAPTISM OF BLOOD	K. N. Kostov	£1.25
☐	THE BERLIN BUNKER	J. P. O'Donnell	£1.50
☐	STRIKE FROM THE SEA	Douglas Reeman	95p
☐	WITH BLOOD AND IRON	Douglas Reeman	£1.00
☐	TORPEDO RUN	Douglas Reeman	£1.50
☐	GO IN AND SINK	Douglas Reeman	£1.75
☐	DEATH OF A DIVISION	Charles Whiting	75p
☐	SS WEREWOLF	Charles Whiting	£1.50
		Postage	
		Total	

ARROW BOOKS, BOOKSERVICE BY POST, PO BOX 29, DOUGLAS, ISLE OF MAN, BRITISH ISLES

Please enclose a cheque or postal order made out to Arrow Books Limited for the amount due including 10p per book for postage and packing for orders within the UK and 12p for overseas orders.

Please print clearly

NAME ....

ADDRESS ....

....

Whilst every effort is made to keep prices down and to keep popular books in print, Arrow Books cannot guarantee that prices will be the same as those advertised here or that the books will be available.